BLINDFOLDED

INNOCENCE

BLINDFOLDED

INNOCENCE

Alessandra Torre

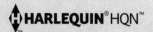

Recycling programs
for this product may
not exist in your area.

ISBN-13: 978-0-373-77828-7

BLINDFOLDED INNOCENCE

For questions and comments about the quality of this book, please contact us
at CustomerService@Harlequin.com.

Printed in U.S.A.

This book is dedicated to Joey,
my best friend and soul mate. I love you forever.

BLINDFOLDED

INNOCENCE

Prologue

I knelt on the floor, a pillow underneath my knees. Blind-folded, I listened intently, waiting for a sign of what was to come. Only the hum of the hotel air conditioner met my ears. Seconds passed, then a minute. Finally, I heard the door open and then click shut. Footsteps, muted on the carpet, behind me. I felt, rather than heard, a male presence pass by my side and come to stand in front of me. Close, so close. I leaned backward slightly. The sound of a zipper being drawn down filled the silent room.

One

Four months earlier

I decided to break off my engagement on a Wednesday night at 2:20 a.m. I was drunk past the point of walking a straight line, but not yet to the point of slurring my speech. Drunk wasn't the best mind-set to be in to make a life-altering decision, but a thin curtain had finally been ripped away and a truth that I had evaded for the past two years now stood front and center in the middle of my head, waving its arms and screaming.

Luke was not the one for me.

I met Luke as a sophomore in college. At the time I was emotionally vulnerable, recently dumped by the first "love of my life" two weeks after he took my virginity. That asshole ditched poor deflowered me to run off with a seventeen-year-old blonde, pink-toenailed California princess. Luke was different—quiet, brooding, a sensitive soul who seemed absolutely terrified of me. I was bubbly, beautiful and determined to get over my heartbreak the college way—partying myself into oblivion. I hunted Luke down the way a lioness would a defenseless baby antelope, making my sole occupation getting him to fall completely and hopelessly in love with me—which he did, putting me on a pedestal and worshipping daily at my whim.

I demanded a proposal within six months, which he gave me willingly—I think—and we began to plan a life together. This life plan was hampered slightly by the fact that Luke was a dreamer with high goals but little follow-through. He enjoyed spending time with me, and not much else. He worked in construction—not in a management capacity, as I had originally thought, but as a laborer. My bubbly persona started to turn into more of a nagging mother role. It wasn't long before my subconscious started poking me with a sharp, pointy stick. I ignored the annoying pokes for twelve months, then my subconscious had enough of waiting.

It is weird the things that enter your head during a breakup. I sat on my bed with Luke sitting next to me, and I wondered why I had never purchased a chair for my bedroom. I had a desk and the typical bedside table, but no chair. A chair would have made the situation easier. Sitting next to Luke on the bed was too intimate—his pain was too close—and I knew I would have to fight to keep from reaching over to comfort him.

I stood up, wobbled slightly and turned to face him. I took a deep breath and delivered the bad news. I think my dramatic breakup speech was hampered slightly by the fact that we were both drunk, but I tried my best to be compassionate, coherent and firm. I accomplished at least two of those objectives.

Luke turned out to have a streak of stalker in him. Despite all the poking and prodding that he had needed to bathe, balance a checkbook and show up for work, it turned out he needed little or no encouragement to spend every waking moment trying to convince me to come back to him. In retrospect, maybe I should have spent less effort trying to get him to fall in love with me. I might have overshot that objective.

After two weeks of avoiding my home, work and anyplace I had frequented during the past two years, I decided to leave my crappy apartment and even crappier job and start fresh. It was good timing. Intern season was starting.

Two

My internship at Clarke, De Luca & Broward began on a Monday morning at 8:00 a.m. I sat in the Human Resources offices with eight other interns and waited for my attorney assignment. Our internships would last for one semester. During that time we would be assigned to an attorney and, for the most part, would be their personal bitch for the next ten weeks.

I had heard the stories. Liz Renfield, one of the junior partners, once made an intern cover her gynecology appointment. The intern had to sit in the cold stirrups and undergo a full exam just so Renfield could make a deposition and continue her birth control uninterrupted. Hugo Clarke was apparently the dream assignment. He was known to take interns under his wing and pretty much guaranteed them a salaried position after graduation. Brad De Luca was a skirt chaser, Robert Handler a drunk, and Kent Broward drowned interns in work. There were a few new attorneys that hadn't yet built up reputations, but I was sure that they would have them soon enough.

"Miss Campbell," the throaty-voiced receptionist barked, waving her hand, beckoning me. I stood, smoothed my skirt and strode to the front. I was nervous, but tried to appear calm and collected. I came to a stop in front of her and waited. "You will be assisting Attorney Kent Broward," she stated. "After orientation, report to his office, fourth floor." She dismissed me by turning back to her stack of forms and calling the next victim, Jennifer Hutchinson. I turned and walked back to my seat, passing Jennifer on the way. She gave me a tight, nervous smile, which I returned.

I sat down on the plastic-wrapped seat and exhaled, releasing the breath that I had not been aware I was holding. Attorney Kent Broward. I could have gotten worse. Broward worked long hours and expected his interns to do the same, but at least I would get good, solid training. If I impressed Broward, I should have no problem getting a strong recommendation for law school. Word was that Broward was tough, but not unreasonable, and fair. I heard Jennifer's assignment called out in the background. She received Liz Renfield. Tough break.

Orientation passed slowly, a boring drone of questionnaires, forms and informational videos on topics such as equal opportunity and sexual harassment in the workplace. We had a catered lunch in an empty conference room—cold ham-and-turkey sandwiches with chips. I munched on a Frito and listened to the idle chat. The conversation seemed to center around drinks after work and where everyone wanted to go.

"Hops Grill. Julia, that work for you?" Trevor, a lanky redhead, leaned toward me as he asked the question.

I shrugged noncommittally. "Hops works for me, if Broward lets me out in time," I said. I didn't expect to make many happy-hour events, at least not for the next ten weeks. I could probably cross off any social events, period, until my internship was over.

"I'm sure Broward will let you off early today. It is the first day, after all." The optimism came from Todd Appleton, a handsome, athletic type, as he stared into my eyes from across the table.

I smiled at him, trying not to stare at his perfect grin. Hmm…that view will help the next few months pass quickly. "Maybe. Who'd you get?"

"De Luca," he responded breezily. "Should be fine. The guy apparently parties more than he works."

I glanced at Jennifer. She was typing furiously into her phone, probably updating her boyfriend on her day. "Jennifer, you going for drinks?" She glanced up, nodded and resumed her texting.

Jane, the Human Resources receptionist, a petite white-haired woman, who would have seemed motherly if not for her piercing stare and gravelly smoker's voice, strode into the room. "Okay, interns, let's move!" she commanded, clapping her hands. "Report to your attorneys and bring all of your things with you!" She clapped her hands again and began herding us out. Todd caught up with me on the way out and held the door for me, pressing his hand gently on my back to guide me through the door. I tried not to smile, but felt a flush hit my face. I headed for the stairs and prepared myself for the fourth floor, and Broward.

Broward was in his forties, tall and bald—shaved bald, in an obvious attempt to hide a receding hairline. He looked like a runner, thin and in shape. He had his jacket on and was seated behind his desk when I came in. He stood as I entered and came around the desk to shake my hand. "Julia." He beamed, pumping my hand. "Nice to meet you." I liked him immediately. He seemed intelligent, approachable and trustworthy. Plus, it appeared he had excellent taste in interns. Looking around, he grabbed a set of keys and a stack of files. "Come with me. I'll show you your office and start you working."

★ ★ ★

Four hours later, I paused in my typing and leaned back in my chair. I stretched my arms and legs and rolled my head, trying to get the kinks out of my neck. I looked around my office, taking my first real appraisal of the space. It was a nice office, more than I had expected as an intern. Dark wood-paneled walls, plush cream carpet and expensive, heavy furniture—the room had a definite masculine sense, a cigar bar–type feel. I didn't mind. Girlie, flowery and pink don't exactly inspire fear in the courtroom.

My desk was filled with legal briefs, all covered with Broward's handwritten notes. They all needed to be summarized and to have his notes implemented. I sighed. Long nights were going to be the norm, mostly filled with menial work that would do nothing to further my work experience. Welcome to the world of internship. I leaned back over the desk and started in again.

An hour later, there was a soft knock on my door and Todd Appleton stuck his gorgeous blond head in. "We're heading out for drinks," he said. "Still room for you, if you're interested." He looked carefree and relaxed, happily done for the day, his tie already loosened.

"I think I'll be here awhile," I said from behind the stack of briefs. "But thanks for checking."

His gaze traveled from my full desk to the crammed cardboard file box on the side of my desk. His smile faded slightly. "All right…I'll take a rain check." He tapped his hand on the door frame twice and then left, closing the door behind him.

I rubbed my eyes and focused again on Britley v. Russell Properties, an exciting legal battle regarding a dispute over water rights on a condominium project. Thrilling. At least Broward was still there also. I could hear him on the phone, his seat creaking occasionally when he stood up, usually to pace. I bet a track had been worn on his plush carpet from the constant pacing. My stomach growled. The next day I would know to pack a dinner. Damn Todd and the other interns, with their light workloads and happy-hour drinks. I grumbled a little longer and then tried to refocus my mind.

At 10:00 p.m. Broward knocked on my office door and entered. Tie undone, shirt rumpled, he looked at my exhausted face with a gentle smile. "Come on, Julia. Let's go. You've put in a good first day."

I smiled at him wearily. I was so hungry I was ready to start chewing on a Post-it note; I was certain my butt had officially fused to the leather seat, and my hands were cramping from the nonstop typing. I wanted to come across as a road-hardened legal warrior, but I was too tired to keep up the facade. Besides, he looked tired also.

"All right, boss," I said, grabbing my jacket and shrugging into it. "I won't argue with you, seeing it's my first day." I picked up my purse and followed him down the hall, waving to the quiet, round, Hispanic housekeeper who waited at the entrance to Broward's office armed with disinfectant and a trash bag. She smiled at me and waited until we passed before scurrying into the office.

"I'll walk you to your car," Broward said—a statement rather than a question. "You don't need to be in the parking garage alone." I nodded my thanks and tried to walk without stumbling.

We got on the elevator. Muted music filled the car. I tried to think of something moderately intelligent to say.

Broward broke the silence. "I buried you in files today. I didn't give you a proper introduction to the office. Tomorrow I will give you a tour and the basic background information on everything that you will need. Week after next I will be in Fort Lauderdale, so I want to get you as acclimated and self-sufficient as possible."

"Sounds great," I said. Thank God, a week of normal hours. I gestured to the ten-year-old gray Toyota Camry, my mom's old car, now one of two cars in the parking lot, the other a shiny black Lexus, which I assumed was his. "This is mine," I said a bit unnecessarily. "Thank you for walking me." I awkwardly stuck out my hand and he shook it.

"See you tomorrow, Ms. Campbell." Broward smiled and released my hand.

"Good night, Mr. Broward." I nodded, and headed for my car.

Three

Six in the morning came way too freaking early. The day before, I had bounded out of bed, excited about my internship, but today it took two snooze cycles before I lifted my head. My alarm still sounding, I fumbled to turn it off just as pounding started on the wall beside my bed. "It's off!" I shouted. Zack, my stoner of a roommate, stopped beating on the wall, probably already halfway back to sleep. He'd had friends over till past 3:00 a.m., and they had made no effort to be quiet. I had no doubt there would be plenty of fights in the upcoming months over our sleep routines.

After breakfast and a shower, I grabbed a blue sweater-dress out of the closet and pulled it over my head, cinching a brown belt around my waist. Grabbing small faux diamond stud earrings and a purse, I surveyed my shoe options. All sexy and over three inches tall. Seeing long hours ahead, I realized I would need to buy some shoes that emphasized comfort over fashion. For now, I grabbed some gorgeous leather-and-gold stilettos and slid them on.

I arrived at the office at 7:30 a.m. Pulling open the heavy teak doors, I entered the lobby, nodding to Dorothy, the ancient receptionist. "Good morning, Miss Campbell," she said creakily. "Here late last night?" Her bemused expression had no trace of pity.

"Not too late," I replied breezily. She grinned at me, her wrinkles accentuated by the motion.

"Have a good day," I heard her call as I pressed the door to the stairs and headed for the fourth floor.

The fourth floor—or power floor, as the staff referred to it—was divided into three different wings, one for each partner. Each partner had two secretaries, two paralegals and one intern. Brad De Luca was the exception, with four secretaries and three paralegals. I remembered from orientation that his caseload was double that of any other attorney, including the other two partners. Broward's secretaries were Sheila and Beverly, neither of whom, judging by their empty desks, arrived till 8:00 a.m.

Broward was already in his office, phone to his ear, when I passed his closed door. I waved at him through the glass and entered my office. Setting my purse by the door, I switched my cell to Silent and then started in on the pile stacked on my desk. I was halfway through the first brief when Broward appeared in the doorway.

"Good morning," he said distractedly.

"Good morning."

"Did you make coffee?" His question caused me to look up from my computer.

"Coffee?" I stalled. *Is that part of my duties?*

"Yes, the kitchen with the coffeepot is on the third floor. I'm sorry I didn't give you the proper tour, but I thought they might have covered that in orientation." A phone began ringing in his office, and he glanced back at me with agitation.

"Yes, I'll get it now." I stood quickly and smoothed down

my dress. He disappeared, and I heard him answer his phone a few seconds later.

Coffee. Okay, I can do this. Are Trevor and Todd brewing freaking coffee?

I found the third-floor kitchen without too much trouble and stared at the complex stainless steel coffeepot. I came from a noncoffee family. I had never desired to attach myself to a caffeine habit, and had treated coffee the same way I treated cigarettes, drugs and—until I was nineteen—sex. I stayed away from them, and they stayed away from me. Therefore, my coffee education rivaled that of a newborn.

Should I admit weakness and ask Ancient Dorothy for help? Nope. I started opening drawers in the kitchen, hoping to find a user's manual for the coffeepot.

My butt was saved by a short, round woman with spiky red hair and an I Love My Labradoodle sweatshirt. Sarcastically, I wondered if the sweatshirt classified as business attire until my subconscious smacked me across the face. Who was I to judge salvation?

"Good morning!" Labradoodle woman chirped happily, bustling past me and settling her orange-and-blue polka-dot lunch box in the fridge.

"Hi!" I blurted out enthusiastically. Probably a little too enthusiastically. She gave me an odd smile before heading to the sink to wash her hands.

I cornered the Labradoodle-loving stranger by the sink. "My name is Julia," I said. "Today is my second day, and Broward just asked me for coffee, and I've never made coffee before, and I can't find a user's manual for the coffee machine, and I don't know how it's supposed to taste...." My rush of words faltered and I looked at her in desperation. *Please,* have some *compassion!*

She beamed at me and patted my arm reassuringly. "Now,

now, that is no problem! I don't drink a lot of coffee myself, but I'll show you how to fix it!" With purpose, she bustled over to the cabinet and pulled out a jug of ground coffee. "Now, the way I fix it is to put three teaspoons of coffee grounds in…and then fill the water canister to eight cups." Three teaspoons, eight cups. Sounds easy enough.

I followed her instructions and had a pot of watery brown liquid brewing in no time. I didn't trust myself with a taste test, but poured Broward a cup and stuck one of the prepared containers of sweeteners, creamers and stirrers under my arm. I carefully navigated my way through the halls to the elevator and used my elbow to press the button. The doors opened to Todd Appleton's perky good looks. His glowing skin and enthusiastic "good morning" spoke of a full night of rest. I stepped into the elevator with him and watched his eyes travel up my legs and stop on my shaky coffee cup and creamer selection. I had already sloshed at least a fourth of the coffee around the rim, and could feel some drops running down my fingers. Great.

"Making coffee for the office?" he teased, his gaze finally reaching my face.

"Very funny," I responded. "Did you know our duties include coffee prep? Something I have never attempted before," I added dryly.

"Maybe for you," he shot back. "De Luca has Le Croissant bring up a full spread every morning, with coffee, fruits and a bunch of pastries. They deliver at 8:00 a.m." He paused, glancing at his watch. "Hence my early arrival. I want to get some while they're fresh."

The elevator pinged and stopped at the fourth floor, doors opening slowly. Todd bounded off, apparently never having been taught by his doting mother that ladies go first. I exited carefully, trying my best to keep every last remaining drop of coffee in the cup, and traversed the three turns and two straightaways until I stopped in front of Broward's door. I bumped the door gently with my knee, and then pushed it in.

I could feel tendrils of my hair coming out of my French twist, and felt completely out of sorts when I tried to gracefully place—and more like dumped—the cup and ceramic container on Broward's desk. He was on a call, discussing what sounded like an environmental issue, and held up one finger to indicate that I should stay. I chose one of the two heavy leather chairs facing his desk and sat, waiting for his call to finish.

While he droned on about the impact of what sounded like a nature trail, I discreetly checked out his office. It was decorated in the heavy, ornate, masculine fashion that all our offices seemed to share. He had stacks of files everywhere and file boxes lining any free space on the edges of the walls. Six file cabinets lined one wall, and a six-person conference table took up the right side of the room. It was a large office, more than twice the size of mine, but what I would have expected for a firm partner. The table didn't look as though it was used for many meetings. Every inch of it was buried in stacks of papers, with hundreds of small and large Post-it notes covering them. My head spun with the enormity of his workload. I had naively assumed that I was making some headway with the measly fourteen hours I had put in the day before. I grew stressed just sitting in his office.

His desk was the cleanest place in the office. He had three legal folders on its surface, one open to the file he was discussing on the phone. He had a large digital clock, no doubt to help him keep track of billable hours. He had two framed photos next to his phone. I couldn't see them from this angle, but assumed they were of his wife and kids. Those photos were probably the most he ever saw of them. My snooping was cut short by the sound of his phone handset being returned to its rightful place. I looked up and into his blue eyes.

"I didn't know how you liked your coffee, so I brought it black," I said, gesturing to the accompaniments in the ceramic holder. I stood up and slid the coffee cup toward him until it was in easy reach.

"Just light cream and Equal," he said, standing up, grabbing the creamer box and flipping through it.

What defines "light"? And how much Equal? I watched him closely, noting how much he added of each to the cup. He looked at the color of the coffee a moment longer than what I would define as normal, and then, dismissing whatever thought was in his head, brought the cup to his mouth.

Gag would be too strong a word for what happened next. An involuntary wince perhaps? His blink was a bit forced, his mouth curled into an unpleasant grimace and there was a slight shudder that he tried hard to cover. An involuntary giggle popped out of me and I slapped a hand over my mouth. He looked at me in confusion, trying to figure out if I was trying to play a joke on him. His expression looked somewhere between mad and amused.

"I'm sorry," I gasped, fighting the ridiculous hiccuping laugh that was fighting tooth and nail to come out. "I don't drink coffee. I've never made it. I was stumbling through trying to figure it out when someone downstairs was kind enough to show me how...." My voice trailed off as my giggle urge left and I felt despair creeping in. "Is it...horrible?" I whispered.

"A little," Broward admitted, a wry smile coming to his lips. "But, no worries. I'll have Sheila walk you through it tomorrow morning. In the meantime, I need a file couriered over from Rothsfield and Merchant. Could you stop by Starbucks on the way back?"

I nodded rapidly, some relief flowing into my body. He didn't seem mad. Yes, I had looked inept, but it seemed to be okay.

"If you prefer," I ventured, "I think Mr. De Luca had some breakfast delivered. I could grab some coffee from their conference room?"

His face darkened. Okay...maybe not something he'd prefer. Did I say something wrong?

"No," he said sharply. "Brad orders that for his secretaries, intern and his clients. We don't mess with, or borrow, from his staff, and I expect the same from him." His glowering tone softened slightly at my pale face. "Sorry," he muttered. "Maybe now is when I should go through the office background." He stood, shut the file on his desk and pressed the call button on his phone.

A delicate, professional voice sounded through the speakerphone. "Yes, Mr. Broward?" It sounded like Sheila, his secretary. *Why wasn't Sheila getting his coffee?* That seemed a secretarial duty.

"I will be indisposed for the next...ten minutes. Please hold my calls."

"Yes sir, Mr. Broward."

"Can you please shut the door?" Broward asked as he sat down. I quickly walked to the door and shut it softly, then returned to my place in front of his desk. Broward leaned back in his chair and tapped his finger to his chin, mulling something over while looking at me. I fought the urge to fidget.

"Okay, to begin, let's attack the elephant in the room." He leaned forward and met my gaze firmly, his almost-stern expression reminding me of when my father used to lecture me on the importance of high school English. What elephant in the room? Is this about the coffee?

"Brad De Luca," he began. "Brad is, without a doubt, the best divorce attorney in the south. His waiting list is over ten months long, and many unhappy wives prolong a marriage for the sole reason of waiting to have Brad represent them." His voice was matter-of-fact and slightly wry. "Brad is a shark in the courtroom and has no problem splattering the walls with blood. He also takes very, very good care of his clients."

His tone and expression led me to believe that "taking care" of his clients might mean a little more than one would think. I nodded to indicate that I got the point.

"You will no doubt notice the daily breakfast platters, be invited on the Bahamas work weekends and hear the drone of excessive and unnecessary celebrations going on in that wing of this floor." His stern gaze moved up in intensity to level six. "Julia, I don't want you to have any part of that. Brad runs his part of the office that way—I run mine in a more...professional and efficient manner. There is a reason that you were not assigned to Brad. Stay away from him." The approachable, friendly Broward was gone. In his chair sat a dictator speaking to me in the manner one might use on a bad puppy.

I was contrite and didn't even know why. "Yes, sir," I said, firmly but quietly.

"Great," he said briskly. "Now, moving on to the other partner, Hugo Clarke. Clarke focuses on criminal law. His clients are mostly white-collar, though if a case has enough publicity, he will take on the bloodier ones. He is a great source of knowledge, and is always happy to help our interns. He has a young grandson who often spends time here at the office. If you see a two-year-old wandering around, that would be Clarke's."

I waited for another death glare and a warning that Clarke sold black market organs, but Broward seemed to be off his soapbox and was now almost jovial. Good lord, it was like dealing with a menopausal woman.

"I focus almost entirely on corporate law—all civil matters. Our work has a lot less emotion involved, but is exciting all the same." Right. Every law student can't wait to dive into corporate reform.

Broward skimmed over the other attorneys and reviewed the billing procedures and his general expectations. They all seemed reasonable, though I suspected his general reference to my expected sixty-hour weeks would probably be more of a seventy- or eighty-hour commitment. He signaled the end of our conversation by pressing Sheila's extension on his phone and indicating that I should open the door.

Her melodious voice came through the speakerphone. "Yes, sir?"

"Please give Julia a tour of the office. Apparently Jane didn't do a proper job in orientation. Also, she will be running over to Rothsfield to get the Danko file, so please explain the mileage system and petty cash."

"Certainly."

Sheila appeared in Broward's doorway within seconds. She matched her polished voice—an older woman, in her sixties, with a blue sweater set, gray wool dress pants, perfectly coiffed silver hair and a string of pearls. She smiled kindly at me and ushered me out of Broward's office, closing his door softly behind her.

Sheila's tour of the wing was in-depth and informative. I met over twelve secretaries, six paralegals, and Attorney Liz Renfield. I nodded at the other interns as we passed through their areas, but didn't have any conversations. I figured out early why Sheila didn't bring Broward's coffee. Handing me the petty cash key, she had an extreme shake to her hands. She was a talker, and I learned as much about her as the firm. She had been there twenty-two years, since it was just Clarke Law Firm and they had to occasionally miss a paycheck if it had been a slow month. By the end of the tour I had learned that Liz Renfield and Robert Handler had once shared more than a case, and that recently Chris Hemming, a civil attorney, had been caught embezzling funds and had been fired.

Sheila led me up a vacant and stale stairway leading to the attic file storage, pausing at the top, key pointed toward the lock in her shaky hand. She glanced at me, somewhat casually. "Did Mr. Broward mention anything about Brad De Luca?"

Four

Sheila and I were alone in the attic, a stuffy room with rows and rows of file boxes. At my initial estimate, there seemed to be over twenty rows, each over fifteen boxes deep and eight or nine boxes high on each side. Fluorescent lights above us made it a well-lit but hot area. The lights combined with Sheila's question made me feel like a prisoner being interrogated. *What is everyone's obsession with this guy?*

"Yes, Broward—Mr. Broward—told me that their side of the office operates a little differently than ours, and that I should steer clear of it." I mumbled the words like a schoolgirl reciting her daily duties.

Sheila's eyes gleamed with the excitement of gossip, but also with warning. "Mr. Broward was probably too proper to say that Brad is absolutely incorrigible! He stopped being assigned female interns three years ago because he couldn't keep his hands off them. He's divorced due to another one of his…relationships, and is never without some young thing on his arm. He's Italian— You know how those men are." She pronounced "Italian" as if it was some kind of diseased animal, and waved her hand as if that should explain everything. "Bottom line…"

She fixed her steely gaze on me. "You are exactly his type. You need to stay as far away from Brad De Luca as you can get."

Sheesh. *This* is what everyone is worried about? That I am about to become one of a senior partner's latest conquests? First off, I am as sexually unpromiscuous as…probably Sheila! I am a twenty-one-year-old college student who has had a total of two partners. In college terms, I'm practically a saint! Secondly, isn't De Luca like forty? In his late thirties at *least*. Who in their right mind would think I would be attracted to someone that old?

I was more than a little offended by the perception of my low standards.

I met Sheila's eyes firmly and confidently. "Sheila, you have absolutely nothing to worry about. Trust me."

Her return look was less confident.

Five

A bit awkwardly, we finished the tour, and ten minutes later I was in my car with the windows down and "Whatever" by Hot Chelle Rae blaring. It was hot as hell outside but I didn't care. I needed wind filling my car and blaring music in order to get my funk to pass. I wanted to make an impression at my internship, but one as an intelligent hardworker, not as the chick that everyone thinks Brad freaking De Luca is going to bang. My head was properly cleared but I was still a little bitchy when I returned to the office, Danko file in hand, along with a still-steaming cup of Starbucks coffee with "light cream and Equal" in it.

I gave the file to Sheila and dropped the coffee off at Broward's desk. He was on another call and waved distractedly to me. I went into my office and started where I had left off the night before. Within three minutes, my office door banged open and Todd Appleton plopped his body into one of my chairs. *Really? Am I going to get any freaking work done today?*

I looked up over my file with what I hoped was an "I'm busy, what the hell do you want?" look.

"Yes, Todd?"

"Where have you been all day? We've been so busy on the East Wing. This one case, the wife caught her husband doing his boss's daughter! And then we found out that…" His voice droned on and on and I began focusing on his beautiful features as opposed to his words. I snapped myself out of my mind fart and waved my hand in front of Todd.

"Todd, can't talk. I'm busy." I gestured to all the work filling my desk and office.

He glanced around. "I know, but…you've been gone all morning."

"Exactly. Hence my heavy workload. I need to get some stuff done."

"Oh." His dejected face reminded me of the time I told the four-year-old I used to babysit that even though he had asked Santa for a real baby alien, it probably wasn't going to happen.

"Sorry, Todd. I'm just buried right now in superexciting deposition reviews."

"Sure, no problem. Hey, we missed you last night. You'll have to come out with us soon." He grinned that smile at me, scratched the back of his head and then stood up, five-feet-ten inches of classic Abercrombie & Fitch beautiful looks.

I flashed him an apologetic smile and returned to my depositions. It was 11:00 a.m. Only eleven or twelve hours to go.

My first two weeks passed excruciatingly slowly. Other than learning office politics, I garnered few legal skills besides filing, typing and deposition review, most of which I had mastered already. My only solace was thinking about the upcoming week—when Broward would be in Fort Lauderdale. I had already cornered Sheila to get the scoop on office hours during that time.

"Nine-to-five workdays," she promised me, an understanding look in her eyes. "This week been rough on you?"

Her voice had taken on a motherly concern, and I wanted to hug her for showing some compassion. Everyone else in the wing seemed to work with an unending supply of energy. It wouldn't have sucked so bad if I hadn't been hearing about the party life in the East Wing.

The East Wing had their own set of big, dark walnut-and-leather double doors. The only glimpses you got inside came when someone was entering or leaving. It was like a super-exclusive club that I couldn't get into, so my mind created impossibly extravagant fantasies about the world inside. Following closely the instructions—or threats—of Broward, I stayed away from the East Wing and all of its "activities," but drooled jealously from afar.

Often as I passed their big double doors, I'd hear loud laughter and other sounds coming from inside. On Wednesday, there was some kind of a party. At five-thirty, Smith & Wollensky waiters started unloading trays of lobsters, steaks and carts of large silver dishes from our elevators. They were followed with five cases of chilled champagne and sumptuous dessert trays that made my mouth water. Muted music could be heard from behind their doors, and a thumping bass. The bass only lasted about three minutes before Broward screamed some form of profanity, opened his door and stomped his way over to the East Wing. About a minute later, the music was turned down and our floor stopped systematically vibrating. Sheila leaned backward in her chair until she could see into my office and winked at me.

The East Wing, unless they were partying, never stayed past 6:00 p.m. The North Wing, Clarke's domain, worked till about eight-thirty most nights. We, the West Wingers, were the night owls. Most Broward paralegals stayed till about 9:30 p.m. I stayed till Broward left, which normally ended up being sometime between ten and eleven. It was better than manual labor, but still mentally exhausting. I went straight home each night, showered, crawled into bed and fell asleep before my head hit the bed. Eat, sleep and work had been the past two weeks of my life. I leaned my head on Sheila's shoulder and signed dramatically.

"There, there," she said, patting my shoulder. "I promise you, you'll get used to it."

The first weekend of my internship I had wallowed in bed the entire time, eating Sour Patch Kids and watching Cameron Diaz movies. Seeing as how texts and Facebook posts from my friends had started to drop off, I figured I needed to spend this weekend back in the land of the living. Friday evening, getting home at a remarkably early 8:00 p.m., I returned two weeks' worth of missed calls. After begging for forgiveness and promising to do better, I cajoled my two closest friends into margaritas and Mexican food at Los Amigos, a run-down college hangout four blocks from my house. My plan was to get sloshed on margaritas, then stumble home—the perfect "college girl gets snatched by a serial killer" scenario, but at twenty-one years old, it sounded like a reasonably good plan.

At 9:30 p.m., dressed in a blue sundress and heels, my hair loose and makeup subdued, I wrestled through the line outside the bar and made my way inside. My skin was paler than usual due to my recent inability to spend any time outside, but I still turned a few heads. I saw Olivia and Becca perched at a high-top in the corner. The bar was filling up, and it took a few minutes of squeezing through people to get over to them.

"Hola!" I said enthusiastically, giving them both hugs before climbing onto one of the stools. They both had ridiculously huge margarita glasses with goofy straws in front of them, and I looked around for the waiter. He came over shortly, took a cursory look at my ID and then disappeared to get us

some *queso* and chips. Becca didn't wait long to start chewing me out.

"So, seriously," she snapped, glancing at her imaginary watch, "it's been almost two weeks since we've seen you. Unacceptable!" She slapped her well-manicured open palm on the table to emphasize her point.

"Go easy on her, Becca," Olivia chided. "She's working— something you wouldn't understand!" She shot a playful smile in Becca's direction.

Olivia was right—working was something Becca would probably never understand. Her wealthy parents and their generous funding pretty much guaranteed Becca an easy ride to whatever wealthy husband she'd eventually marry. With Becca's perfect body, classic bone structure and disarming personality, she had basically won the genetic lottery.

Olivia was more like me—from working-class parents, barely surviving on student loans and part-time jobs. I was especially tight at the moment, due to my full-time unpaid internship. We were all prelaw students, but I was a semester ahead of them, and therefore the first to undergo the intern experience.

"Really, Jules, how's it going?" Olivia said.

I shrugged. "So far, it's a lot of menial work. My boss is okay, just a complete workaholic."

"Oh, please!" Becca said. "Tell me what he's really like. Is he Mr. Sexy-Aggressive Attorney, or the nerd you'd like to bang some freakiness into?" She grinned at me across her margarita.

"Uhh…neither. Try happily-married-plus-I-wouldn't-hook-up-with-someone-at-the-office sexuality. If that even exists." I smirked at her, taking a big swig of my drink.

Olivia laughed, and Becca's eyes rolled. She leaned forward and pointed at me. "Don't give me that high-and-mighty routine. You make it a profession to tease half the men in this town into drooling oblivion, and leave them high and dry. Don't tell me you would pass up the opportunity to have the upper hand in the office."

I pasted an offended look on my face. "Why, Becca! I can see why you think it's easier to 'actually' have sex with guys, but I enjoy the chase more than the actual rewards. If I slept with every guy I made out with, can you imagine my reputation? Not to mention I'd be pregnant with six kids!"

Olivia cut in. "Sweetie, you have a reputation anyway—as the biggest tease this side of the interstate. There's not a guy on campus who doesn't know your game by now."

They were right in their harassment. I teased guys all the time—got them worked up to the point of excitement and then stopped the action. My methods may have been frowned upon, but it allowed me to preserve my relative innocence and get a confidence boost at the same time. "I assure you, there are plenty of guys on campus who have yet to find out about my teasing ways. I'm not going to fuck guys just because they're worked up."

Becca snagged a chip, dipping it into the cheese, and shrugged at me. "At least suck them off, Jules. Then they're not left hanging, and you can sorta retain your moral high ground."

"Becca, then she wouldn't have the power over them. She wants them to continue wanting her. Wants them to imagine 'what could have been.'" Olivia nodded knowingly.

"Oh my lord—are we done with my pysch evaluation?" I asked. "Why does it matter that I'm a tease? I don't see us giving Becca the third degree when she decides to bang half the lacrosse team!"

Becca was in the middle of a strong rebuttal when I felt an arm slip around my shoulders. "Hey, beautiful," a voice said in my ear. I pulled back and stared into Todd Appleton's face.

"Todd!" I said, surprised to see him out of the office. I hadn't seen much of him in the past two weeks since I was banned from entering the East Wing. He had stopped in once or twice, but I'd always been too busy to chat.

"This seat taken?" he asked, gesturing to the empty stool.

"Not at all!" Becca said, smiling brightly. She flipped her brown hair over her shoulder and leaned forward, flashing Todd her best megawatt smile.

I looked to Olivia for approval, and she rolled her eyes good-naturedly and smiled agreeably at me.

Todd introduced himself to my friends, and then slid onto the stool. He motioned for the waiter, and then leaned back, drumming his fingers on the table. Grabbing a handful of chips, he turned to me.

"All the interns have been going out a few times a week," he said, biting down on a chip covered in cheese. "You should join us sometime."

I shot him a look. "Sure, I'll just swing by on one of my three bathroom breaks."

"Oh, so Julia's been ignoring you, too?" Becca said, leaning forward and showing her ample cleavage.

"Aw, I'm just kidding her," Todd said. "I know that her attorney buries her under work." He brushed the back of his hand gently down my arm, sending a shiver through me. I moved away, catching myself before I smiled at him. *Flirting is fine, but I'm not about to take it further…even though you are so damn hot!*

Becca shot me an inquisitive glance and I sent back a "he's all yours" look. The waiter swung by with a platter of dirty glasses and plates, and Todd put in a drink order.

"So," I said casually, "what's it like working for De Luca?"

Todd snorted and nodded enthusiastically. "It is awesome.

The guy is an absolute animal! You should see him in the courtroom. He rips these guys to shreds!"

"The courtroom?" I interrupted him. "You've been to court?" *This is bullshit! Todd gets plush hours and courtroom experience?*

"Yeah! He took me with him last Monday. It was awesome!"

Five minutes with Todd and I was already a little sick of the word *awesome*. Maybe I was just bitchy about my current situation. Either way, I tried to appear cool and offhand. "What was going on there Wednesday?"

"Wednesday?" Todd's face scrunched up, as if he was concentrating hard. *Seriously!* I wanted to scream at him. Smith & Wollensky, lobster, music, *two days ago,* and you can't remember?!

"Oh!" He slapped his head. "The Hatfield deal! You know the Hatfield family—the media tycoon? Mr. Hatfield finally settled so De Luca threw a mini celebration for the missus."

"*That* was a *mini* celebration?" The words popped out before I could stop them.

Todd looked at me, surprised. "Yeah, well, you know, De Luca throws some big parties. We have a huge client party planned out at his house this weekend." He shrugged as if it was no big deal.

"Are you going?"

"Of course!" He snorted again. "It's going to be, like, awesome! I heard he's hiring strippers!"

WOW. Super Classy. De Luca seemed to live up to the reputation. I took a big sip of margarita and thanked God I hadn't been assigned to him.

One giant margarita later, Todd was still hot, but now not quite as annoying. My drunken haze had turned his juvenile antics into sexy cool. I was starting to weaken, letting his hands do some roaming, when Olivia pulled me aside.

"Seriously, Jules, I'm going to do you a big favor and send you home."

"Whaat...? Why?" My slurred voice sounded drunk, even to me. I waved my hand in front of my face, stopping Olivia from responding. "Never mind, you're right. I'll go." I moved over and hugged Becca, gesturing over the music that I was heading out. She blew me a kiss and waved goodbye.

I hugged Olivia and Todd goodbye. He held the hug a few seconds longer than necessary, then gave me an extra squeeze. Olivia walked me out and offered to call a cab. I waved her away and pulled off my heels, starting the drunken stumble home.

Six

In every successful swinger relationship, there must be a set of rules so that everyone knows their place, and so that no one is offended or taken advantage of. Different couples practice different rules depending on their own preferences.

Seven

Tuesday, 10:00 a.m.

A file folder sat in the center of my desk. I walked into my office and stopped short, staring at it. I instantly knew it didn't belong. It was red. Files on my desk were usually in the blue or green folders that were used for civil litigation or corporate filings. I picked it up hesitantly and thumbed through it. Immediately, I could tell it was a divorce file—Custody and Division of Assets were prominent tabs. I closed the file and tapped it on my desk, thinking, *What to do...*

I could call Ancient Dorothy, tell her that a file had been misdelivered, but that was just silly. I was less than twenty feet from the East Wing. I could just walk over there and deliver it to the first secretary I saw. It would take less than a minute, and then the file would be properly handled. It was the obvious and responsible course of action.

Except that Broward doesn't want you going to the East Wing, my conscience nagged with a know-it-all tone. *What am I, five?* I countered, getting irritated at my conscience. *I'm perfectly capable of returning a file without getting into any trouble.*

Decision made, I grabbed the file and strode out of my office, ducking past Sheila and practically jogging past the remaining open doors. I felt as if the red folder was a giant *Look at Me!* sign advertising my destination. Which, of course, it kind of was. I tucked the folder under my arm and willed myself to be invisible. My concern was unnecessary. No one even looked up, everyone absorbed in the ever-present pile of work. Broward being out of town didn't mean the presses stopped.

I took a last-minute detour into the restrooms located just to the right of the elevators and appraised myself in the mirror above the sink. The light in the bathroom was muted, but it was bright enough to show me that it was not my best day. Whether intentional or not, my knowledge that Broward would not be in this week had caused me to dress down and not put as much effort into my appearance. I was wearing khakis, a pressed white button-down shirt and one of my new pairs of sensible, low, open-toed heels. My hair was, as always, up in a bun, and I had opted for glasses instead of my normal contacts. Some people think of glasses as sexy. Those people haven't seen my glasses. Coke bottles would be a more apt description.

I had neglected to put on makeup, which meant I had pale, untouched skin and dark circles under my eyes. I knelt and opened up the sink cabinet and fished around behind a tampon box, reaching into the dark depths and feeling blindly until my hand bumped against what I was looking for: my small cloth makeup bag.

My first day I had packed an emergency makeup kit, one that included mascara, lip gloss and concealer. I had stored it there in case I ever needed to freshen up before a big meeting, or hadn't had time to do my face before work. I sent a silent thank-you up to God for blessing me with such incredible foresight, and hauled myself back up to a standing position.

Three minutes later I looked reasonably presentable. I still had my thick glasses, but I had long, plump lashes behind them and my lips had some color. The dark shadows were still present, but minimized by the concealer.

I grabbed the red file folder, opened the door and scolded my nervous butterflies. Then I straightened my shoulders, pulled open the heavy bathroom door and headed for the East Wing.

Eight

Rule 1: She is kept blindfolded for the first meeting. If the blindfold is to be taken off, it must be done by her alone.

The heavy East Wing double doors opened to a sea of noise and activity. People were everywhere, and everyone seemed to be very important, very busy or very emotional. I stopped just inside the doors and tried to get my bearings.

The room was large, dominated by three oversize curved secretarial desks that created a semicircle at the back of the room. To get to the secretaries, there was a wide path flanked on either side by leather seating clusters. Both seating arrangements were full. One seemed to hold a meeting in progress; the other had two leggy blondes and an older man in a suit, apparently waiting for something. To the right was a large glass conference room, another meeting in progress. I could hear muted tones of what sounded like an argument coming from that side. On the left were offices, probably holding paralegals and Todd. Behind the secretaries was a large office with floor-to-ceiling windows through which I could see the downtown skyline. I could also see a man standing at his desk, a phone to his ear. Judging from the size of the office and its view, I assumed it was De Luca's. Okay, Julia. Get in, get out, and stop gawking.

I moved quickly and—I hoped—confidently toward the secretary cluster. Their three desks were elevated, and I felt like a defendant approaching the judge. The secretaries all seemed cut from the same cloth: old, dignified and spicy. Headmistress-style seemed to be De Luca's preference. Or perhaps HR's preference for De Luca. The center headmistress wore a red suit and had a brass nameplate on her desk that indicated her name was Carol Featherston.

She looked up as I approached and her sharp gaze immediately locked on the red folder held in my now-sweaty clutches. She skipped a greeting and held out her hand. I passed the file meekly over. Her phone started to ring, but she ignored it and flipped quickly through the file, then snapped it shut and looked back at me.

"Where did you get this?"

"I'm Julia Campbell, from Broward's office. I—"

"Where did you get this?" Her piercing gaze and shrill voice told me to get to the point.

"It was on my desk, ma'am."

"All right, I'll handle it. Thank you." The snappy response seemed to indicate that I was done. I couldn't imagine this woman planning stripper-filled parties. Todd must have been exaggerating. I smiled politely at her and turned to leave. My exit was interrupted by a loud rapping of knuckles on glass. I paused midturn and glanced back at Ms. Featherston. She held up a finger and glanced over her shoulder. I followed her gaze.

A bear of a man stood at the glass partition of the large office with the view. He had the build of an ex-athlete—impossibly broad shoulders and muscular arms that his thousand-dollar dress shirt couldn't hide. He had olive skin and a thick head of hair—strong, handsome features. He would have been too good-looking if it weren't for the fierceness of his features. He looked like the kind of man who chased confrontation down and then ate it for breakfast. Phone to his ear, his knuckles were still rapping the glass when my eyes met his. He pointed one finger at me and then motioned for me to come, turning his back and pacing away without waiting for a response. *Uh-oh.*

I must have had panic on my face when Ms. Featherston turned back to me. Her stiff expression softened slightly; her tone was a little kinder, but still firm.

"Go on in," she said. "He wants you."

Ms. Featherston returned her attention to the file. I glanced around, looking for an escape, and then, wobbly, made my way around the secretary stand to the door of the office. Brad De Luca was printed on a brass nameplate in the center of the door. *Broward is going to kill me.*

I opened the door without knocking and walked in, shutting it quietly behind me. I stood by the entrance, hands together in front of me, and waited for De Luca to get off the phone. His office was long, and there seemed to be a silly amount of space between where I stood and where he paced. *I'm not moving a damn step closer to this man if I can help it.* I seemed to be having trouble breathing. My chest was tight. Beads of sweat were forming on my upper lip. I tried to discreetly wipe them off. *What the hell am I so nervous about? He's not going to eat me, for Christ's sake.*

He finished his conversation and hung up the phone, staring at me. Looking into his eyes, I felt my knees buckle slightly. There was this draw to him, this indescribable pull that I couldn't break from. He emitted, even across the large office, a wave of power, intelligence…and sexuality. *No freaking won-*

der everyone talked about this man. Seeming to be completely at ease, he picked up a stress ball and squeezed it, never breaking eye contact. I felt like an innocent little fawn stuck in the lion's gaze. I stayed quiet and waited for his gorgeous self to say something.

"I need a car," he finally said. His voice was sexy and deep, definitive. He sounded like a man who had never second-guessed a single action his entire life. I, on the other hand, was second-guessing every predisposed opinion I had made about him. Maybe Broward and Sheila were right to be worried.

"A car?" My voice came out a little higher than I had intended, almost a squeak. *I definitely needed to get my shit together.*

"Yes. I know the casino typically handles my transportation, but I plan to go on a side trip this weekend, and want a car." He picked up his phone and started to punch in a number, as if to indicate that our conversation was over. Then he paused, looking at me again, closer, his eyes narrowing slightly, his gaze sweeping over my body in an obvious perusal. I bristled slightly, crossing my arms over my chest, feeling my cheeks warm.

When he spoke, his tone was slightly confused. "Have you done something different?"

"Different?" I didn't really know what to say. This was the strangest interaction I had ever had. I'm sure he was blown away by my verbose and witty conversation.

He came around the desk slightly, eyes locked again on mine. *Please don't come closer.* "You look…different."

I felt as if I was in Crazy Town. Has he seen me before? "I'm wearing glasses."

De Luca looked at me again, then something flipped in his eyes, a moment of understanding. He turned away from me, continuing to dial a number, and I understood that our interchange was over.

That was freaking weird.

I walked back to the center desk and waited for Ms. Featherston to look up. She did, after a moment.

"Mr. De Luca asked me to reserve a car? For this weekend?" I sounded inept, even to my own ears.

Featherston looked confused, and then her expression cleared. Her mouth curved into something resembling a smile. "He thinks you're Tiffany," she said wryly.

"Who?"

"Tiffany. The girl downstairs who handles travel arrangements. You look like her…slightly. He must have gotten confused. I'll make sure she gets the message." She shot me an amused look and then refocused on her computer.

I turned on my heel and headed for the doors, wanting to get back to the normalcy of the West Wing. *Wow, talk about an ego check. What a…jerk! So caught up in his own world he mistakes me for someone else—like all of us are bland, interchangeable slaves waiting around to jump to his ridiculous travel needs?* I could feel my irritation building. I pulled my shoulders back and straightened my head, enjoying the anger coursing through my body. It felt good having some of my backbone again.

Back at my desk, I pulled out my cell and sent a quick text to Olivia. Dinner and drinks tonight?

Her response was quick, and affirmative. We agreed, through a series of texts, to meet at 8:00 p.m. at Café Salsa, a downtown tapas bar known for their great bands. I locked my phone and put it back in my purse. I planned on enjoying this Broward-free week, and damned if I'd let that asshole De Luca affect it. I attacked my pile of files with new gusto.

★ ★ ★

A few moments after the double doors closed behind that delicious ass, Brad dialed a second number, watching the stately secretary outside his office answer her phone.

"Yes, Mr. De Luca?"

"Who was that?"

A soft chuckle sounded in his ear, and she spun in her chair, meeting his eyes through the thick glass. "*That* was one of the interns. Kent Broward's." She looked at him with a glare that would melt a lesser man's skin. "I trust this will be the last I see of her?"

He met her glare and smiled, turning away and walking to his desk. "I'll think about it."

That night, I dressed to kill, picking out a red minidress and sky-high nude stilettos. I straightened my hair and carefully applied my makeup. Putting on my sexiest lace bra and a matching thong, I shimmied into my dress and then dusted bronzer over my legs, chest and arms. A small black purse in hand, I stood in front of the mirror and gave myself the once-over. *Hot damn, woman. You are looking good.*

At five minutes before eight, Olivia pulled up outside my apartment in her old gray Ford Explorer, blaring Katy Perry. I skittered out on my heels, navigating the overgrown path with care. Entering Olivia's SUV was like crawling into a bubblegum bubble. It smelled yummy and completely feminine, and said *girl* as loud as the feather boa hanging from the rearview mirror could scream.

We sang and car-danced the ten minutes to Café, my spirits rising with every chorus. At the restaurant, we got a great corner table with a view of the dance floor and bar.

"So, give me the goods," she demanded as soon as we sat down.

"What goods?"

"You know! On your new job, life, everything! I haven't seen you in over two weeks, and last weekend didn't count! Becca was there, and that prevents any real conversation from occurring." She giggled to soften her point, but we both knew she meant it. Becca was wonderful, but Becca was all about Becca, twenty-four hours a day. "Any word from Luke?"

I rolled my eyes at her reference to my ex. "No, thank God. He doesn't know about my internship, and I don't think anyone has told him where I live. Has he called you anymore?"

She shook her head in response. "Just that one time. I think I made it pretty clear to him then that he wasn't going to get any information from me."

I brought my martini up to signal a toast. She followed suit.

"To new beginnings."

"To new beginnings," she parroted. We clinked glasses and both took generous sips.

"So, tell me about the new job." Her eyes glimmered. "Anything going on with you and that gorgeous hunk we saw at Amigos?"

"Todd?" I grimaced and shook my head. "No, he's too...I don't know...immature. Besides, I don't want to get involved with anyone at work. It's too complicated." I thought of De Luca and my face flushed.

Olivia caught the tell. "What? What is it?"

I told her about De Luca, Broward's warning and today's interchange. She started to giggle and then clamped a hand over her mouth at my glare.

"It's not funny," I hissed.

"Oh, come on! It is funny! You trotted in there thinking that he would bend over backward to woo you, like every other guy you come across. Instead he gave you a menial task and sent you on your way!" She smiled affectionately at me, and patted my arm. "It's okay, Jules. Not everyone is susceptible to your charms."

I shrugged and was on the verge of a witty comeback when a server materialized at our table with two martini glasses filled with blue, glowing liquid. "Ladies, these drinks are from the table by the stage." He deposited the drinks in front of us and disappeared before we had time to formulate a response. I drew my blue martini close and tried to glance discreetly over my shoulder. Three suits by the stage nodded and raised their drinks. I gave them a quick smile and turned back to Olivia.

"What do you think?"

Olivia leaned to the side and spoke over the sugary rim of her new drink.

"Fairly cute. They look successful, a little old."

"How old?"

"Umm...late twenties? Maybe even thirty." She said *thirty* as if it was ancient. Which, for us, it was.

"Any wedding rings?"

She tried discreetly to squint and instead came off looking as if she had discreetly farted.

"Stop that," I snapped. "We can look up close." *What the hell, I put on this dress for a reason, right?* I turned in my chair, flashed my best smile and gestured for the guys to come over. Time to have some fun.

Two hours later

Screw Becca and Olivia's opinion, I was a cock tease, and wasn't about to be ashamed of it. The chase gave me purpose, excitement; it was my favorite part of being single. Sex or a reputation were things I didn't need or want. For me, teasing was more of a conquest thing, and it gave me an instant ego boost when I needed one.

I definitely needed one tonight. De Luca, having me—even if it was a rumpled, dorky version of me—in his office, and not even giving me a second glance. Worse, mistaking me for someone else! He was old, for Christ's sake, even if he did radiate sex from every pore on his gorgeous body. As a rumored horndog, he should have smiled, flirted or asked me out—even if I had planned on saying no. Yes, I definitely needed an ego boost, and my evening's prey waited in front of me.

Bob, a twenty-nine-year-old tax accountant with a bird chest and moderately muscular arms, lay flat on his back on top of his bed, gazing at me in drunken adoration. Stripped down to my black lace bra and thong, I straddled him. My hair fell loose down my back and I leaned forward, nibbling and kissing his neck. He moaned, and I could feel his erection pushing at his dress pants, begging to get out. His hands roamed down my back over the curve of my hips and grabbed my ass. Continuing to tease his neck, I reached down and slid my hand underneath his pants' waist and felt the hardness of his cock. It was pretty nice compared to the ones I had previously touched. I grabbed it firmly, jacked him up and down twice and let him think for a minute that I was going to do more. Then I slyly bit my bottom lip, shook my head at him and pulled my hand out.

The fire in his eyes died a little and he looked at me with intense yearning. *Right there, that is what I want to see.* My confidence felt that familiar swell, but it was brief this time. It sank again quickly, almost as low as before. I gritted my teeth in irritation, pushing back against my subconscious, trying to feel that satisfaction I normally experience. But it was gone.

I leaned forward, kissing Bob gently, then climbed off him, reaching for my dress, half listening to his sputtering words. *Sorry, buddy, you're done.*

Nine

Wednesday, 8:15 a.m.

Brad De Luca's cell rang for the seventh time that morning.

"De Luca," he snapped into the phone.

"Julia Campbell," his cousin Tony's voice rang through the phone. Tony was a forty-year-old divorcé, with three kids, who drank full-time and painted houses as a hobby. Brad couldn't remember the last time he had spoken to Tony before 11:00 a.m. He must need money. He groaned silently and waited for more.

"You know her?" Tony asked.

His mind searched his recent clients, conquests and acquaintances and came up blank.

"No, don't believe I do."

Tony's voice slurred a bit. "She's an intern at your office."

"Oh. She's probably with Broward or Clarke. They keep the female interns away from me."

Tony laughed so hard he began to hiccup. "I bet they do, man! You'd be slaying them!"

Brad glanced at his watch impatiently and willed the man

to get to the point. "Who's she to you, Tony?" His voice had taken on the rough brogue of his Italian childhood.

"I got a call this morning from Bob Hanstle—the yuppie guy whose kitchen I'm painting? He's trying to get information about her. He knows she works for your firm, and, given my last name…thought I might know someone over there."

"Your last name isn't De Luca."

"Yeah, well, I might have mentioned that we're related." Brad's patience waned. Tony probably "mentioned" Brad's name at every job opportunity he got, in hopes of increasing his credibility.

"I don't know anything about her." He tried to convey a tone of wrapping up the conversation, but Tony wouldn't let it go.

"Come on, Brad, give me something. This guy is desperate over this chick. She must have a magic pussy, man."

"Sorry, Tony. Never met her before." He hung up the phone. *So…it must have been Broward's intern. And she had another man hot on her trail.* He really needed to get to the office.

I woke up buried in the soft sheets of my cozy bed. I stretched, rolled over and winced at the hangover headache that was pounding in my temples. I pulled my eye mask up and glanced at my bedside clock. Holy shit! 7:45 a.m. I attempted to jump out of bed and was squashed back down by the invisible stakes that were piercing some important cerebral mass in my head. I tried again, slower this time, and ended up on my feet. Glancing into the mirror next to my door, I saw a face smeared with makeup and a distinct floral skin design that I recognized from the embroidery on my pillow. Ugh.

I grabbed powder-blue capris, a white cardigan-camisole set and some tan heels. I didn't have time to shower, so I scrubbed my face as quickly as I could and threw on some light makeup.

As any party girl will tell you, one-day-old going-out hair looks pretty damn good, so I ran my fingers through it and headed out the door.

I was in the fourth-floor kitchen, buttering a stale biscuit and licking some melted butter off my fingers when he walked in.

Whoa.

It was as if every ounce of extra air left the room in that instant, squeezing all the space out with it and putting me front and center in his laser beam. Damn. We locked eyes and neither one of us moved. In his office there had been a long, empty expanse between us, and even then there'd been a sizzle. Now, there in the small kitchen, the full force of his… essence…was magnified tenfold. It scared the crap out of me.

His eyes were a normal dark brown color, not anything special, but they blazed with a powerful intensity. He smelled of…something. I don't know how to describe the smell, but it was intoxicating and animal. The man reeked of masculinity and sex. He seemed to be a big, tight ball of controlled energy and I could just as easily imagine him ripping someone's head off as dipping me backward into a kiss. As I stood there, frozen, his sexy features curled into a smile and he looked as if he wanted to eat me. I backed up and bumped into the counter. I was acutely aware of the butter all over my fingers—and dripping from the edge of my mouth. I licked my lips and said the first thing that popped into my mind.

"I'm not Tiffany."

His smile faltered slightly, and he shook his head and chuckled. "I know."

"I'm Julia. Julia Campbell. Broward's intern."

"I know."

"You do?"

"Yes. I just asked Sheila where to find you. She said you were in here."

"Oh." A pause. His eyes never left mine. "Why were you looking for me?"

"Would you like to go to lunch?" He turned on some powerful, magical force, and radiated with intense sexual heat. I almost swooned, but caught myself. *Keep it together, you damn woman!*

"Umm, no."

"No?" His grin increased and he looked almost incredulous. He glanced around as if wanting someone to witness this.

"No." My voice grew in strength and confidence. *Cocky prick.*

"Why?" He moved closer and I lost all sense of reality. The man was like no one I'd ever met. I could see why divorcing wives would throw apart their legs and beg him for more than lawyerly duties. The man was walking, breathing sex. I had never found bodybuilders or large men attractive. I had pined for and worshipped the rail-thin, pretty look of male models. But this man was built like a god, with the disposition of Satan. I couldn't imagine being an intern to this man and not doing more than filing his briefs.

I would have moved back farther, but the kitchen counter rail was already digging into my ass and no doubt now leaving a bruise. I met his amused gaze and tried to portray nonchalance.

"For one thing, you're a little old."

His eyes flickered a bit at that, but he kept his thoughts to himself. "And?"

"*Annnddd,* I'm not supposed to talk to you." Even to my ears, that sounded juvenile.

His egotistic smirk was back. "Ahhh…yes. Broward wants to keep you all to himself."

I didn't like that response, but kept my mouth shut and let my eyes communicate my silent retort.

"Let's go to Centaur."

"No. I have work to do."

"Come on—I'll have you back in a flash. No one will even know you're gone."

"I—"

"Julia!" Sheila stood in the doorway, glaring at De Luca. He had the good grace to look sheepish, which also looked ridiculously sexy. *Good lord. Someone needs to take this man out back and shoot him.*

I fled to the safety of Sheila's side, taking my buttery fingers with me and leaving my plate and knife behind.

"I need Julia," Sheila said. "Are you all through with whatever it was you needed her for?" Her expression painted her opinion clearer than any billboard could.

De Luca nodded a goodbye to me and strode out of the kitchen, winking at me and patting Sheila on the shoulder as he passed. I could suddenly breathe a lot easier. Sheila turned and affixed me with a steely stare, all evidence of grandmotherly goodness gone. "Is this going to be a problem?" she demanded.

"I don't know what you're talking about."

"Good."

Ten

11:45 a.m.

I didn't know what I had been doing the past two and a half hours, but it hadn't been anything productive. I twirled a pencil around my hand and debated whether or not I should ask someone for an Advil. My phone rang, a shrill sound that drilled into my headache with unsympathetic persistence.

"Julia Campbell."

"It's Beverly." Beverly was Broward's number two secretary, a plump redheaded woman who thought that stripes and polka dots matched, and had an extreme habit of oversharing everything. I mean everything. The second day I met her she "confided" in me that she'd once contracted genital herpes from a gas station restroom toilet. *Need I say anything more?* She would.

"Hi, Beverly."

"We need you to run over to OfficeMax. Rick in IT just called, and apparently they're having some kind of technical crisis that can only be solved by a…T-I44 FireWire cable port, whatever that is. We would go, but De Luca's office is having us run a gabillion copies for some last-minute filing and the—"

"No problem, Beverly. I'll do it now." *And stop by CVS and grab every hangover remedy they've got.*

"Are you sure? I hate to ask you, but if we don't get—"

"Yes. I'm sure. I'll do it now."

"Great! Thanks, Julia. Just run it to IT when you get back. It's on the second floor, next to the—"

"I know where it is."

"*Oh-kay!* Thanks, Julia."

"You're welcome."

I hung up the phone and rose, glad for a chance to get out of the office. I slid my heels on, grabbed my purse and practically skipped to the elevator, avoiding even looking in the direction of the East Wing doors. *Take that, Brad De Luca!*

I took the elevator directly to the parking garage and exited, looking to the right for my car. One of the firm's black town cars was idling near my Camry. The driver's tinted window rolled down as I approached. A twenty-something white kid in a chauffeur's uniform was seated in the driver's seat, and spoke to me as I passed.

"Ms. Campbell?"

"Yes?" I stopped in surprise, staring at him.

"I've been instructed to drive you to the store."

"What?"

"I'll drive you to the store."

"No, I'm fine. Thank you."

He ignored me and got out, walked around to the backseat door and opened it. I glared at him.

"I can drive myself. I'm a big girl."

"Get in the car." The order came not from the pimple-faced driver, but from inside the car. It only took a second for me to identify the deep, authoritative voice, and I shoved Pushy Driver aside and leaned over, looking into the car.

"You listen to me," I hissed, pointing my finger in De Luca's face. "I am not one of your strippers you can order around! I am *busy* at work and—" My tirade was interrupted when De Luca burst into laughter, his entire torso shaking. My finger sagged a bit but remained pointed at him, and I fought the ridiculous urge to laugh myself.

"Strippers! Jeff—did you hear that?" Jeff started to smile, and I turned with a snap and shot him the stoniest glare I could. His smile faded but stayed in his eyes. *They're laughing at me. Dammit. I don't care if he is a partner in the law firm that my future is riding on, I—*

"I don't know what you've heard about me, but I take all the new interns out. Ask Todd. We went out as a group last week, but Broward had you stuck in preparation for that boring-as-hell mediation that he flopped at. I've taken that Asian intern out three times, for Christ's sake—what's his name—Anton Wu? Something like that. So, despite what you think of me, I am just trying to give you the same courtesy I give all the interns—the pleasure of my company and infinite knowledge." He raised both hands in a "trust me I'm innocent" gesture. His cocky smile infuriated me, but my balloon of propriety had deflated.

I stared at him, thinking. My ego, brain and mouth were all totally confused. My headache screamed silently at me, making it even harder to reason. My shoulders finally slumped. "Really?"

He grinned out at me. "Really."

"Okay," I said glumly, getting into the car.

Jeff closed the door once my legs were safely inside. He hummed a little tune as he returned to his rightful place in the front seat. I wanted to smack him. I dreaded doing so, but turned and tried, rather unsuccessfully, to smile at De Luca and convince him to forget the little hissy fit that had just occurred.

He didn't bite.

He relaxed in the car beside me, such a large man that he took up a seat and a half without really meaning to. He looked at me with interest, studying me. I tried to sit as close to the other door as possible without making it obvious. I could feel myself beginning to have trouble breathing again. *Damn this man.* I couldn't think of anything to say, and the silence was starting to get uncomfortable, at least for me. He didn't seem anything other than totally at ease.

"Are we going to OfficeMax?" I finally said.

"No."

"What about the…cable port thingy?"

"We are going to Centaur. For lunch."

"I told you I didn't want to go to lunch. Do you just take everything you want?" As soon as the words popped out, I wished I could take them back. *Firm partner, Julia. Remember that, for God's sake!*

He seemed amused by the question. "Yes, normally. I've found it's easier to ask for forgiveness than permission. Plus, I already asked, and you said no."

Oh, okay. So he's daft. I nodded politely and tried to put a respectful look on my face. I don't think I succeeded.

"Do you like Centaur?"

"I've never been. It's a little out of my budget."

"You'll like it. You do eat meat?"

My dirty mind chuckled to itself, but I kept my tone mild. "Yes, I eat meat."

His mouth turned up slightly, a smirk he tried unsuccessfully to keep in check. I looked away, trying to remain composed, but fighting a ridiculous urge to smile myself. *Keep laughing, De Luca. I plan on putting a porterhouse on this bill.*

The town car pulled through big gates and past freshly cut lawns up to a huge white Southern-style farmhouse with deep porches and thick columns. The entrance steps were flanked on either side by centaur statues. The well-manicured lawn, impressive structure and white-gloved valets screamed *expensive*. An attendant sprang to action when the car stopped, and pulled open my door. I accepted his outstretched hand, swung a leg out and stood up, squinting in the bright sun. My headache was drumming its fingers on my cerebral cortex.

I walked around the car and met De Luca at the base of the steps. He gestured for me to go ahead, and I stepped forward. As I climbed the stairs, he placed a gentle hand on the base of my back. A delicious shiver ran through me and my subconscious smacked it down as if it was a wandering fly.

The maître d' instantly recognized De Luca and beamed. "Mr. De Luca! Come, come, I will put you at your favorite table!" He grabbed two leather-bound menus and led us through the restaurant. It was packed, and as we traversed through the tables, we were stopped several times by different men standing up to shake De Luca's hand and say a sentence or two in greeting. When we finally arrived at the table—a large four-top in the back corner—I sank into the seat in relief. Before I had a chance to open my menu, a tuxedo-clad waiter appeared.

"Mr. De Luca, how are you?"

"Very good, Mimmo."

"The usual?"

"Yes, please."

Mimmo turned and disappeared. I glanced at De Luca over the menu.

"Is he going to ask me what I want to drink?"

"No. Is wine acceptable?"

My headache raised both its hands and waved them around. "I'd prefer just water."

He nodded without responding. He ignored the menu and leaned forward on the table, crossing his arms and gazing at me. His biceps stretched the sleeves of his dress shirt and I raised the menu a bit higher, hiding behind it.

"How are you enjoying the internship?"

I lowered the menu slightly and spoke over it. "It's been quite informative. I feel like I'm learning a lot and getting a great base that I'll be able to build a strong legal education around."

He reached over and gently pushed the menu down so that he could look at me. "Is that what you have prepared as your interview spiel?"

I colored slightly. "Maybe."

"Come on. I'm not going to go running to Broward. How is it really going?"

I sighed, not knowing how honest to be. *Hell, the man practically kidnapped you—you can probably be frank.* His eyes were compassionate and gentle, and I didn't see any blood dripping from his teeth.

"It sucks," I admitted. "Broward works these ridiculous hours, and I am nothing more than a glorified secretary. My duties consist of typing and filing, with an occasional coffee run thrown in. Other than the prestige of the firm's name, I am adding nothing to my résumé. The only thing I have figured out is that I *don't* want to do corporate law. The other interns all seem to be learning and doing so much more— Todd has been to court with you, for heaven's sake! I am just trying to get through these next couple of months and then spend the next three weeks sleeping."

His brow arched and he gave me a conspiring look. "I'm

sure you've been doing something other than sleeping in your time off."

I didn't respond. *Where the hell is that coming from?*

He leaned back as our waiter brought two empty glasses and then filled them from a chilled Voss water bottle. "I know that Kent can be a hard-ass, but keep your morale up. You will learn something, even if it's how to bill ridiculously long hours. If you want to see how the other half lives, you can always spend a day in either my or Clarke's office. We normally sub the interns around a bit—let them see the other disciplines." The waiter held out a bottle of wine for his inspection, and De Luca looked at it and nodded.

"I don't think I'll be spending much time in the other wings. Mr. Broward seems pretty intent on keeping me in our office."

His eyes narrowed. "In your office or out of mine?"

I shifted uncomfortably, my body language no doubt answering the question before my lips even opened. "More likely the second."

He waved away the offer to taste the wine and the waiter took the hint, hurriedly pouring two glasses and then scurrying away.

"I recall you making a stripper comment earlier. I'm not sure what you have been told about me, but I'm not nearly as bad as they make me out to be." His deliciously deep voice carried a little bit of ego.

I'm sure you are exactly as bad as they make you out to be.

"Okay then, let's verify some of the rumors."

The challenge stood on the table between us.

De Luca took a swig of wine, his eyes never leaving mine, and then set it down firmly and nodded at me. *Bring it on.*

I started to open my mouth to speak, and he raised a hand,

stopping me. "Wait. Before I agree, let's make a deal. For every…rumor…you bring up, I get to ask you one question."

I nodded in response. Throwing caution to the wind, I grabbed the second glass of wine and took a sip. I had a feeling I'd need it.

Our duel was postponed again by the overattentive waiter. "Are we ready to order, Mr. De Luca?"

"Sure, Mimmo. I'll have my usual. Julia?"

I had barely looked at the menu, but went with my initial thought. "Porterhouse, please. Medium rare."

Mimmo raised a brow but did not comment on my choice. "Would you care for a salad?"

"No. Baked potato, please. Just butter."

"Certainly." He did a little bow and departed.

De Luca looked back at me.

Okay, let's go. "Have you ever slept with an intern?"

"Yes." The answer was said matter-of-factly, without shame or pride. As if he had answered another question entirely.

"Details?"

"I'll save that for a second date."

"We aren't having a second…date."

"We'll see. My turn. Why did you choose CDB for your internship?"

"It's the best. I have no desire to settle for second best."

"Have you been with the best in the past?"

"I've never had a job before."

"That's not what I meant."

I shot him a look. He put up his hands in feigned innocence and grinned.

"Why do you think I've been told to avoid you?" I asked.

He shrugged and took a sip of the wine. "All good reasons, I'm sure."

"That's evasive."

"I'm an attorney. It's my job."

"And you think you're good at your job."

He raised an eyebrow. "I know I'm good at my job. There's a reason I have a ten-month wait."

"I've heard other reasons that divorcing females might want to wait for your services."

"Meaning?"

"Sex."

"So you think I'm good at *that* job?" His eyes brimmed with mischievousness, and I suddenly had a very good idea of what he would have been like as a ten-year-old boy.

"You're being evasive again."

"Just trying to figure out what you think you know."

"Do you sleep with your clients?"

"Just the female ones."

His blatant and unashamed response floored me, and I stumbled over the next question. He had leaned forward, across the table, and was meeting my eyes dead-on. I felt locked into a stare-off.

"All of them?"

"I'm not a gigolo. I have sex for pleasure. If I am not sexually attracted to the woman, there is no purpose in having sex."

"Don't you think that's bad for business?"

"On the contrary, it is extremely good for business." He leaned back and put one hand to his temple, playing with his pinkie with his mouth. His gaze had started to smolder. "I am very good at pleasing women, Julia."

I blushed and looked away, praying for our food to arrive. It did not, but there was a different interruption: a ringing cell phone.

Brad reached for his cell and touched the screen without breaking his gaze at me.

"De Luca…

"At lunch...

"Yes, you can patch her through."

He looked at me apologetically, and looked around for our waiter. Mimmo materialized at his side with a pen and pad in hand. This seemed to be an old pattern they had. De Luca grabbed the pen, looked at his watch and scribbled "12:33 p.m." on the notepad. He ripped off the top page and returned the notepad, but not the pen, to Mimmo.

Hysterical babble could be heard from the phone pressed to De Luca's ear. To his credit, he listened intently to the hysterics without an eye roll or sign of impatience. At the first pause, he spoke. "Claudia, listen to me. You need to trust that we know what we are doing and we will handle it. I will have him covered by the private investigator. He won't sneak anything by us on my watch, I promise you."

More hysterical shouting, then something that sounded like pleading.

"Those assets are safe. We already have a court motion in place that has frozen those. Please relax, Claudia. Why don't you let me send Alfonzo over? He can massage those worries right out of you."

I tuned his conversation out when Mimmo brought our food. My steak was enormous and smelled incredible. I had my knife and fork ready and dived in the moment the plate hit the table. De Luca shot me a bemused look, which I ignored, chewing furiously. The steak had just enough fat to add flavor, and was tender and perfectly cooked. I liked my steaks bloody, and this fit the bill. I paused in my intake to sip some wine. The glass was full. I stopped and looked at it. *Did I finish the first glass? Or did he refill this early?* I shook my head and pushed it to the side, reaching for the water glass instead. I needed to keep my head clear, given the temptation sitting across from me. Plus, I had broken enough cardinal rules for the day. I didn't want to add Drunk at Work to the tally.

I was eighty percent through my steak and had demolished the baked potato when De Luca finally ended the call. He glanced at his watch again and wrote "12:42 p.m." on the piece of scrap paper. I glanced at it and rolled my eyes.

"You're going to bill her for *nine* minutes?"

"It was nine minutes I could have spent talking to you. And yes, at eight hundred and fifty dollars an hour, I damn sure am going to bill for nine minutes."

"Not ten?"

His mouth twitched. "Not ten. For the same reason."

Well, it looks like the man has some shred of moral fiber. Shocker.

"I've got to get back to the office." He mumbled the words through a hefty bite of steak.

"Do we have time to run an errand?"

"Depends on what it is. Rick in IT is not expecting you to return with a…cable port thingy? I think that's how you referred to it."

"I need to go by CVS."

"For what?"

"If you must know, a pregnancy test." I kept a straight face and he blinked, taken aback. He squinted at me, trying to figure out if I was serious. I kept my iron facade. For about four seconds. Then I burst out giggling. "God—you are easy! I need headache medicine. But you, of all people, with your stable of women, should know to never ask a woman what she needs at the drugstore."

He grinned. Reaching for his phone, he unlocked it and then pressed a number into the phone. "Jeff. We will be ready for pickup in about five minutes. Check the car for some Advil or Tylenol. If there isn't any, go grab some. We'll see you in the valet area in a bit." He hung up the phone and returned to his steak.

"I could have picked up my own medicine."

"We're already short on time. They'll wonder what's been keeping you."

"Scared of Sheila?"

He grinned again, looking up from his steak. "Terrified. That woman is worse than my mother."

His steak was already half-gone, and the remaining bit didn't have a chance. The man didn't believe in wasting time. Mimmo appeared at my side.

"Ms. Campbell. I've taken the liberty of wrapping a few of our house truffles for your enjoyment later."

How does this man know my name? I nodded my thanks and placed the small, exquisitely wrapped package into my purse.

He left, taking a handful of our plates with him. De Luca stood, shoveling a few more pieces of meat into his mouth, and then reached for my hand.

"Let's go."

I stood quickly and grabbed my purse. "Shouldn't we wait for the check?"

"I have a house account. They know what to tip." He wiped his face with the cloth napkin and tilted his head, indicating that we should leave. I allowed him to lead me out, but pulled my hand free as we approached the front doors. A doorman held the door for us, and we exited into the hot summer air.

The town car sat in front, Jeff standing by it. As he opened my door, he handed me a small plastic bag. Giving me a casual smile, he gently shut the door once I was fully inside. I peeked into the bag and pulled out a small bottle of Advil and a bottle of water. *Sweet salvation.* My headache jumped up and down, cheering. I twisted open the Advil bottle, popped three in my mouth and sucked down half the bottle of water.

De Luca spent the ride back to the office on the phone. I leaned back in the seat, the heavy food and wine making me sleepy. We were back in the garage before I knew it, and I glanced around before reaching for the door handle.

"Relax." De Luca spoke from the other seat, having disconnected his call. He reached over and grabbed my knee, trying to reassure me—I think, but the connection of our bodies was a shock to my system, and I stifled a gasp.

I swatted his hand away. "If Broward finds out I—"

"Do you always do as you're told?"

I gave him a death glare, but his demeanor didn't waver one bit. "Yes, I typically do."

"You should learn to bend the rules."

"You should learn to follow them!" I retorted, smiling a bit. "Good afternoon, Mr. De Luca. Thank you for the ridiculously expensive lunch."

"I enjoyed it."

I didn't know how to respond to that, and opened the car door. Jeff was standing there, and I gave him a small smile and rushed to the elevators. I pressed the button and waited, glancing back at the black car. It stayed there, idling, Jeff once again in the driver's seat. The bell dinged and the door opened. Thankfully, the elevator was empty. I entered, pressed the button for the fourth floor and leaned against the wall. I felt as though I had dodged a bullet, had skipped across glowing coals and then had tied myself securely to the tracks of an oncoming train. The bell dinged, sounding eerily like a far-off train whistle.

Eleven

Rule 2: She is mine and not yours. Remember that.

Day three of no Broward loomed ahead of me and I woke up early in nervous anticipation. Knowing full well that I was headed straight to hell, I dressed for success in a navy wrap dress that hugged my ass perfectly, and leather-and-gold Prada stilettos that had been a gift from Becca. I added a chunky gold necklace and put my hair up in a messy bun. Taking extra care with my makeup, I made sure that I looked amazing before trotting out of the house.

At 7:40 a.m. I slid into my chair, turning on my computer and checking my voice mail. One from Broward.

"Julia—this is Kent. Just checking in to see how things are going. You must have already left for the evening. I sent you a few emails—give me a call if you have any questions. I will be in court all morning tomorrow, so try me in the afternoon if you need me."

I deleted the voice mail and stared at my computer's opening scripts, willing them to hurry. I wanted to take care of Broward's emails first, and then try and finish some of the legal research that I had been putting off. My phone rang.

Ancient Dorothy's voice creaked through the phone. "Julia, you have a delivery. Is it okay if I send it up?"

I checked my watch: 7:45 a.m. Early delivery. "Yes, Dorothy. Thank you." I assumed it was FedEx bringing an 8:00 a.m. express package. My computer finally loaded the log-in screen and I quickly entered my credentials. Scrolling through to my first email from Broward, I heard a light knock at my door.

"Julia?"

A moderately attractive man stood in my doorway in a gray suit and blue tie. He held a large arrangement of lilies and orchids. I squinted at the man, who looked familiar, and then it hit me. Billy, Ben, no—Bob. From the other night. *Oh, Jesus. This is bad.*

"Bob!" I tried to interject some hint of pleasure into my voice, but I think I missed the happy tone and ended up with more of a strangled croak.

"I hope it's all right that I stopped by. I remember you saying that you interned here. I couldn't get through on the number you gave me, and I sent you a friend request on Facebook—and I stopped by yesterday but you were out...." His rushed speech faltered and I think he realized how desperate he sounded. "I just wanted to stop by and give you these." He took two steps forward and thrust the flowers into my desk space. The glass vase hung from his outstretched hands as if it would slip at any moment. I had no choice but to take them.

"Bob, these are beautiful. Thank you." I buried my face in the arrangement and sniffed, trying to think of what else to say. They *were* beautiful, and judging by the size of the arrangement, expensive.

"Would you want to go out sometime? I know a great Italian place, just around the corner, not a far trek from here."

"I can't, Bob. I just got out of a bad relationship, and I'm just not ready yet." *My oldest and most faithful letdown.* His face fell but he maintained his smile.

"Hey, I understand. Can I leave you my number, though? So when you're ready...just in case you lost it before."

I didn't lose it, Bob. I tossed it in the trash. Similar to the way I denied your friend request.

"Of course. I'll save it. If things change I'll give you a call."

His pathetic response, an face-splitting grin, made me wince inside. He came around my desk with his arms out, and I stood. *Oh, great.* Bob went for a kiss, but I turned my head and gave him a hug instead. We were pulling out of the hug when De Luca appeared in my doorway.

He leaned against the doorway with his arms folded, filling the entire space with his enormity. He had a dark look in his eyes, and radiated power and masculinity. His gaze went from us to the large arrangement on my desk, then back to Bob and me. "Am I interrupting something?"

Bob paled. I'd hate to see what would happen if we were dating and I was attacked on the street. He'd probably duck into the nearest Starbucks and order a scone to calm his nerves.

"No. Bob was just leaving. Bob, this is Brad De Luca. He is one of my bosses."

Brad's eyes locked with Bob's, and he moved forward and shook his hand firmly. I think I saw Bob wince. My office seemed incredibly small at that moment with Bob, Brad, the ridiculous flowers and me. Bob squeaked out a hello.

"I need to speak to Julia if you both are done here."

Bob smiled shyly at me and fled the office. I crossed my arms and stared at Brad stonily.

"What, pray tell, did you need to speak to me about that couldn't wait?"

"Who is he?"

"Bob. He is a—"

"I know who he is. I meant who is he to you?"

Why does this man think he knows everything? "He is nothing to me."

"Are you dating?"

"Is that any of your business?"

"It is if he's visiting you at work."

"Oh, please! Don't even pull that card."

"Are you dating?"

"No."

He studied me, his eyes possessively roaming down my body and up again, and I felt myself flush. *Thank God I dressed up.* The magnetism he put out was ridiculous. This office was way too small for the two of us.

"Come to Vegas with me this weekend," he said.

"What?"

"I'm going to Vegas this weekend. Why don't you come?" It was more a directive than an invitation.

"Are you serious?"

"Dead serious." He looked serious. And tempting.

I smiled. "I appreciate the offer, but I'll have to pass."

"Think it over. I'll have you back safe and sound by Monday."

"I appreciate the offer, but no."

He raised his eyebrows and looked at me appraisingly. "No boyfriend?"

"No."

"Think it over." He gave me a ridiculously sexy parting smile, turned on one heel and sauntered out.

I sank down in my seat. This was way too much excitement for 8:08 a.m. I tried to focus on Broward's first email, which was still open on my screen.

From: Kent Broward
Subject: ADMA/Bakers/Turner Development
Date: June 12 9:27:22 PM EST
To: Julia Campbell
Julia,
Attached is information for three new S corps. They need corporate documents created.
Two of these S corps—Adma LLC and Bakers Investments Properties will be JV partners on a development. Please prepare an initial draft of an operating agreement between the two. You can use the Henderstone Land JV OA as a template.
KB

I was both excited and dismayed. Excited that this seemed to be the first real legal work I had been given, dismayed that I didn't have the experience or knowledge to complete it. Also dismayed because I had three other emails from Broward and I wasn't sure what other nuggets of goodness those held.

The next two emails were tame by comparison, menial tasks that I would be able to quickly knock out. The last email was only two lines and gave me at least three new wrinkles.

From: Kent Broward
Subject: De Luca
Date: June 12, 2012 11:08:03 PM EST
To: Julia Campbell
Julia,
Sheila said that De Luca was speaking to you in the kitchen. Has he been bothering you? Please keep your distance.
Kent

I groaned silently. *Note to self: Sheila is a rat.* "Has he been bothering you?" *Ummm, don't know how to answer that.* "Keep your distance"? *Wow. I seem to be following that advice superbly.* I marked the email as Unread and vowed to reply to him later.

The rest of the day passed in a blur. I recruited/begged/ bribed Beverly to help with my corporate documents, and stumbled through the operating agreement on my own. I was grinding through the legal research when I glanced at my phone and saw the time: 8:30 p.m. My stomach was growling loudly when salvation appeared at the door. De Luca stood in the doorway, pizza and a six-pack of soda in his hands. I tried not to smile but failed miserably. He beamed back at me.

"I'm not happy to see you—it's the pizza," I said, pushing back from my desk and rubbing my eyes.

"Come on. I already had Todd scope out the office. This whole wing has left for the night. Your dangerous secret will be safe. Let's eat in the conference room."

I stretched and stood up. I was barefoot, and considered putting on my heels, but then decided against it and padded after him. I yawned. "Where's Todd?"

"I sent him home once he gave me the lay of the land."

"Does he know you're over here?"

"I don't know or care. Todd is a smart guy. I'm sure he can figure it out."

Great. Just what I need.

"I'll eat with you because I'm starving and not finished with work, but this is the last time I'm going to have any type of interaction with you."

"Really?"

"Yes, really. Broward is already smelling something. He sent me an email about it today."

"Ahh, yes. I got one of those also."

"And?"

"And what? Do I seem the type to follow Broward's directives?"

I shrugged in response. We had entered the West Wing conference room. The fluorescent lights were in the process of warming back up, so the light was still dim. I wrestled two of the Dr Peppers from the six-pack, placing them on the table. I put the other four cans in the minifridge and grabbed a roll of paper towels. Brad sat down and flipped open the pizza box, taking two slices and spinning the open box to me. I glanced in. Half pepperoni, half meat lover's. I grabbed a slice of each and sat down, the two of us taking up one corner of the long table. There was silence for a moment as we dug in.

He spoke first. "So, this is the last time, huh?"

I nodded in response, my mouth full of pizza.

"You really think you'll be able to stay away from me?"

"Oh, my lord!" I groaned and looked to the ceiling in mock exasperation. "Does your ego have no bounds? As I see it, you've been the one who can't stay away." I waved a pizza crust at him to emphasize my point.

"I take an interest in all of our interns. You are the future of our company."

"Bullshit. Are you telling me you are bringing dinner to your favorite intern, Wu?"

"I'm not attracted to Wu."

"And you are attracted to me?"

"Of course." He had locked his ridiculously sexy stare on me and spoken softly, but with absolute confidence and conviction. I swallowed. I wanted this man so badly it hurt. Knowing I couldn't have him made it that much more delicious.

"Well, if this is truly our last encounter, we might as well make it count."

"Meaning what?" I squeaked.

"I want to know about you. Let's finish our conversation

from lunch. You can ask me anything you want, as long as I have the same privilege."

"I'm not as exciting as you are."

He turned that over in his mind, shaking his head gently as he thought god knew what. I started the game.

"I was told you were recently divorced. True?"

"Yes."

"Details?"

He gave me a wry glance, put his hands together on the table, looked down at them and then at me.

"I have only been married once—to my college sweetheart. We were together eleven years, married for seven of those. Hillary is a great girl, but we were too different, too incompatible. I think we both realized our mistake early on. But we stayed together and miserable, hoping...I don't know...that something would change. Nothing changed, and we separated."

"Who represented her in the divorce?"

He smiled slightly. "No one. We both did it unrepresented."

"That's a little unfair."

"It would have been if I hadn't given her everything. There is nothing more she could have gotten. I'd say it was extremely fair."

"Why did you give her everything?"

"I've seen divorce pull too many people to shreds. It turns people into horrible things, gets them to the point where they hate themselves as much as their exes. It happened to my parents, and is one of the reasons I went into this business. I make sure that I am the animal, the horrible one. I don't want them to become that person. This way the couple stays civil and a fair arrangement is made." He shrugged, taking another slice of pizza. "At least that's the plan. It often goes astray."

"I'm not buying the nobility you paint divorce attorneys with."

"Hey, it normally works for chicks at the bar." He grinned.

"Were you faithful?"

"To Hillary? No. I had an affair that lasted the last year of our marriage. It ended before my divorce, but was the straw that broke the camel's back."

"She found out?"

"I didn't make much of an effort to hide it. I think I wanted to get caught, wanted a way out. She overlooked it for a while, until my affair started leaving her voice mails describing our indiscretions."

"Why?"

"She wanted a relationship. My wife got in the way of that. I tried to break it off and she got mad, thought that she might have a chance if Hillary dumped me. Can we discuss something else?"

"Why did your parents divorce?"

His expression became even more pained. I was obviously choosing the wrong topics. "She disagreed with my father's business practices, and it divided them. She eventually left us to be with a man she felt was more suited to her moral compass."

"Us?" At his confused look I tried again. "You said she left us."

"Children were a nonnegotiable in my father's eyes. Family loyalty is of utmost importance to him. She knew that by leaving him, she would be leaving us, as well. I haven't seen her since then."

"Why didn't you reach out to her as an adult?"

"I felt abandoned as a child. As my father's son, she regarded me with the same level of disdain. It pissed me off as a teenager, but as an adult, I appreciate the unintended effect it had on my life."

"And what effect is that?"

"I am driven by the need to always be the best. Whatever insecurities I got from her dismissal have helped me strive for, and attain, success. In both my personal and professional life."

"I don't see screwing strangers as a successful personal life."

He met my scornful look solidly. "Don't knock something till you've tried it. This lifestyle is what I want right now. I'll know when I'm ready to settle down."

"I take it another side effect was your inability to accept rejection?"

"If you're referring to your resistance to spending time with me, I don't view it as rejection, just an unawareness of the allure of my charms and the inevitability of our friendship." He grinned at me confidently.

I took a bite of pizza and tried not to stare into his gorgeous features. "I have a feeling your friends turn into jilted ex-lovers more often than not."

"I'd love to show you how wrong you are." His eyes practically sizzled my skin as they roamed my body, and I had to stop myself from choking on my food. He took mercy on me, though, and changed the subject. "My turn to interrogate. What's the deal with Bob?"

"Bob is a guy I met the other night at a bar. That's about the extent of the story."

"Did you sleep with him?"

"What? No!"

"Really." His voice was laced with disbelief.

"Yes, really. I went home with him, but all we did was make out. I took a taxi home afterward. I'm not a slut—I had just met the guy!"

"Yet you made enough of an impression that he tracked you down at work?"

I looked at him cockily over the half slice in my hand. "I

guess I make quite an impression." His eyes darkened and he looked so fucking hot I had to look away. *Easy, Julia.*

"How many men have you slept with?"

I swallowed hard, willing the chunk of pepperoni down my throat while my mind raced. I pretended to chew and waved my hand in front of my face, making the "wait a minute" sign. He looked on with amusement, enjoying my discomfort. *Damn man. What is the rule with this? I multiply the real number? Or is it divide? Holy hell.*

In my panic, I just decided to go with the truth. "Two."

His look was slightly confused, and then sharpened. "Two? How old are you? Did you have a long-term relationship?" His questions came out in a clump, and faster than I was able to answer them.

"Yes, two. I am twenty-one. I was nineteen when I lost my virginity, and was engaged to the second guy I slept with. We broke up about six weeks ago."

He nodded slowly, wiping his mouth with a napkin. He missed a big glob of marinara, and it stayed on the corner of his mouth. "Two people, huh?"

"Yes. I don't believe in sex without commitment and love." I tried to keep a straight face, but he looked ridiculous with the red sauce that was beginning to drip down his chin.

"And you loved those two?"

"I thought I did. I was young."

"And you are so old and wise now?" He grinned.

I handed him a paper towel and indicated the offending area. "I'm wiser. Still young and vibrant," I said tartly.

"Do you enjoy sex?" The atmosphere in the room changed, the gradual buildup of sexual tension reaching a peak from where there was no going back. *We were really having this discussion.*

"Of course." And I did. I enjoyed the power and control it gave me.

"Then why would you limit yourself? Why require that love be attached to the act? There is no sense in living a dry, sexless existence while you wait the years it could take to find your next 'love,' in the meantime missing out on some of your peak sexual years." I opened my mouth to object, but he plowed on. "Most people don't truly ever fall in love. As you admitted yourself, your first two loves probably weren't 'loves' at all. If you follow the 'love before sex' thought process, you will probably just get sexually frustrated and convince yourself that you love someone simply so you'll allow yourself to sleep with him, which will only end in an unnecessarily long relationship that will end with someone getting hurt." He looked at me in frustration, his pizza forgotten.

That was quite a speech. "Look, for you sex might be a sexual release, but I don't function the same way. Sex for me is more of an emotional thing, not anything that I *need*."

"Bullshit. Everyone needs sex."

"That is a man talking. You have a need to release your... stuff. We don't operate that way, or at least I don't. Like I said, it's emotional, not physical."

"You make love, but don't fuck." The expletive sounded dangerous and incredibly sexy in his voice.

"No. I fuck. I just do it more for the control aspect rather than the physical." This was the most honest conversation I had ever had with anyone—I was revealing all my secrets. There was a certain freedom in knowing that this was the last time I would see him, and that nothing I said could be used against me.

His eyes narrowed, a flash of understanding in them. "You've never had an orgasm."

"What?"

"Orgasm. Have you ever had one?"

I didn't really know how to answer the question, and it wasn't because I was being evasive. I rolled my paper towel on the table until it formed a strawlike shape. "I don't think so. Sex feels good, but the way I hear orgasms described, it seems to be this earth-shattering experience, and I feel like that is something I wouldn't be unsure of having." I shrugged nonchalantly, my face starting to burn. "Some women can't orgasm. Like fifteen percent of the population. I've tried, both through sex and on my own, and nothing happens. My gyno says not to worry about it. Sex can still be enjoyable, and it is."

He chuckled to himself and then placed both hands flat on the table and leaned forward, looking at me. "You can orgasm."

"Oh, because you know so much about the inner workings of my body in the forty-five minutes you've spent with me."

"All women can orgasm. Your gynecologist and whatever women's magazine you got that ridiculous statistic from don't know what they are talking about."

"You are so bullheaded! You don't know everything about everything!"

He leveled me with a confident stare. "I know everything about sex, and pleasing a woman."

I'll bet you do. "I'm sure you don't. Maybe your conquests were faking."

He smirked at me, nothing but ego in his face. "They weren't faking."

"How would you know?"

He sighed, exasperated. "I don't need to try and convince you of something that I could easily show you, if you weren't so obtuse on the whole idea."

I would absolutely love to have you show me. I tried to keep a blush from my cheeks, tried to not picture his hands on my body, that mouth on my skin. "Whatever. My turn. You just had like nine questions." I pushed the pizza box away from me, worried that I would keep eating it if only to keep my hands from reaching over to him. I grabbed Brad's can of soda, feeling its weight, and got up to get us both fresh Dr Peppers. I mulled over my next question as I bent over the mini-fridge, reaching in to get our drinks. Feeling eyes on my ass, I quickly glanced over my shoulder, and caught him staring. A normal individual would have averted his eyes and played it off, but he let his eyes linger, smiling slightly and letting me see his appreciation. *Pig.*

"Has anyone ever sued you for sexual harassment?"

He was offended. "That would assume that harassment had occurred. I assure you, I don't make advances unless the women are clearly receptive."

I stalked back to the table with the sodas and slammed them down on the table. "Do I seem *clearly* receptive?"

He shrugged, a sheepish smile on his face. "I figure you're a work in progress."

"Uh-huh. Would you allow that to fly in court?"

"Point for the prosecution." His teasing tone was back.

"You're making my points for me. Remember what I said earlier, about your inability to accept rejection? You are proving it with bullshit like that." I sat down, unable to keep a grin off my face. The damn man exuded this ridiculous magnetism that I couldn't stay away from. He was the kind of person who, when talking with someone, made them feel like the most important thing in his world. For the first time this evening, I wondered if this was indeed the last time that I would be seeing him. I didn't entirely trust myself to stay away.

"So, why does Broward hate you so bad?"

"I think a better question is, why does Broward want to protect you so much?"

"Evasive."

He sighed and opened the can. I cringed, wondering if my dramatic slam of the soda earlier would cause it to foam or explode, but it opened with little fanfare.

"I hate to use the whole 'everyone hates me because they're jealous' bit, but I think Broward looks at my life and compares it to his. He buries himself in work to, I suspect, avoid his home life with his sweet and intelligent but incredibly boring wife. He chose a dull focus, corporate law, and I think he is burned out. He sees my wing as 'not real work.' We play as hard as we work, and I think that irks him. He also has access to the billing and payroll system. My income dwarfs his and, considering we're equal partners and I work half the hours he does...the dislike is understandable."

"Do you envy yourself?"

He looked at me quizzically, but I knew he knew exactly what I was referring to. "I live the life, Julia, the life I chose for myself. The women, the parties, the power, the money. It's everything I always wanted."

"Is that why you're sitting here eating cold pizza and talking to me? You could be elbow-deep in pussy at the Silver Nugget."

He chuckled. "It's the Gold Nugget. And you are a conquest. It's part of me mixing it up." His honest and offensive answer should have angered me, but it didn't. I knew what he wanted. I was just beginning to worry that I wanted it, too.

"Would you ever remarry?"

"No. The type of woman I need doesn't exist. I fooled myself when I was younger, but I know better now. It's not fair for me to promise happily-ever-after to a woman that I would be unfaithful to."

"Why? Are you a sex addict?"

"That's a bullshit clinical term. I love sex. I don't believe in restricting myself in order to conform to society's standards."

"Sheila thinks you're a sex addict."

"Sheila and I have had sexual tension for the last five years."

I gaped at him and he started shaking with controlled laughter. "God, Julia. You're too easy."

"From what I hear about your standards, it's not like Sheila is out of the question," I retorted.

He stopped laughing and looked at me with a grin. "Come with me to Vegas."

"No! This is supposed to be our last hurrah. My wild days are over. Starting tomorrow, I'm back to being a good girl." I slapped my hand on the table to emphasize my resolve. But my subconscious was already packing a bag and choosing the proper shoes.

He slapped the table back at me. "Start Monday. Have you ever been to Vegas?"

"No. My parents preferred exciting vacation locales such as Palm Springs and North Dakota."

He reached across the table and grabbed my hand, pulling it to him. He looked solemnly into my eyes, and desire curled in my belly. "Come to Vegas with me. Please. I promise not to sexually harass you. I just want to get to know you better. I promise you won't regret it."

I couldn't find anything to say and stared wordlessly into his eyes. I had so many conflicting thoughts running through my mind and didn't know which one to listen to.

I glared at him. "No."

Twelve

"You're going to Vegas?" Olivia's shocked expression increased my stress level.

"Yes. I mean, I think so."

"When?"

"Tomorrow, after work. Our flight leaves at six forty-five."

We were in my living room, a bottle of wine open on the coffee table. When I'd opened the door and Olivia had seen my face, she'd walked straight past me into the kitchen, grabbing the first bottle she had seen. We were now taking turns swigging from it. Super Classy.

"What do you know about this guy? I mean, other than the dire warnings from all members of the CDB staff."

"That's really about it. I looked him up in the state bar directory. He's active, so he has no criminal history."

"Yet! A rape, kidnapping and murder charge might be added after this weekend!"

I rolled my eyes at her. "I called you over to calm me down, Olivia. If I'd wanted hysterics and gross exaggerations, I would have called Becca."

"Did you look him up on Google?"

"Of course. But the first five pages were all news reports about big cases. I didn't want to look through eight million Google results."

"All right then, let's focus. If you're going, then we just need to make sure you do it right. Have you packed?"

I grinned at her. This was more like what I had in mind.

One hour and another bottle of wine later, we were surrounded by sequins, leather and pink. Half my closet was on the floor, more clothes were on my bed, and we had both come to the same conclusion. I had nothing to wear. My clothes fit one of three genres: business attire, college-bar dressy and theme-party costume. Too bad we'd never had a Vegas-themed event.

"Maybe I shouldn't go." I flopped down on the bed and promptly sank through three layers of girliness.

"Or maybe we should call in reinforcements."

I looked at her in dread. "Becca?"

She nodded firmly. "Becca."

Becca's family was just a few decimal places short of Rockefeller money. Her parents' generous monthly allowance supported two main things—alcohol and clothes. Becca lived in a two-bedroom apartment, and one bedroom was solely dedicated to clothes and shoes. Olivia and I took a brief appraisal of our intoxicated states, and then called a taxi. We planned on showing up unannounced with a large suitcase and a bottle of cheap wine, the only thing left in the fridge.

It was a Thursday night and one in the morning, so we didn't have to wait long for a cab. By one-fifteen we were ringing Becca's bell. A habitual night owl, she answered the door with music blaring in the background and a phone pressed to her ear. Her gaze traveled from our sweats to my suitcase to the bottle. "Jen, I gotta go." She snapped the phone shut and threw the door open.

It took about five minutes to fill Becca in on the situation, and I was surprised to see that she was in full support of the trip. I should have known that stupid, impulsive decisions would resonate as logical with her.

We walked into the magic of her closet a few minutes later. Becca and I had fairly similar body types, but I was a lot taller than her. However, that was no problem, since pants weren't a big Vegas fashion statement. Other than wearing the same top and dress size, we shared one very important characteristic—shoe size. It was a quality that caused me pleasure every time I opened my tiny closet. Though I was perpetually broke, you'd never know from seeing my shoes. Becca bought, wore and gave away designer shoes as if they were tissues. It was one of the reasons we got along so well. It's easy to forgive almost anything when an apology is coupled with a pair of barely worn Manolos.

Becca was also the most traveled of our group. Having been to Vegas countless times, she kept up a running monologue as we sifted through her cedar-lined racks. She listed more restaurants, shows and stores than I could possibly remember, especially given the fuzzy state of my mind. I had pretty much tuned her out when I realized there was an expectant silence in the room. I turned to find them both staring at me.

"I'm sorry—what was the question?"

"Sex. Are you planning on having sex with him?" Becca said slowly, as one might to a child.

"No!" I said scornfully, while somewhere inside me a little woman jumped up and down and screamed, *"Yes!"*

"He's flying you up there," Olivia said carefully. "Spending a lot of money on you. You might want to clue him in to that fact."

"What, that she's a tease?" Becca put both hands on her silk-clad hips. "Yeah, Jules. You know, some guys don't respond to that very well. You've gotten lucky so far, but one day a guy isn't going to stop when you tell him to."

"I don't think Brad's like that." I hung the silver mini I had been considering and continued flipping through the hangers, hoping that Becca and Olivia would move on to a different subject.

"Really? College girls thought Ted Bundy was a pretty nice guy also," Becca said a little too cheerfully for the subject matter.

Maybe it was a topic I should broach. But didn't I communicate that to him last night? *I don't have sex with people I'm not in love with. He knows that. He just doesn't understand it.*

"Why are you such a prude anyway, Jules?"

"She's not a prude, Becca. She just doesn't believe in giving it to every guy who buys her a *mojito*."

Becca stuck out her tongue at Olivia in response. "At least expect to suck his dick. You'll be lucky if you make it out of the weekend with just that act."

"Um, how about we leave me and my sexual future alone?" I suggested. "I promise you, I am a big girl, and I will make it through the weekend without being raped, tortured or killed." Discreetly, I reached back in Becca's closet and tapped on the cedar wall, hoping that I had not just jinxed myself.

Thirteen

"Phone away, sir." The meticulously manicured flight attendant shot Brad a stern look as she passed by. Her tone was softened by the lingering glance and hand as she patted his shoulder. I reached down in my bag and unlocked my phone, tripled-checked that it was on plane mode, and then stuck it back in my bag. Brad, with a resigned sigh, finished typing out an email, then turned his phone off and set it on the armrest. I pulled out a piece of gum, double-checked my seat belt and looked out the window.

The day had passed quickly at work. Brad had stayed in his wing, and I in mine. I had accomplished all the tasks that Broward had left for me, and looked forward to not thinking about work for the next two days. The first-class stewardess walked back by, pausing by our seats.

"Champagne?" she offered.

"Yes, please," I replied. Brad nodded. We certainly seemed to be traveling in style. I had never been in first class before and felt ridiculously giddy about the experience. I took both the pillow and blanket the stewardess offered, then stretched out in my roomy seat, a glass of champagne in hand. Brad had

BLINDFOLDED INNOCENCE | 93

taken the aisle seat and his enormous frame made the spacious seat look tiny. It was impossible to ignore the energy he radiated, and I became suddenly nervous about the upcoming trip and how it would go. There would be no escape there, no way to distance myself from his sexuality, the power that emitted from his every move. The thought of the two of us alone for two days... I had no idea what to expect. And I hoped I hadn't made a mistake by agreeing to come.

Fourteen

*Rule 3: You may not know what will occur until you arrive.
We reserve the right to change the events according to her desires.*

Landing in Vegas was an experience in itself—not the landing, but the walk through the airport. We had each packed only a carry-on, so we headed straight for the exit once we left the plane. The airport was crowded with cleavage, diamonds and tourists, its walls covered with digital screens advertising different shows, casinos and restaurants. We fought through the crowds and finally walked past the exit, hitting the taxi and limo lines. It was chaos, with a long line for the taxis and all the drivers shouting and waving. Brad spotted our driver first, an older black man in a tuxedo. He went over and shook his hand. "Hey, Leonard," he said, pumping his hand enthusiastically.

"Hey, Mr. De Luca," the driver said in a thick New York accent. "How ya been doing?"

"Great, Leonard, just great. This is Julia," Brad said, holding out his arm and drawing me toward them. I shook Leonard's hand and smiled. He was a large man who looked as though he might have been a bouncer in his younger days. He was missing a tooth but still managed to look dignified.

"Hi, Julia. It's a pleasure to meet you. That bag all you got?"

"Yes, sir, but it's a heavy one."

"Awww, it'll be no trouble to me. Besides, the big guy can always help me out." He clapped Brad on the back.

"How's Jeanne?" Brad asked, following Leonard to a white stretch limo. The driver limped a little when he walked, so it was a slow trip. I lagged behind and watched them chat.

"She good man, real good. She been playing with the grandkids all day while school's out."

"I bet she enjoys that."

"She do—but I'm starting to want my house back! Those kids watch too much cartoons, not enough baseball." He chuckled good-naturedly as he swung our bags into the trunk.

Leonard held the door open and I ducked into the limo, sliding all the way over to the other side. Brad crawled in after me and shut the door. It was quiet inside the limo, and we waited for Leonard to make his way to the driver's seat.

"I take it you come often?" I said dryly.

He grinned at me and grabbed my knee, giving it a squeeze and leaving his hand there. Now that we had landed, his intensity had lightened, and he seemed playful. "I try to come up about every other month. Clears my head, and sometimes my wallet."

"You typically come alone?" I hated asking, but I wanted to know.

"Depends on whether I'm seeing anyone, or what kind of trip I'm in the mood for."

"And what kind of trip are you in the mood for now?"

He slid his hand up my bare leg until it reached my upper thigh. "Haven't really figured that out yet," he said. His hand on my bare skin lit up every sensor in my body, sending a streak of arousal through me. I looked at him, at his ridiculously sexy profile, his gorgeous lips curving into a sinful smile. I had done it, yielded to his demands and come on this trip. *What on earth would I do now?* In this city of sexuality and sin, where secrets were made and affairs carried out. I fought the impulse, tried to focus on anything but the feel of his flesh on my thigh, his fingers moving gently, teasing my skin.

Fuck it. I leaned over, grabbed the back of his head and kissed him.

Our first kiss began tentatively. It was not a planned event, and I wasn't sure how he would react. He responded immediately, reaching a hand between my body and the seat, hooking it around my waist and pulling me tight to him. He deepened the kiss and used his other hand to brush my hair away from my face, and then trailed his fingers down my neck and cupped my breast through my thin T-shirt. His hands on my breast and tight around my waist were electrifying, and I moaned, feeling arousal take over my entire body. Our tongues combined perfectly, teasing and tasting each other until we finally pulled apart, gasping. I stared into his eyes, frozen. *What the hell have I gotten myself into?*

He leaned back, sliding his hands in all areas they shouldn't be until they were back in his domain. I scooted back in my seat also, nervously biting my nails and trying to think of what to say. *God, did Leonard see that?* I glanced toward the front and saw that he had closed the privacy screen. *Thank God.*

"Come here."

I looked up. Brad was patting the seat next to him. The space I'd just scooted out of. Hesitantly, I slid over again, and he used his arm to spin me away from him, so I was facing the door. "Move down," he said. I slid my butt out until I was lying down, my head on his leg.

"I've got to make a call," he said. "You relax. We have a

thirty-minute drive ahead of us." He began to run his fingers through my hair, and I did relax. I tried to figure out what was going on between us, and what I would do once we were alone in the room, and what...

Instead, with his hand gently playing with my hair, and the hum of the car on the road, I drifted off to sleep.

I woke up to the sound of Brad talking on the phone.

"I told you I would take care of it...."

"No, for Christ's sake, don't get him involved...."

"I can't handle it on this trip. I'm not alone...."

"Just a girl. No one you know...."

"She's not that type, too straitlaced...."

I lay still, with my eyes closed. His fingers were still running through my hair. *Has he been doing that the entire time?*

"Look, I have to go. We're almost at the casino. I'll call you next time I'm in town. Tell Jenny I said hi."

The limo swayed as we rounded a curve. Brad gently shook my shoulder. "Julia."

I pretended to sleep on.

"Julia." Louder this time.

I stirred, and then opened my eyes. He was looking down at me, bemused. "Hi."

I stretched, as much as I could in the backseat of a limo. Then I sat up slowly, rubbing my eyes.

"Are we here?"

He chuckled. "Yes, we're about to pull up. You might want to check your makeup."

I blinked at him, and then reached into my bag and pulled out a compact. Peering into it, I saw that my mascara had smudged, and I had a bit of dried drool running down the side of my mouth. *Great, Julia. Really sexy.* I quickly grabbed a tissue from a built-in dispenser on the dash and wiped away the offending items. I was sliding my zippered bag back into my purse when the limo pulled up to the casino.

Bellagio was gorgeous, a massive cream high-rise with a lake in front. Brad gestured to the water. "Our room will have a view of the fountains. I think you'll really enjoy them." We pulled into a massive portico with black-vested valets everywhere. Leonard stopped at the curb and one of the attendants opened our limo doors. The employee recognized Brad immediately and tipped his hat to him.

"Mr. De Luca. Welcome back, sir."

"Thank you. Our bags are in the trunk."

"Certainly. They will be waiting in your room."

"I appreciate it." Brad pulled a thick wad from his pocket and peeled off a one-hundred-dollar bill. He handed it to the man, who pocketed it.

"Thank you, Mr. De Luca. Let me know if I can help with anything else, sir."

Brad nodded at him, grabbed my hand and pulled me toward the building. Inside was a sea of activity. Colors and sounds were everywhere. The lobby ceiling was a mass of handblown glass flowers in every color I could imagine. There was a line of easily a hundred people waiting to check in. The front desk was at least ninety feet long and had more than ten agents posted behind it. I expected us to head toward the line, but Brad veered to the right and we entered a small private lobby on the way to the casino floor.

Decadence seemed to be the theme the decorator had picked for this space. The walls were covered in gold-print wallpaper, with cream paneling covering the lower half. There was a leather couch and chairs surrounding a low table with various desserts and finger food positioned on it. A seventy-inch flat screen showed ESPN, and a beverage stand occupied an antique table set along the right-hand wall. Two attractive women in skirt suits stood along the wall, ready to spring into action if a guest needed help. Two more beautiful women were behind the desk, one of whom was on the phone. Brad indicated for me to sit on the couch, and he stepped up to the desk. I helped myself to a bottle of water and a mini–key lime pie. I had just popped the bite-size dessert into my mouth when Brad finished at the desk and came back to me, a key packet in hand.

"Ready?" I nodded my response, my mouth filled with deliciousness. He took my hand and led me into the madness of the casino.

I had never been to a casino before, but this one seemed very comparable to every Vegas movie I had ever seen. The colors were brighter, the smell of smoke invaded my senses, but everything else seemed the same. There were excited screams coming from somewhere, old ladies in fanny packs sitting at slot machines and depressed-looking men fingering their dwindling chip stacks. Brad looked longingly at the blackjack tables, but continued through the space until we reached a set of elevators, where he pressed the up button.

The elevator seemed uncomfortably small, but I think it was just because I was so aware of Brad's invasive presence. Classical music was playing and, looking up, I saw a security camera fixed down at me. I quickly looked away. At the twen- tieth floor, the doors slowly opened, and we exited.

I expected a typical hotel room, but should have known better. The first hint was the door, or doors, to our room—a double set made of mahogany. Next to the doors was a brass plate with 20E printed on it. Brad swiped the key card and opened the doors.

It was a two-bedroom suite that screamed luxury. The doors opened to a large living room with floor-to-ceiling windows showing an impressive view of the Strip. Brown suede couches with silk pillows, plush cream carpeting and a leather-and-walnut desk occupied the room. A dining table sat off to one side, with a large floral arrangement at its center. I roamed the suite, seeing a large fruit-and-chocolate platter in the master bedroom along with a card. The master had a huge king bed, an ottoman at its foot and fresh flowers on its bedside tables. The master bathroom was the size of my apartment at home. It had a huge Whirlpool tub, as well as a walk-in steam shower with multiple body jets and a huge rain head. Heated marble floors led to a large vanity with his-and-hers sinks, and a dressing area. There was the standard toilet room—I never understood those—and a large walk-in closet. Our suitcases were already in the closet; several of Brad's suits already hung up. I wondered if they had opened my suitcase. I also wondered why it was in here versus in the other bedroom. I wandered over there to check it out.

The second room was noticeably smaller, but also well appointed. It had a queen bed, an upholstered chair and a dresser. The bathroom en suite would have put a Hampton Inn to shame, but was puny compared to the one in the master. I walked back to the living room, where Brad was dumping the contents of his pockets onto the counter.

"I need to go down to the casino and speak to my host," he said without looking up. "Do you want to dress for dinner?"

I looked at my watch, surprised. It showed 11:40 p.m., but it was set to eastern time; it was either 8:40 or 9:40 in Vegas. We had eaten here and there—both in the airports and in first class—and I had assumed that those snacks had comprised dinner. Apparently not.

"Umm…okay. I'm not really hungry."

"Dinner here is just as much about the experience as it is the food. Are you tired?"

"Yes. I mean no…." My nerves were fried. I was tired, but

wasn't ready to face that situation yet. I was terrified of going to bed, or not going to bed, with this man. "I don't know," I finished lamely. This suave man in a suit riffling through hundred-dollar bills in a gold-laden Vegas suite wasn't the same guy who had grinned at me through a mouthful of pepperoni pizza yesterday. I tried to breathe normally while thoughts of escape flooded my mind. *What have I gotten myself into?*

He looked up at me and froze. I could see thoughts flitting through his mind, showing themselves on his face, but he stayed in place, silent and unmoving, and I did the same. I tried to force my face into a casual smile, but my lips didn't move. Unexpectedly, I burst into tears.

He was at my side in an instant, his hands in my hair, pulling it out of the way, and his face pressed against mine, his lips soft on my forehead and cheeks. He lifted me up and carried me to the big room, laying me on the bed. He smoothed my hair back, and brushed at my tear-soaked cheeks. My body shook and I was sobbing like a child. He shushed my sobs, and kissed the back of my hands, which I had brought up to cover my face.

My sobs were starting to slow, and I tried to sniff them back, but just ended up with a throat full of phlegm. I swallowed hard. Brad kissed my forehead gently and lay on the bed next to me, propped up on one arm so that he was above me.

"What's wrong?" His deep voice, impossibly gentle, almost sent me into another crying spell. I fought it as hard as I could. *He's going to think I'm mental. Maybe I am mental.*

I had no good answer to give him, so I just shook my head mutely. His eyes were pools of concern and confusion. I felt so impossibly stupid and childish.

"Is it something I did?"

I couldn't bear the expression on his face, the confused,

searching look. I hiccuped, my throat filled with tears, and I finally spoke. "I don't— It's just… I don't want to have sex with you." The words came out broken and strangled, and I cringed at the adolescent sound of them. His laughter broke my shame and I looked to him quickly, anger winning the roulette spin of the emotional mess that was my current state.

As soon as he saw my face, he held up a hand in defense. "Julia, please. I'm sorry." His face was clear, his eyes strong and confident again. "I wasn't expecting you to have sex with me. Is that what you think I brought you here for?" His voice dropped all trace of laughter, and was now concerned and gentle. He brought a hand up, pushing my hair out of my eyes again. I turned my face away, wanting to see anything but his pity.

"Julia. Sex is not something I need to woo someone for. I brought you here because I can't stand traveling solo. I hate to be by myself, hate to be reminded of the fact that I'm alone." The words were so raw, so honest in their imperfection that I turned, meeting his eyes, looking for and finding truth in their depths. "I want you sexually. Trust me on that. But that's not why I brought you here. I brought you because I like spending time with you, and would like to get to know you without you having to fear Broward or the office finding out."

I tried to speak, tried to move my mouth and have some kind of intelligible thought emerge, but nothing came out. I felt so much at one time—embarrassed, relieved and, in some crazy way, aroused. I reached for him, and he shook his head, keeping me at bay, my arms falling limply to the bed. He grabbed my wrists and stood, pulling me to my feet. I tried to think of something to say, some response to his assurances, but my mind was wiped by the feel of his hands. They gripped the hem of my shirt and pulled up, dragging it over my flat stomach and the swell of my breasts, up and over my head. Tossing the shirt to the side, he wordlessly ran his fingers down the sides of my body until he hit the top of my skirt. He followed it around to the back, slipped his fingers underneath the material and unzipped it. His movements were efficient, purposeful enough that I relaxed against his touch, numbly moving to assist him. He let go of the fabric and it fell silently to the floor. I stepped out of it as well as my flats. I stood in front of him in my plain cotton bra and panties, my cheeks still wet from the tears. *After that speech, he's really going to try and have sex with me?*

He bent over and picked me up, his huge muscles making my weight seem negligible. He carried me to the bed, drew back the blanket and set me down softly on the silky sheets. He pulled the cool sheet and down comforter over my body, enveloping me in luxury. He kissed my lips gently and then moved up and kissed my forehead. Reaching over, he switched off the bedside light, plunging the room into soft darkness. Standing up, he looked down at me, his expression unreadable. He pulled his shirt off, exposing a tan, muscular chest and huge shoulders and arms. He went around to the other side of the bed and I heard a zipper. I stiffened, still unsure of his intentions. Moments later, he was in the bed, his arms surrounding me. He turned me to my side, away from him, and spooned his hard body against mine. I shifted, fitting tighter into him, and then relaxed into an exhausted and deep sleep.

Fifteen

I woke up once during the night. I rolled over and reached out, feeling for Brad, but the bed was empty. I raised my head and softly called his name. Hearing no response, I pushed back the blankets and stood. I went into the bathroom, used the toilet, washed my hands and padded back to bed. I didn't need to check the other rooms to know he wasn't there. The man had a presence that filled a space—if he was there, I would have sensed it. I glanced at the clock on my way to the bed: 2:45 a.m. I lay back down and was asleep before my head even hit the pillow.

I was awakened by Brad's mouth on my neck doing incredibly delicious things to my body. I was wet before I even opened my eyes. The sunlight was streaming in through a crack in the curtains—the gorgeous room glowed a soft yellow. The blanket tented over our bodies, Brad on top of me, his legs on either side of mine, his weight supported by his knees and one arm. He paused, his mouth leaving me, moving to my ear, whispering in it. "This isn't about sex, I promise you." His words tickled my ear, and I squirmed against him, giggling softly. His hand roamed, skimming the top of my bra, over my small cleavage, traveling down my stomach. When it reached the top of my panties, it tugged down, softly swiping fingers over my pubic area, teasing the bit of hair there.

"If this isn't about sex, what are you doing?" I said softly, biting back a groan of pleasure.

He moved above me, shifting his body, the brush of his skin against mine sinful. "It's about proving you wrong… and pleasing you."

His fingers continued their sweep of my pelvis, running up and down my mound. I moaned with desire and responded immediately, pulling my long legs free and wrapping them around his waist. I leaned my head back, opening my neck even more and arching my back, pressing my breasts into him. He took advantage of my arched back to move his free hand underneath, grabbing my butt firmly, squeezing it hard, almost to the point of pain. I gasped in surprise, grinding against him, loving the feel of his strength. He instantly moved his hand, taking it up and grabbing the back of my hair, drawing my head back so I was staring up into his deviously playful eyes.

Swiftly, I leaned up and kissed him until he responded, pushing down with his head, pinning mine to the bed. We kissed long and hard, as he moved his arm so that it matched the other, his weight resting on both elbows on either side of me, his body lying softly on mine. I could feel his dick—ridiculously hard and ridiculously big—so much that I second-guessed whether it was him. Maybe it was his cell phone, or some other object? Then it twitched, and I had no doubt in my mind. *Good God.*

I pushed on his shoulders, trying to roll him over so I could assume my normal dominant position on top, but he didn't budge. He continued teasing my mouth with his tongue and grinding into me. I wrapped my legs tighter, digging my heels into his ass. I touched his muscular back with one hand and reached down with the other, trying to feel his hardness. He sat back on his knees, taking his mouth off mine, and grabbed both of my hands, pinning them together and holding them down with one hand above my head. He swiveled out of my legs and lay to the side of me, my body now stretched out beside him with my hands captured. I bucked off the bed, glaring at him, hating the restriction of my hands. He leaned over and kissed me gently, with a bit of tongue, softening my anger slightly. Then he pulled back again.

His eyes took a greedy and unapologetic tour of my body, his free hand leading the way. He pulled down the tops of my bra, allowing my breasts to be free and exposed, my nipples erect in the morning air. He ran his hand down and over the top of my panties this time, feeling the wet silk at my opening. His grin grew and he teased my pussy through my panties, running his hand from my clit to my ass, back and forth. Then he slipped a finger past the fabric and inside me. His eyes changed at the feeling of my tight wetness, growing darker and losing a bit of their control.

"Oh my God, Julia," he breathed. "What am I going to do with you?" Wonder and desire filled his voice and eyes, and I stared at him, wanting his mouth on me again. I arched my back, pressing my sex into his hand, wanting some kind of release for my overwhelming desire. Is this what it's like? The men I torment with my teasing. Is this what they go through? This blatant need for release? I had never experienced it before, and suddenly understood the desperate look in their eyes. I was sure I had it in mine. *I'm going to have to change my teasing ways. This is pure torture.* The realization sent a blaze of anger through me and I ripped my hands free, catching Brad off guard. My eyes flashed with what must have been a combination of lust, anger and a hunger for the power balance to be restored. I needed to see in his eyes what I had in mine. I tried to roll on top of his body, but he held me at bay, his strong arms too powerful. I tried to reach for his cock, but he moved my hands away and resumed his previous position on top of my body.

"I want to suck your dick," I breathed, injecting desire and longing into my voice. This would cause a normal all-American man to immediately roll over and unzip, but Brad shook his head at me and clicked his tongue.

"This is about you. I want to please you."

"What will please me is having your big dick in my mouth!" I shouted back. *What man turns down head? At 9:00 a.m., no less.*

"You said you can't come."

"Yeah, so?"

"I'm going to make you."

"You can't. It's been tried."

His expression turned scornful. "By who? Nineteen-year-old frat boys whose version of foreplay is having you give them a blow job?"

I silenced. He did have a point. *Damn him.* "Seriously, let's just drop it. I've accepted it. You need to do the same."

"Do I look like a man who gives in easily?" He looked like a man who was too damn gorgeous for words. His bare torso was that of a Roman gladiator's, knotted with muscles that flexed and popped when he moved. His waist was thick and strong, and my hands couldn't seem to stay away from his massive arms. He pushed me back on the bed and moved, sliding down my body until his face was at my stomach.

My mind realized what he was about to do before my mouth did. "*Waaa…* Stop!"

My shrill voice caused him to raise his head and look at me. "What?"

"What are you doing?"

"What do you think I'm doing?"

"I…er…don't do that." As a matter of fact, no one had ever done "that" to me. I had always been self-conscious about the thought that a man would be placing his mouth on my most private part. What if it smelled, or tasted bad? What if I didn't like what he did? Would he be offended if I told him to stop? It just seemed easier to skip the act altogether. And I had never gotten any pushback about it. Truth be told, I think college guys were as scared of the act as I was.

"Don't do that, or haven't done that?"

"Both."

"Julia. Trust me." I looked down at his eyes and saw a hint of it—the pleading look. He really wanted to do it—wanted it the way I had needed the earlier release. It wasn't the power trip that I had been looking for, but it was as close as I would get. I nodded mutely, closed my eyes and steeled myself for disaster.

Brad slowly rolled down my panties until they reached my knees, and then pulled them off. He spread my legs and paused, breathing in the scent of me and letting me feel his hot breath. I felt so incredibly exposed, my legs open, and him staring at me, my lips, that close up.... I'd looked at myself in a hand mirror once and had been scared to death at what I saw—all the different colors and shapes....

I tried to breathe normally but felt as if I was about to hyperventilate. I glanced down. He was focused, not looking up at me. The sight of his muscular, manly body in between my legs was erotic, and I felt my moistness grow. He leaned down and I braced myself.

The first feel of his mouth on my sex startled me. I had been expecting it, my body in nervous anticipation, but it still surprised me. I expected to feel a tongue pushing and protruding. Instead, he placed his whole mouth on me, a blanket of wet hotness. I tried to figure out how he was making the sensations I was feeling, but all thought left my head the moment he started moving his tongue. I lost all sense of feeling except between my legs. It was as if every sensory receptor on my body immediately fled their posts and converged *there*. A sensation similar to an itch started to grow between my legs, with pressure building behind it.

I wrapped my legs tight around Brad's head and grabbed his hair with my hands. From some other plane I heard my voice saying "oh fuck, oh fuck, oh fuck" over and over, but I had no consciousness of speech or of how to get myself to stop. My shyness had fled, and I knew nothing but undeniable pleasure. He continued whatever ridiculously delicious thing he was doing with his mouth and the itch grew stronger, my body twitching to keep it under control. A wave of intense sensation grew, swelling. I was unable to control it. I tucked my pelvis up, grinding my sex into his face and hearing my voice grow louder.

Holy shit, it's actually happening. I'm about to have an—

My body exploded. I arched my back, spread my toes, and felt the earth, stars and moon collide. The core of my body shattered in a feeling I can only describe as the most incredible experience of my entire life. The itch was satisfied in the purest form of pleasure, so pure that I felt almost pain at the intensity of it. Waves, sweet and incredible, radiated out from my sex. *"OH FUUUCCCCKKKKKKKK!"* I screamed so loud that I'm sure people four rooms over could hear, but I couldn't spare any possible brain power to tell myself to quiet down— all my senses were overwhelmed by the ecstasy of the orgasm.

It lasted almost too long, my body at the verge of breaking, then faded, some delicious tendrils hanging around a little longer than others. My body was shaking uncontrollably, sensual waves of pleasure still gently washing over me, gradually disappearing by the time Brad took his mouth off my body. I lay back on the bed, delirious and twitching with aftershocks. My eyes were closed, and I kind of heard him moving around. I didn't have the energy to open my eyes. I was spent, naked and lying there, legs spread, exposed, and I didn't give a damn. The man had drained all reasonable thought and feeling from my body. It took a good two minutes before I felt that I could move again.

I tested my legs, moving them one at a time, and then lazily rolled over, propping myself up on one arm.

Brad was leaning back in a soft chair, his legs sprawled out in front of him, one hand playing with his mouth. He watched me, a small smile on his lips.

I looked at him through drugged eyes. "Pretty proud of yourself, aren't you?"

He spread his hands, palms up, shrugged his shoulders in a "hey, what can I say?" gesture.

"I faked that."

His outburst of laughter surprised both of us, and I joined in, giggling and rolling over on the bed. He stood and ambled over, dropping down next to me. The whole bed shook with the extra weight.

I glanced at the clock: 9:18 a.m. "How long did it take me?"

"About four minutes."

"Damn."

He was amused. "You wanted it to take longer?"

"No! I didn't want to give you any more fodder for your big ego." I snorted. "Not that I accomplished that."

He reached over and tucked a lock of hair behind my ear. "Do you regret it?" he said softly.

I flopped onto my back. "Are you kidding? That was the single best moment of my entire life! I've never been so happy to be wrong." I rolled over again, my face inches from his, and looked at him with seriousness. "Thank you. I owe you one."

He leaned forward and gently kissed my lips. "Don't mention it."

Sixteen

My limbs felt ridiculously loose and lazy, and I wandered, still mostly naked, to the bathroom. I closed the door, stripped off my bra and dropped it onto the floor. I reached into the shower and turned every jet to full force. Steam quickly filled the bathroom, and I gingerly stepped into the hot spray. It felt like a thousand little fingers massaging me, and I stood still for a good five minutes, letting the spray warm and awaken my body. Finally, I stopped being lazy and grabbed the small shower gel bottle, squeezing a generous amount into my palm and running my hands over my body. I heard the door click open and, through the fogged glass door, saw Brad's head lean into the bathroom.

"Julia, I'm ordering in breakfast. What would you like?"

"Umm…two scrambled eggs and fruit please."

His head disappeared and I heard the door shut. I used the shampoo and worked my hair into a lather, loving the warm water hitting me from all directions. *This is the life.*

Five minutes later, I reluctantly turned off the shower and stepped out onto the plush white bath mat. The bathroom was a steamy sauna, and I wrapped my hair in a fluffy towel and walked to the closet. I remembered seeing bathrobes there, and I snagged one off the hanger and pulled it on. I washed my face at the sink, then reached for my toothbrush. I blushed, thinking of our deep kiss just a half hour earlier, wondering how bad my morning breath had been. I brushed extra long and hard, hoping to make up for any stinkiness I had exhibited earlier.

When I was finally satisfied with my teeth, I unwound my hair and tried to towel dry it as best I could. I got it somewhat unwet, fluffed it and walked back into the suite.

Brad was sitting at the dining table, a phone to his ear. He was facing away from me, looking at the Strip. His legs stretched out, one hand spinning a water bottle on the table, he looked every bit the powerful man he was. He wore a baby-blue polo, faded jeans and new white-and-silver Nike runners.

"Tell her to stay in the house, change the locks and don't answer if he knocks. If he pesters her, call security. The dues they pay in that gated community should more than cover a security guard intelligent and experienced enough to write a decent police report. First thing Monday we'll file an emergency injunction against him. Tell her to relax. Anything he does right now will only help our case. And for God's sake, keep her away from the pool boy! I want us surveilling her day and night—for her protection—but also to keep an eye out for other P.I.s. I have a feeling they're trying to catch her in something, and I want to have a head start on them...."

"Exactly...."

"If you need a good guy, call Romanelli. He owes me one...."

"You, too, brother."

He hung up the call and turned to stand, pausing when he saw me in the room. A smile broke out on his face. "Have a nice shower?"

"Amazing. I want to pack that shower up and take it home with me."

"Tomorrow you should try the bath." His voice had turned slightly sexual, and I fought back a blush.

There was a polite knock at the door. Brad pulled out the leather dining chair to the right of his seat, and indicated I should sit. He strode to the door and swung it open. A petite Asian woman with a large room-service cart entered, wheeling it toward the table. I started to rise, and she shook her head and hands.

"No, no. You sit." Her broken English was accompanied by a sweet smile, and she scurried around the cart, unloading the dishes. Brad returned to his seat, pausing on the way to kiss the top of my head. *The damn man was an enigma.* The server made quick work of the loaded cart, and before long the table was filled with small plates of breakfast items. She left a small vase of yellow flowers in front of us, made a slight bow and left.

My requested eggs and fruit were present, along with yogurt, orange juice and milk. Brad had ordered a full breakfast for himself, and heaped bacon, hash browns and a waffle onto the large plate already containing an omelet.

We ate in silence for a few minutes, then Brad said, "We have dinner reservations at Prime tonight, and tickets to a Cirque du Soleil show at 10:00 p.m. That leaves the day pretty much up to you. I'll leave Philipe's number for you. He's my host. He can arrange anything you're interested in."

I blinked, halfway through a biscuit that I had snagged from one of his gabillion plates. "You're leaving me?"

He laughed. "Oh, how many times I've heard that one."

"Ha. Ha." I glowered at him and took another huge bite of biscuit.

"I have stuff to do. Mainly gambling. Stuff you won't be

interested in. I'll regroup with you at dinner. Trust me, you'll have a fine time without me." He winked and went back to eating, apparently done with the conversation.

I felt the happy bubble that had enveloped me since my first orgasm begin to deflate. I don't know what I had envisioned, but his leaving me in the room while he handled his "stuff" all day wasn't it. *What was the point of a trip to "get to know each other" if we spent the whole time apart?* I grumbled to myself and jerked open the lid to the yogurt with unnecessary vigor. He eyed me carefully, sensing my irritability. It wasn't that hard to sense—I was practically beating him over the head with it.

"You're not going to start crying again, are you?"

This thought struck me as so absurd that I burst out laughing. I laughed until tears threatened and milk started to drip from my nose. I grabbed a napkin and shook my head, still shaking slightly. "That was a onetime thing, I swear. I'm typically not a crier. I don't know what came over me." *Plus, now I don't have to debate about having sex with you. I know what I want.* I could feel the bright red color of my face and I studiously avoided his eyes, focusing really hard on finding the perfect scoop of Dannon strawberry yogurt.

"Any guesses?"

I set down the yogurt and met his eyes. "If I want a shrink, I'll use the ridiculously long day stretching before me and ask 'Philipe' to send me one. Now, if you'll excuse me, I think I'll go to my room to start my sentence!" Knowing full well how juvenile I was acting, I tossed down my yogurt and stomped off, heading toward the other room. Brad caught my arm as I passed his chair, and he stood, spinning me around and holding me by the shoulders. He kissed me, firm and hard, and then released me.

"I'll see you tonight." He cheerfully sauntered into the master bedroom, and emerged twenty seconds later with a room key in hand. I stood there, arms crossed, feeling rather silly in my plush robe and wet hair, and watched as he winked at me and left the room. The door shut quietly behind him.

Fuck. That just made it pretty freaking clear who had the upper hand. I flopped down on the sofa to lament my woes, and then grabbed my cell off the coffee table and punched in Olivia's number.

She answered on the second ring. "Please tell me you're alive and safe."

"Very alive and pretty safe," I teased.

"Having a good time?"

I wandered through the suite and pondered her question. "Pretty good. We didn't do much last night, just checked in and went to bed." I decided to leave out my hysterical crying fit.

"Bed? Or *bed?*"

I giggled. "Just normal bed, Olivia. He has been a gentleman, and we have a two-room suite." *Not that the second room has been used.*

"So you slept separately?"

"Yes. Kind of. There was some cuddling."

"Wow. You are so wild and crazy," she monotoned. "Cuddling? On the second date? Becca would tear you a new asshole if she heard this."

The room phone rang, and I glanced over my shoulder and frowned at it.

"Olivia? I'll call you later."

Seventeen

I looked at the phone, unsure of whether I should answer it or not. Finally, I bit the bullet and picked up the receiver. It was the concierge, confirming our 7:00 p.m. dinner reservation at Prime. I hung up the phone and sat back down at the table. Munching on a few breakfast potatoes, mulling over my day, I decided to hit the hotel pool and then spend the afternoon at the spa. I fingered the card that Brad had left and dialed Philipe's extension.

A male voice answered on the second ring, stiff and businesslike. It warmed dramatically when I identified myself. "Ms. Campbell! How can I help you?"

"I was thinking about going to the spa this afternoon. Could you help me to book some services?"

"Certainly. Just let me know what services you would like."

"I was thinking about a massage?"

"Julia, in Vegas, you need to go big. Let me put you down for a full treatment. Make that beautiful man treat you right."

I smiled into the receiver. "You're the boss, Philipe."

"Shall I put you down for one o'clock?"

"That would be perfect. Thank you." I was preparing to hang up when he spoke again.

"What are you doing between now and one?"

"I was going to go to the pool."

He clicked his tongue into the receiver. "You don't want to go to the hotel's pool. It is a zoo. Give me a call when you're ready, and I'll have someone escort you to our VIP pool."

"You rock."

I could hear his smile. "Yes, as a matter of fact, I do."

"Talk to you soon." I hung up the phone and moseyed to the bedroom, flipping on the clock radio when I got to the room. My outlook had brightened considerably after speaking to Philipe. *Why was I pissed to spend the day alone?* I pushed a few of the presets until I found a top-forty station. I turned up the volume and walked into the closet, unzipping my suitcase and flipping it open. I had only packed one bathing suit, an electric-blue bikini. I dropped my robe and stepped into the suit bottoms, tightening the side ties. A Rihanna song started on the radio and I sang and danced my way into the bathroom. I brushed my teeth again, then applied some waterproof mascara and lip gloss. My hair was still damp, so I ran a big comb through it and pulled it into a low knot. Becca had loaned me a sheer white cover-up, and I took it and my bikini top out of my suitcase. I put them both on and picked up the bathroom phone. I dialed Philipe's extension.

"Already ready?"

"Yes, sir."

"Someone will be there shortly."

"Thanks."

Five minutes later, as I was pulling on a pair of bejeweled sandals, there was a knock at the door. I grabbed the bag I had packed, complete with tanning spray, magazines and a white hotel towel, and went to the door. An attractive blonde in a gray suit stood there and flashed a friendly smile.

"You Julia?"

"I am!" I reached out my hand, and she shook it.

"I'm Rayne. Philipe asked me to show you to Cypress. You ready?"

"I am. Let's go."

Rayne kept up a steady stream of chatter as we traversed the halls, elevator and four different buildings. I was grateful she was there and more than a little worried about finding my way back. Finally, we arrived at a pool entrance, which was roped off with a line of people waiting to enter. She breezed by the line and waved at the security guard. She pulled me with her by the hand, moving through throngs of people until we arrived at a white cabana with linen curtains. We ducked inside and I saw a couch, television and wet bar, a wicker basket next to the couch with sun oils, magazines and towels. The wet bar had a bowl of fresh fruit and an ice bucket with bottled waters, sodas, beers and mixers. In front of the cabana, in a roped-off area, were two chaise lounges, ready with additional towels and pillows.

I flopped down on the couch and smiled blissfully at Rayne.

She laughed and crossed her arms. "I take it this is acceptable?"

"Girl, you are gonna have to drag me out of here!"

She laughed and took the seat next to me on the couch. "I wish I could stay here and relax, but I have a whale up in Privé that is dying to grab my ass again. If you need anything, Dmitry will get it for you."

"Who's Dmitry?"

"Oh, you'll see." She winked teasingly and sauntered off. I looked around the cabana and grinned to myself. I set my useless bag down on the floor and unzipped my cover-up. Pulling the garment over my head, I tightened my bikini strings and then started looking at the oils in the basket.

"Hello." A gorgeous blond stuck his head in, then the rest of his body followed, wearing a tight white Bellagio polo and short white shorts. A little too short. My suspicions were confirmed when he stood up in the cabana and sashayed rather than strode over to me. The man's features were Ken-doll perfect, and he had gleaming white teeth. I assumed this was Dmitry. "Ms. Campbell, I am Dmitry," he confirmed with a Russian lilt, something I'd never heard from a gay man before.

I stood up, smiling, and shook his hand. "Hi, Dmitry."

"Would you like me to spread some lotion on you?"

I blushed, and nodded. Twenty minutes later, I was stretched out on one of the outside chaise lounges, earbuds in, listening to Beyoncé, a frozen hot-pink drink next to me. My body was glistening with coconut oil, which Dmitry swore was the crack cocaine of tanning products. My hair was twisted up and had been sprayed lightly with an SPF protectant and moisturizing treatment, and I had a stack of chilled towels in a silver ice chest next to me. Dmitry had wanted to put cucumbers on my eyelids, but I had drawn the line at that. Every ten minutes, fans above me sent cool mists of moistened air down to me. In total bliss, I closed my eyes and drifted off to sleep.

Dmitry woke me up, shaking my arm gently. "Ms. Campbell." I blinked sleepily and tried to focus on his beautiful face. "I was told you have a 1:00 p.m. spa appointment. It is eleven-forty. Would you like me to order you some lunch?" I had fully woken by then, and nodded. Stretching, I removed my earbuds.

"Hot dog and fries, if they have it."

Dmitry's face took on a look, as if he had eaten something bad. "A hot dog?"

I grinned at him. "Not fancy enough for you?"

His pained look answered my question. "I suppose you'll be wanting a chocolate milk to drink?"

"No, smart-ass, a lemonade would be great." I batted my eyes at him sweetly. "Please?"

"Your wish is my command," he said, mock bowing.

"Thank you, dahling."

I decided an hour on my back was long enough and flipped over, lying on my stomach. A band had started playing poolside and I decided against the earbuds, pulling them out and undoing my bikini top. I balled it up and put it next to my chair, lying back down. Dmitry reappeared, my lemonade in hand, and frowned at me.

"You need a pillow—let me get you one." He strutted over to a wicker chest and bent over, opening it. Seconds later he had a small white pillow in his hand; he positioned it for me, fluffing it dramatically first. "It'll be about fifteen minutes on your...snack. I'll bring it over as soon as it's ready."

I nodded, feeling the warm sun on my bare back, already starting to doze. I dreamed of being on a crowded street. It was hot and muggy, and I was being bumped in all directions. I finally escaped into an oyster bar and ordered a dozen raw ones. But the more oysters I ate, the more appeared, and I began to stress over the mounting pile. I had just called for the—

"What the hell are you doing?" The voice was loud enough to wake me, and I jolted out of my dream. I opened my eyes and saw only terry-cloth white—the cushion of my chaise. The voice had been deep, and sexy, and...Brad. I rolled over and saw him standing over me, hands on his hips, looking down on me with an expression of mock irritation. I saw his eyes wander to my bare breasts and I raised my hands quickly to cover them. "What?"

"A hot dog?" His eyes flashed with humor, but he kept his stern expression. "I'm dropping ten K an hour at the blackjack table, they are instructed to wine and dine you to subliminal bliss, and you're ordering a hot dog and fries?"

He sat next to me on the chaise lounge. I had to slide over in order to accommodate him. I still had both hands cupping my breasts, and he reached over with one hand and traced a line on my skin down the center of my chest. My breathing quickened. He pulled down one of my hands, then the other, leaving me completely exposed. I pulled my hands back up, looking around quickly to see if anyone had noticed. They had. One guy gave me a thumbs-up. *Great.*

"Don't cover them up," Brad said. "They're beautiful. I want to see them."

God, he is hard to say no to. "No!" I hissed.

"Why?"

"I don't flash my tits around. Besides, they're little."

"I fucking love them. They're perfect. Let me see them, Julia. Please."

I rolled my eyes and cursed him under my breath for being so damn irresistible, and for having the power to control my damn actions. I dropped my hands and he dropped his eyes, drinking in the sight of me bare and exposed. "God, baby." He shook his head, running his hand lightly over my stomach, my skin tightening at his touch.

Dmitry chose that moment to reappear and I blushed. He didn't give me a second glance, just stared at Brad, his expression adoring. *Yeah, buddy, I feel your pain.* "Hi, Mr. De Luca," he purred. Brad nodded at him, smiled and then focused back on me. Dmitry started straightening up the cabana, all the while looking over at Brad. I guess his magnetism didn't limit itself to women.

Brad leaned forward and kissed me, putting his hand on my right breast and squeezing it gently.

"Brad!" I pushed him back and swatted his hand away.

"What?"

"You can't grope me in public! Me being topless is bad enough!" I looked around furtively.

"Did I mention the amount of money I'm spending? I could fuck you right here on this chair and they wouldn't say anything." My jaw dropped, and despite my best effort I could feel my pussy practically pant with anticipation. He leaned down and kissed me again, keeping his hand to himself this time, then leaned forward and whispered in my ear. "Let them all look. It turns me on when men drool over you." I frowned, trying to think of an intelligent response, when he kissed my neck and rose, looking around for Dmitry. The man practically sprinted to his side and beamed enthusiastically.

"Is her lunch ready?"

"Yes, sir, they're bringing it now. Can I get you anything to eat?"

"No, I'm fine. Thank you."

"*Oh-kay.* You be sure and let me know."

Brad leaned over and lightly brushed his hand over my nipples, making me shiver. Feeling braver, I bit my lower lip and stared at him. He froze, his eyes flashing at me, and then he gave a slow grin. He kissed my cheek and then whispered in my ear. "Your body is killing me. I want to take you up to the room right now." I gave a slow smile in response and rolled over. I pretended to adjust and get comfortable on the lounge, pushing my ass up teasingly. He groaned and grabbed my ass with his hand, squeezing hard. Releasing it, he then gave it a hard slap—so hard I yelped. I lowered my ass and lay down flat, glaring at him over my shoulder. He chuckled.

"Have a nice day, baby. Enjoy your damn hot dog. Order a second if you're feeling really crazy."

I growled at him through the terry cloth.

Eighteen

6:15 p.m.

I sat in the spacious master bathroom, putting on makeup at the counter seat. The spa had been wonderful. I got a ninety-minute Swedish massage, a facial and a mani-pedi. I showered at the spa and left feeling deliriously relaxed and polished. The radio played from the bedroom, and I sang along while I blow-dried and straightened my hair.

I debated calling Olivia back, but there was too much to discuss and I didn't know when Brad would be returning. I also wasn't ready for her questions.

I didn't know how I felt about Brad. Half the time he pissed me off with his arrogance and sexual misdoings, and the rest of the time I wanted to shove him down and rip his clothes off. I was used to being the aggressor, to being in control of the relationship. That wasn't going to be possible with Brad. But then again, a relationship wasn't a possibility anyway.

Having only had sex with two guys, the prospect of Brad being the third scared me. What did it say about me if I had sex with someone that I sometimes didn't even like, much less love? What had been the point of my waiting until I was nineteen for sex if I was just going to jump into bed with strangers now?

I dusted nude shadow on my eyelids and then reached for the bronze. I couldn't resist the incredible attraction I felt for Brad. I wasn't naive enough to think that this animal attraction was something just the two of us shared. I could see the look in every passing woman, in every waitress, room attendant and grandma that walked by. I remembered this morning's orgasm, and a twinge of pleasure zipped through my lower body. I wanted, even needed to have sex with him. I couldn't remember ever wanting to have sex with anyone unless it was to show my love and to preserve a relationship. Sex with Brad would be different—dangerous, passionate and… and…I didn't know what to do.

I blinked and looked in the mirror, examining my eyes. They looked good. Adult, sophisticated and sexy. I leaned forward to apply a second coat of mascara. I was just about ready.

I was in a lace bra and panties, had slipped on some heels for the hell of it, and was spritzing on perfume when Brad walked in. His grin widened, and he walked into the bathroom and leaned against the door, whistling under his breath. He must have come up and changed at some point during the day. He now wore a white button-down shirt with dress pants and a jacket.

"Not the outfit I would have expected for dinner, but you look mighty fine, Ms. Campbell."

I sauntered over and placed both hands on his lapel, pulling him gently to me and kissing him on the lips. "Very funny, smart-ass. I'll be dressed in a minute."

He grinned wickedly. "I'll watch. Want a glass of wine? I can grab some out of the wine cooler."

"No, thanks."

He stayed in his position, arms crossed, and watched me as I went into the walk-in closet and shut the door. Becca had blessed me with three different dresses, all ridiculously short and sparkly. According to Becca, everyone in Vegas glittered. From what I had seen so far, she was right. I grabbed a nude strapless minidress that sparkled when the light hit it, paired it with my highest stilettos and rubbed some lotion on my legs. Fluffing my hair, I prepared to make my grand entrance to Brad. Swinging open the doors dramatically, I put on my sexiest pout and walked out. To an empty bathroom. *Cool, Julia. Really cool.*

Shaky on the plush carpet in my ridiculously high heels, I made it to the living room without turning an ankle and sat in the first chair that I came to. Brad whistled at my wobbly entrance and let his eyes linger on my legs, tanned and freshly shaved. I pretended to glare at him. I had worked pretty damn hard to look this hot and was glad it was getting the proper attention. He walked to my chair and leaned over, placing his hands on the armrests on either side of me. His scent invaded me and I got wet just from smelling it. That, and his beautiful face, and those dark, sexy eyes with their thick lashes. He nudged my legs apart with one knee and moved it in a bit, his dress pants scratchy against my smooth skin. His mouth so close to mine, he brushed my lips sweetly and then moved to my ear.

"I want to fuck you in that dress."

I inhaled sharply, his knee moving farther in between mine. Fuck dinner and the damn show. *I want him right now, right here in this suede chair.* I leaned my head back, and he nuzzled, nipped, then kissed my neck. I smiled. "Want to skip dinner?"

His eyes lidded as he shook his head. "A man's gotta eat. Plus—" he moved his hands from the armrests to my waist and lifted me to my feet as though I weighed nothing "—you'll need fuel for tonight's activities." He nuzzled my neck again and squeezed my ass. Hard. I loved it.

I pasted an innocent look on my face. "What, the Cirque du Soleil show?"

"Get your ass out the door," he growled, smacking me.

We arrived at Prime a few minutes before seven. Brad stopped just outside the restaurant, reaching into his pocket to answer his ringing cell. I wandered to the side, seeing a balcony with a view of the lake. Just then I heard something, a few soft, haunting notes. Brad tapped my shoulder and I turned. "Out," he whispered, the phone still pressed to his ear. "On the balcony. Watch the fountains." I made my way to the balcony and leaned on the heavy marble railing, the water starting to move in front of me. The music began again, softly and then increasing in volume until every note was clear and beautiful. The fountains increased with the music, swelling and falling, thousands of different jets under the lake creating a beautiful dance that made my heart ache. I stood there, transfixed and swept away by the perfect harmony, as the last note lingered on the lake.

I became aware of Brad's presence behind me. Touched by the display, I turned and hugged him, holding him tight and feeling his strength. He smoothed my hair and looked out on the lake. "It's beautiful, isn't it?" I nodded and backed away from him. He turned and offered his arm to me. "Shall we eat?"

I beamed and nodded, accepting his arm as gracefully as I could. "Yes, we shall." *And Cinderella arrived at the ball.*

Prime was incredible. Decorated in navy and cream silk, it was elegance to the *n*th degree. The restaurant was located right on the lake, and our seats were in a private alcove with a full-length window showing the view in all its glory. Brad began by ordering a thousand-dollar bottle of Dom Pérignon, which was delivered to our table before the waiter had even finished his initial speech. I took a sip timidly. It was the first restaurant, other than Centaur, I'd been to that had more than three utensils. Brad sat across from me in his suit, playing with a fork and looking devastatingly handsome. My nervousness from the night before returned.

"Don't worry about the etiquette." Brad must have seen my study of the four forks at my setting. "I still don't know my way through these utensils."

I doubted that, but grinned at him.

The first food brought to our table was a seafood tower, almost four feet tall, with four levels of white meat. Crystal-clear ice chips with colossal shrimp, oysters, clams, crab legs and lobster stacked its silver shelves. The minute it was delivered to our table by two black-clad waiters, Brad rubbed his hands together in glee and pounced on it. He filled the white china plates set in front of us, plucking succulent items from each level. I waved him off, but he ignored me, piling on more seafood. I stared, aghast, at my plate.

I did not eat seafood. Not that I didn't *eat* seafood, but I didn't really like seafood. I had a very limited palate. I grew up eating chicken, rice and vegetables. The chicken was prepared in different manners, but the rice was always brown and the vegetables always overcooked. The only seafood I had been exposed to was imitation crabmeat that smelled disgusting and often occupied a portion of our fridge. I have no idea what my mom did with the crab, but I think she ate it straight out of the package. *Yuck.* I had tried shrimp before, and didn't mind it, but it wasn't anything that rocked my world.

I stared at my heaped plate with a mixture of digust and dread. The waiter was busy affixing a white bib around Brad's neck; a second waiter headed toward me with the same intent.

I held up a newly manicured—*damn, those look good!*—hand to ward him off. He halted with surprise.

"Ma'am, your dress." He held up the bib as if it was a burnt offering. This exchange drew Brad's attention, and he stopped, midcrack, his head coming up and peering at me over his bib, causing an unladylike giggle to start to rise from me.

I swallowed it down and looked at him. "I, er…don't like seafood."

"Lobster? King crab?" His face twisted into an unbelieving scowl.

"Well, we didn't eat a lot of seafood growing up and—"

"Have you ever had it before? Lobsters, crab, oyster?"

Cinderella was about to be exposed. "Well, no. I've had crab before, and didn't like it." *Imitation crab, but crab's crab.*

He beamed and reached across, pushing my plate closer to me and waving the bib-carrying waiter forward. "I, er—no, really…" I said feebly as the waiter affixed the ridiculous bib around my neck.

Brad pushed a ceramic bowl with a candle that heated melted butter toward me. "Dunk the pieces into the butter, and then eat," he urged, his hands already covered with dripping butter. "You'll love it." Hesitantly, I pulled a piece of the soft meat out of the precut lobster shells and dipped it in the butter. His eyes never leaving me, Brad followed the meat to my mouth to be sure that I ate it. I tentatively put the meat on my tongue and gently chewed. The feathery consistency didn't sit well with me and all I tasted was butter and bland meat. I swallowed, the blob of buttery meat slipping down my throat with a thick glug. *Ewww.* I fought a grimace and smiled in my best ladylike manner. "Hmm…" I said.

"That's the best lobster in town," Brad beamed, beside himself with glee. "Go on! Try the crab!" He dug into his pile with reckless abandon.

The waiter came and refilled our champagne glasses. I took a generous sip of champagne and faced the plate again. Looking past the ridiculous plate, I gazed with despair at the tower—made for four and towering on the table in between Brad and me. I practically had to lean around it to see him. The bottom rung of the silver tower was empty when they had delivered it, but was now being filled with the empty lobster and crab-claw shells.

Lightbulb.

Fifteen minutes later, Brad sat back with a satisfied groan. "I have been dreaming of those claws for weeks." He met my eyes with a Cheshire grin. "Well? Was I right or what?"

I smiled at him over my champagne and empty plate. "It was very good, Brad. Thank you."

"I don't know how you look so put-together. I always feel like I need a bath after eating this stuff." He wiped his face with his napkin and pulled at his bib, breaking the plastic tie. "Should we get another or do you want to go ahead and order dinner?"

"Dinner, please," I said quickly.

Brad's eyes trained on me for a moment, then he shrugged. "Sounds good to me."

The waiter appeared and began pulling the silver trays off the tower, starting with the top one. *Uh-oh.* I had anticipated his taking the entire tower at once, as he had brought it to us. My mind raced for something to distract Brad.

Shrimp platter gone.

"I was thinking, Brad…"

Clams and oysters level gone.

"…maybe tonight, after the show…"

Lobster level taken.

"…we could, ahh…" *Don't look down!*

The large silver platter that had housed the tangled pile

of snow and king crab legs was lifted, exposing the plate of empty shells…and expensive meat of crab and lobster I had carefully hidden under the guise of placing my shells on the plate. The meat, which had been strategically hidden from the side view, was now fully exposed, crab and lobster stretched out like bathing beauties on South Beach. Brad completely ignored my sentence—not that it was going anywhere—and stared at the shell plate in bewilderment. The waiter leaned over and examined it, puzzled.

The lightbulb went off in both their heads at the same time and they turned in unison to stare at me. Eyes wide, frozen in my seat, my hands twisted in my lap as I tried to think of something to say. Brad broke the silence before my head found a solution.

"You hid that?" he asked, his head tilted to the side, his eyes unreadable.

"I didn't really like it," I lamely responded. "You seemed so excited and my plate was so full…" I trailed off.

"Jesus, woman!" he quietly and happily thundered.

He's happy? I was confused.

He grabbed his bread plate and quietly scooped up the offensive pieces, plopping them onto his plate. He moved the still-lit butter stand back in front of him. A second waiter appeared with a replacement bib and Brad sat up so that he could tie it on. Once the trash plate had been rummaged through, by both Brad and the server, who shot me a look of sophisticated disdain, it was carried away and Brad and I were left alone. Just us, my leftover seafood and the glow of drawn butter. Brad was beside himself with amusement.

"Why didn't you just say you didn't like it? I would have been more than happy to eat it all myself, Julia."

"You were so pushy about me eating it, and so enthusiastic about it, I didn't want to disappoint you." I sounded like a freakin' child, but it had come out of my mouth—no point in trying to put it back in.

"I'm not your father, Julia." His grin faded slightly but he kept his tone light. "You don't have to do as I tell you."

I set my chin and stared at him. "I know, Brad. I don't do everything you say." But I doubted my own words. I had let him talk me into a lot.

"Does our age difference bother you?" His face was so serious, I tried to keep from grinning, but seeing him peering at me over his plastic bib with butter dripping off his fingers, my grin broke through. "What?"

"Nothing. No, our age range doesn't bother me. It did… before I met you. I envisioned you old, wrinkly, with gray pubic hair…." I grinned wickedly at him.

"How do you know I don't have gray hair down there? I could have a whole forest."

I wrinkled my nose and tossed a piece of bread at him. "Gross! Besides, I sneaked a peek last night while you were drooling in your sleep." He laughed and grabbed my hand, bringing it to his mouth for a quick kiss.

"I can't keep my mouth off of you," he murmured. A stream of deliciousness shot through my body. I took another sip of champagne and met his sexy eyes across the table. *God, this man is tempting.*

"Another bottle of Dom Pérignon, Mr. De Luca?"

Another? What happened to the first? I looked at my now-empty glass.

"Yes. Are you ready to order, Julia?"

"You go ahead. I'll know in just a moment." I quickly scanned the menu. The prices made my eyes widen. The seafood tower Brad had just demolished was three hundred and fifty dollars! I tried to find something relatively inexpensive, but gave up on that mission. Most of the items on the menu I didn't even recognize. I finally settled on a filet, which was something I at least knew I liked. I heard Brad order a prime rib and three side items, then the critical waiter's eyes were on me.

"Filet, please, medium rare." I smiled sweetly and handed him my menu. He nodded primly and left. I leaned forward and whispered. "This place is ridiculously expensive! Do you know how much that lobster I was throwing away costs?"

His eyebrows rose at my indignation and he smiled. "Julia, it's all comped. All this—" he gestured around "—is on the casino. Their focus is on gambling, and I pay them royally for it. This is your first time in Vegas and I want you to have a good time." He smiled good-naturedly at me. "But I appreciate your concern for my wallet." He raised his glass for a toast. "To bigger and better. May you enjoy this weekend." I raised my glass and clinked it to his.

My eyes floated through the room. We were tucked in a beautiful little corner and had a nice view of the other tables. My eyes froze on a couple by the window. "Brad—that's George Clooney!"

Brad glanced over his shoulder and shrugged. "You'll see a lot of celebrities this week. Vegas is their playground, especially Bellagio."

I saw George Clooney reach across the table and rub his date's hand, a platinum-blonde in a blue dress. I tried not to bounce in my seat with excitement and forced my eyes away from the actor. *Becca would never believe this.* I wondered if I could sneak a photo with my iPhone, but dismissed the thought. Brad was watching me, a smirk on his handsome features.

Our food came, sizzling steaks on white china with melting butter on them. Brad had ordered creamed corn, mashed potatoes and mushrooms, and a group of waiters brought out the plated dishes. We both dug in, and other than occasional moans, there was silence for the next few minutes. I finally took a break and sat back with my champagne. Blissfully, I closed my eyes and let the food settle a bit in my stomach.

"Enjoying yourself?"

I nodded without opening my eyes. "Immensely."

I felt his hand underneath the narrow table, caressing my knee. My eyes opened and I moved my knee out of his reach. His eyes turned playfully mournful.

"I haven't decided whether I'm going to let you have that. I'm trying to be a good girl."

"Good girl?" He swallowed a swig of champagne. "I haven't seen that side yet."

I harrumphed and leaned forward on my elbows, staring at him. "I'll have you know I am a *very* good girl, even if I have had weak resolve lately around you. I plan to go back to my prudish ways, starting tonight." *Maybe.*

He leaned back in his chair, his hand on his chin, rubbing appraisingly. "Is it for religious reasons, this attempt to abstain?"

I shrugged. "Not really. I have a healthy relationship with God, and I don't particularly think he cares if I choose to express my love in a sexual manner. But that's what I feel I am doing with sex, expressing my love—not for religious reasons, just for my own. I hear about women who feel used or guilty after sex, and I've never felt that, and don't want to start."

He leaned back, regarded me seriously. "I think most of the women who feel that way are having sex in order to accomplish something, to win a man's affection, impress him, gain financial security…." He waved a hand generically. "The man they are sleeping with is fucking them for one reason—pleasure—not because he loves them, or wants to love them, or wants to pay their light bill, but because he wants to get off, and they are conveniently around. After sex, they all of a sudden have a boatload of expectations, and get their feelings hurt when nothing has changed on his end. Women think sex is this magic act when in fact it isn't. And there are too many women ready to hand it over too easily."

I glared at him. "You make us out to be so...pathetic. Is that how you view women, as disposable receptacles to stick your dick into?"

He rubbed his head exasperatedly. "Julia, I am being honest about sex. Your college boys probably don't know enough about sex or how they're feeling yet. I am a mature man trying to explain to you how we, as men, work. It's a point of view that most women never know."

"So that's why you sleep with your clients? To get a sexual release? Don't you think that you risk too much for something you can get from all of the sluts lying around waiting for you to fuck them?!"

My voice had risen a little too high, and Brad glanced around before answering. "Julia, the clients I do fuck are adult women, most of them mature, who realize what we're doing and what our roles are in it."

"What are your roles?" I asked, my tone sharp.

"Julia, don't attack me because you don't believe in my lifestyle choices. I have absolute confidence in my sexual relationships and don't need to explain them to anyone. I am choosing to explain them to you because I hope to fuck you in the future—" he placed careful emphasis on the word *fuck* "—and I don't want to do it with any misplaced expectations on your part."

I bit into a mushroom and chewed slowly, putting off a response. *Damn man.*

His voice, taking on a gentler tone, continued. "Our roles,

when I am with a client, are pretty defined and simple. We don't screw at the office. I come to her house—she is never in mine. When I take my clients on business dinners, it's for just that, business. If she's interested in sex and I am sexually attracted to her, then we meet later, have sex and I go home."

"It sounds awfully cold and heartless to me. Don't they feel used?"

"Most men fuck in a way that might make a woman feel used. They spend the majority of the time getting oral sex, or taking what they want in the position that they want it. As I mentioned earlier, the reason for their sex is to get off, not for any other purpose. I don't fuck that way. I am more about the woman's pleasure. Did you feel used this morning?"

His sudden question caught me off guard. Midchew, I quietly swallowed the hunk of tender filet I had been savoring and wiped my mouth. I sipped the glass of ice water and looked up at the gold-leaf ceiling, thinking. Had I felt used? *Used* hadn't even crossed my mind. I had felt elated, relaxed, sleepy, but not guilt or regret. Then again, a guy going down on you was a lot different than sex, right?

"No, I didn't feel used. But I think what we did and sex are two different things. Sex is me giving a part of myself."

He snorted. "Says who? Every woman-lit book out there? Your parents? The church? Society has this hang-up with the idea that women are losing a part of themselves every time they fuck, and it's bullshit. So a man can be with twenty different women and have a normal, healthy self-esteem, but a woman sleeps around and she's emotionally destroyed? Women attach feelings to sex because society tells them to. They think that they should feel for a guy before sleeping with him, so they manufacture a relationship or emotions and that only screws them up later on. It provides justification that later bites them in the ass when they try to look in the mirror and come to grips with 'what they've done,' when 'what they've done' is nothing to be ashamed of. The act of sex is healthy, normal, God-given. It's the emotions and entitlement that everyone attaches to it that are harmful."

I looked at him, listening to his words, and tried to remind myself that he was an attorney, born and bred to convince juries, lonely housewives and me that what came out of his mouth was fact. I felt as if I was in a Twister game and could no longer tell whether I was upside down, or lefty, or right side up. Part of what he was saying seemed completely logical, although it went against everything I had ever been taught or told. But who was I to blindly follow what I was taught or told? It made sense that the church or my parents would tell me to wait for sex, that I should only sleep with my husband, the person I loved. I was sure I would tell my future daughter the same thing.

Brad poured more champagne. "If sex is only for procreation, then yes, only have sex with your husband—it would be wrong to create young with total strangers. That mindset thinks of sex only as a tool for reproduction. It ignores the essence of sex—the passion and enjoyment."

"I don't think sex should be saved for marriage—that's not what I'm saying. I just think that I should love the person I have sex with."

"What is love?"

"What?"

"What do you consider love to be? Not love for your family, but the love you're talking about, toward a partner. What do you consider it to be? How do you know when you're in love?"

"I don't know. I do know that I need to be more careful, not put a label like love on a relationship before I'm sure. Before, I felt like if I loved someone, then I was obligated to have sex with them. I wasn't manufacturing feelings of love to justify sex, as you seem to think women everywhere are doing. I thought I was in love and felt like that was expected of me. Plus, I didn't want to enter into marriage without knowing if I was sexually compatible with the person."

"Who were you thinking of marrying?"

I toyed with a hunk of soft white bread before deciding to butter it. I wanted something to keep my hands and eyes occupied, anything to avoid looking in his intense brown eyes and strong face. One hundred percent of his attention was on me, and I felt as if I was under a microscope. He was asking me things and making me look at ideas and feelings that I hadn't had a chance to examine, and I didn't know what or how I felt yet.

"I was engaged to a guy named Luke. We dated for six months, I thought I was in love, and I probably was. It was just… He was just the wrong guy for me. I wanted too many things from him, and he didn't have the skill set or work ethic to provide them."

"Material things?" His voice seemed a little dark.

"Eventually. I want to live my life a certain way. One that doesn't involve unpaid bills and run-down apartments. Luke was older than me, twenty-seven, and couldn't keep a job and had no aspirations. I was looking at a future of me working constantly and nagging him all the time. I didn't like the person I was turning into and couldn't accept the person he was. I had deep feelings for him, but I felt like if he was my true love, I wouldn't have been trying so hard to change him."

"And the other?"

"Other what?"

"The other love you had—your first."

"Oh. That guy was a jackass. He was the first guy I wanted more than he wanted me. He promised me the world and then dumped me two weeks after he took my virginity. We had been together six months and had sex on my nineteenth birthday. I hate thinking about him. There wasn't even anything great about him. He was a weak, pathetic, silver-spoon asshole." I grinned suddenly and looked up at Brad. "Do I sound a little bitter?"

"A bit. It's okay. Early loves can be a bitch."

"Did you love your wife?"

"I met my wife in college, and yes, believed I loved her."

"And now?"

"Do I love her now?"

"No. In retrospect, do you think you were in love with her?"

"I think love is a Hallmark idea that society has created. I cared very deeply for her. All of the books and movies adore the phrase, 'I loved her—I wasn't in love with her.' I think for a marriage to work, both parties have to understand that it's not about being 'in love.' Both people need to care deeply about the other person, to put the other's needs before their own, and to make a daily commitment to that person to stick it out. Hillary made that commitment to me, and probably would have stuck it out till we were old and gray and dead. I wasn't committed and dropped the ball. But what I should have added first is that choosing the correct person is the most important step. There's no point in putting all of the daily time, effort and commitment into a lifelong marriage with the wrong person. Hillary and I were the wrong people."

"But you said on our first date that you wouldn't get married again."

"All of my beliefs about what makes a marriage work are based on my work experience and marriages I've seen that do work. A woman who can meet my needs sexually wouldn't fall into the same criteria that I would want in a wife. It's a catch-22." He shrugged his shoulders and tilted his head at me. He drained his glass and set it down, staring at me with hungry eyes. "You look breathtaking."

I laughed and leaned forward, shaking my finger at him. "Ah-ah-ah, you are not going all Rico Suave on me. We haven't finished this conversation."

"Fine. What else do you want to pick my enormous brain about?"

"God, you are cocky. Okay, last question."

"Shoot."

"How many women have you slept with?"

"What?"

"You heard me! If I'm even going to think about sleeping with you, I need to know what number I'm going to be."

"So you are thinking about sleeping with me?"

His hand was back on my knee. The unexpected touch caused my breath to hitch. I swatted his hand away again, but slower this time, looking at him through lowered lashes. "Kind of. You are very persuasive, though I don't want to know how many times you've given that 'sex is society's blessing' opening statement."

He laughed and removed his hand, but lingered as he did so, grazing my inner thigh with his fingers. I waited for his response expectantly, and he rolled his eyes. "God, Julia. I don't really know."

"What? Of course you do! Don't guys notch it into their bedposts or something?"

"Not gentlemen."

"Oh, please, don't pull that. Okay, rough estimate if you're too 'gentlemanly' to give me an exact."

He thought for a while, pulling on his ear, his eyes getting hazy. He finally shrugged. "If I had to guess, probably in the hundred-fifty-to-hundred-eighty range."

I think my eyebrows hit a new high on my forehead. I

had been expecting something high, but this took the cake. "Bullshit."

"I have no reason to brag to you. If I calculate about two a month—there were probably ten before I got married—I've been divorced five or six years.... It's got to be in that range."

"You pig!" I sputtered.

"Why? Because I love sex and enjoy having it with beautiful women?"

"I don't know—it just seems wrong. Haven't you had any relationships in the last six years?"

"Of course I have, but they weren't monogamous, on either side."

"Then that's not a relationship. The whole definition of a romantic relationship is exclusivity—monogamy. Otherwise you're just two friends who fuck."

He waved a hand at me, dismissing my point. "There are couples who have a loving, normal relationship and aren't monogamous."

"I don't think you are a good authority on how a loving, normal relationship works."

"Don't judge me when you don't know me. Just because I currently choose to be single doesn't mean I can't be a good husband."

I stared at him in stony silence. I couldn't even process his contradictory words; I was too stuck on the number of women he had slept with. That was way too many. I didn't have any good reason why. For the same reason I didn't have any good response to his argument that women should have carefree, emotion-free sex. He had bended my thinking on that, but I'd be damned if I was going to let him know. I finally sighed and relaxed my angry shoulders. "I'm still hungry. Are we ordering dessert?"

He laughed and leaned forward, cupping my chin in his

hand and kissing me. "Yes, we are, but not here." He gestured to our waiter, who had been waiting for a lull in our conversation. He presented the check, which Brad quickly signed. "Come on, let's go." He stood up and held out a hand to me. I grabbed my purse and stood, smoothing down my dress. My hand clasped firmly in his, I followed him through the restaurant, past George Clooney—*oh, my God!*—and outside, onto the balcony.

The balcony, where I had watched my first fountain show, now had several small round tables set up with tablecloths, silver and candles. A tuxedoed man held out my chair, gold with red velvet cushions, and I smiled at him and sat down. Brad took the seat across from me and nodded to our waiter, a new gentleman, older and short, with a thick white mustache.

"Monsieur? Mademoiselle?" the man greeted us and poured Voss water into both our chilled glasses. He began to describe their dessert selections. Brad cut him off while he was still on the first dessert.

"How many choices do you have tonight?"

"Four, sir."

"We'll have one of each."

"Yes, sir."

"And a bottle of Dom Pérignon, 1996."

"Certainly, sir." The man left, and I leaned forward and whispered to Brad. "You shouldn't have ordered champagne. I'm going to be drunk if I have any more."

He leaned forward also, our faces now only inches apart, and whispered in a conspiratorial tone, "What is drunk Julia like?"

"Very horny and also very sleepy. It leaves a very narrow window of opportunity."

"Are you horny right now?"

I wet my lips, our faces still very close. "No." *Yes!*

"Then you should drink some more."

"Don't think you can close the deal without me being inebriated?"

"Touché, Ms. Campbell." He waved; the miniature tuxedo was instantly at his side.

"Yes, Mr. De Luca?"

"I think we will hold off on the champagne, please."

"Certainly, sir. I will let the wine room know immediately." He rushed off in a blur of coattails.

Faint musical notes began drifting across the water, and I turned to watch the now-still lake. Brad watched me, smiling at my rapt attention.

I rose and walked to the balcony's edge, leaning on the rail and staring. The notes were louder now, and the initial delicate fountains of water were beginning to grow, shooting higher into the sky. I wanted to stay there forever, in that spot, in that gorgeous dress, my skin glowing, a gentle breeze on my shoulders, watching lights and water dance on a lake to a man singing opera. I felt Brad's presence behind me and he leaned forward, resting his hands on the railing on either side of me, his face next to mine, watching the show. We stayed there, silent, spooned together against the railing, until the last note traveled across the water and the lake went dark.

"It's heartbreaking, isn't it?" he said. "Heartbreaking and beautiful at the same time."

"What is that song?"

"It's Andrea Bocelli. 'Time to Say Goodbye.'"

"It is wonderful. Achingly beautiful."

"That's a good way to put it." He moved his hands from the railing to my arms and grasped them. Pulling on one and pushing with the other, he spun my body until my back was on the railing, my face tilted up to his. I stared into his eyes, pools of so many complex things I didn't understand. I only knew one thing. I wanted him so badly it hurt, ached between my legs. I knew it wasn't right—I knew I was one of hundreds, but I didn't care. I wanted him more than I had ever wanted anything in my life. I leaned forward, closed my eyes and kissed him with everything I had.

He responded instantly, pressing his body hard against me, moving his hands from my arms. One hand grabbed the back of my neck, the other gripped my ass hard, and I hooked one leg around him, crazed to feel more of him against my body. He was hard, and I felt it, liked it. We kissed like teenagers for almost a minute before separating, breathing hard. He kissed me one final time, hard, and let me go. He smiled at me playfully, then we walked back to the table.

Our waiter appeared so quickly I suspected he'd been standing in the shadows, waiting for our make-out session to end. I blushed, but he seemed completely at ease. He was followed by a tall man carrying a large tray loaded with desserts.

Fifteen minutes later, I had eaten small bites of tiramisu, pineapple cheesecake, fruit-loaded crème brûlée and some extremely rich chocolate mousse. We had downed ice water but no alcohol, and I stretched luxuriously, my stomach filled to the brim. Candlelight flickered off the remnants of our desserts and Brad's face glowed across from me in the light. I licked the last bit of mousse off my spoon and played with it in my mouth, eliciting a smile from Brad.

"You are incorrigible," he murmured.

"That I am," I said. I smiled, too, our eyes meeting and holding for one delicious moment. I finally broke the contact, looking away. "Do you typically come to Vegas alone?"

"It's probably half-and-half. Vegas is a wonderful place, but it can be lonely as a single." He shrugged. "It's not a difficult problem to solve—beautiful women fill the casinos."

"You mean prostitutes?"

"I think the preferred title is *escort,* but no, I don't meet with them."

"Never?"

He sighed and looked at me, bemused. "You ask a lot of questions."

"As do you. And I answered all of yours."

"Point made. A previous host I had sent up a girl once. I declined the escort and spoke to the host. They understand to not have it happen again."

"So you just sent her away? Was she pretty? What did she say?"

"She was extremely pretty, young, nineteen or twenty, had too much makeup on and a short dress, something similar to what you're wearing." *Great. I'm dressed like a hooker.* I pulled my dress down a bit, trying to get it to cover more leg. "I had just gotten up to my room and was getting ready for dinner when she knocked on the door."

"What did she say when you opened it?"

"God, I'd hate to sit through the opera with you. Let me tell the story, or I'll really stretch it out. She said that Blake—he was my old host—Blake had sent her up, and then she gave me a look that I think was supposed to be sexy. She asked if she could come in. I asked her if this is what I thought it was, and she didn't answer, she just walked past me into the room."

"And?"

"And...we didn't do anything. I told her I appreciated the gesture, but was not interested. I think I lied and said I was in a relationship or something. It was a few years ago. I offered her a drink, we talked for a bit and then she left."

"Really? Just talked? You, who have been pushing the envelope with me since we met, sat in your Vegas hotel room with a nineteen-year-old girl, had a drink and talked. Then your gentlemanly self walked her to the door and she left." I crossed my arms, shook my head and fixed him with a stare. "I'm not buying it."

He laughed and leaned forward, pulling one of my arms until it was free, and held my hand. "Why do you have such a low opinion of me?"

"You admit yourself that you are a sex fiend. Why would you pass on it when it's right there for the taking?"

"Because it is right there for the taking. That girl rode up that elevator to my room not knowing anything about me and was ready to have sex with whoever opened the door. There's no worse turnoff than that. Now, you, who are fighting me supposedly tooth and nail, that is a big turn-on for me." His voice had lowered. He fixed me with a look that he probably thought was sexy, which it was—deadly sexy—but I wasn't about to admit that.

"Supposedly? I am fighting you tooth and nail. And listen to what you just said. In that line of thought, rape should be right up your alley."

"Don't be ridiculous. You know what I mean. I like the chase."

"Is that the only reason I'm sitting here? Because I'm an intern in your firm, therefore off-limits? And because I said no when you initially asked me to lunch?"

"You're taking this personally. I invited you here because I enjoy spending time with you. You challenge me and make me laugh. And because every time I see you I want to rip your clothes off and put my hands on you." He finished the sentence in almost a growl. My eyes widened and I felt myself get weak despite my resolve to keep him at bay.

"So you didn't have sex with her?"

"No. Believe it or not, I do have some restraint." He lifted his head, catching the waiter's eye. The man scurried over with the bill, which Brad signed. He took a final sip of water, and nodded at me. "Let's go."

We walked out to the big double doors of the casino floor, and I held tight to Brad's arm, balancing carefully on Becca's shoes. The casino assaulted our senses as we entered—mechanical sounds of coins clinking, colors and lights everywhere, and a musical chime of voices talking and laughing. The faint smell of smoke was in the air, and we had to move slowly, crowds of people everywhere. I gripped Brad's arm, giving it a quick squeeze. He looked down at me and smiled. Then he leaned over and kissed the top of my head. He slowed a bit as we passed the blackjack table, his eyes lingering, and I pushed him on, laughing. We finally made it through the casino and lobby, and the exit doors were opened for us by two white-gloved door-men with beaming smiles.

"Mr. De Luca, your car is ready." A suited man appeared at Brad's side and held out his arm, indicating our limo. It looked just like the one that had brought us from the airport, and then I saw the familiar face of the driver, whose name I couldn't remember.

"Leonard," Brad said, shaking his hand.

"Got the car all ready for you. We going to New York, New York?"

"Let's talk in the car. I need to check with the boss."

Leonard grinned broadly and winked at me, holding open a door. "Ms. Campbell, you look beautiful."

"Thank you, Leonard. Good to see you again."

I stepped into the car, sliding over and watching them converse, a brief unguarded opportunity to study Brad unnoticed. He was such an enigma. Thoughtful and sweet at times, the perfect gentleman. Other times he was pure sexual temptation, able to soak my panties with a single look or touch. He was unapologetically honest about his love of women and sex, comfortable and unashamed of his conquests or lack of monogamy. I didn't know how to take it, didn't know what I wanted from him, other than the one overriding sexual desire that had been interfering with my common sense since the moment we'd met.

He climbed into the car, turned to me with a serious expression. "I made show reservations without asking what you wanted to do. If you don't want to go out, we can do something tamer. Leonard can just give us a tour of the Strip and then take us back to the hotel."

I grinned at him. "You and me, alone in this car? Sounds disastrous. Where would Leonard be taking you if you were alone?"

"If I'm alone, I normally go to dinner with Philipe or one of my other friends. We make a guys' night of it."

"Meaning?"

"You know Vegas—cigars, strip clubs, scotch…."

"But no prostitutes?" I teased him.

"You got it." He pulled me to him, kissed me briefly.

"Then let's do it De Luca-style."

He laughed, looking into my eyes, his own dark and sinful. "You really want to jump into the snake pit?"

"Viva Las Vegas, baby."

"Viva Las Vegas."

Nineteen

The stripper's name was Alexis. Not truly. Her real name was Sarah Hinkle, but that didn't sound sexy. It sounded Midwestern and hicky, which is what she had been—all braces and acne until she was sixteen, then the braces came off and she stole enough makeup from the local Walgreens to paint her face and hide her pimples. It took two more years and a girl down the street, Jennifer, showing her the "right" way to put on makeup, for Sarah's beauty to really show. Now, Springfield, Illinois, long gone, she shimmered in light gold body glitter, her skin toned the perfect shade of tanning-bed bronze. Her jet-black hair, grown long and flowing down her back, had just the right amount of curl, and when she flipped her head over, it fell into place perfectly. Her nails were long, with a perfect French manicure, and her nude painted feet had slid into jeweled five-inch stilettos. Naked in the dressing room, perfume filling the air and soft naked bodies everywhere, she tapped a fingernail on her lips and surveyed her outfits. Finally making her selection, she leaned forward and started pulling out hangers.

★ ★ ★

Brad called up front and asked Leonard to head to Baccarat. The driver nodded and pulled a U-turn, heading back into the Bellagio gates.

"What's Baccarat?"

"It's a bar back at Bellagio. We can grab cigars and drinks there, play a few hands. If I'm giving you the Vegas experience, you need to at least try your luck before we head home."

I nodded, grabbing my purse and double-checking that I had my ID. Leonard pulled around to a different entrance, parked and hastened around to my door. We stepped out and made our way through the casino again to a side bar. The opulent theme continued in there. A baby grand was front and center with a distinguished man playing Frank Sinatra. The maître d' recognized Brad and led us to a roped-off area reserved for VIPs. We settled into a plush velvet love seat, Brad taking up eighty percent of it. A stout, dark-skinned man appeared, dressed in all black, and offered us leather-bound menus. Brad waved them off.

"We'll have two Manhattans and a house phone, please." The man nodded and left, appearing again within seconds with a cordless phone.

"VIP reception is extension four-four-two, sir," he said in a European accent. Brad nodded, pressed a few buttons and then waited.

"This is Brad De Luca. May I speak to Nadine?" Brad waited a moment, his eyes catching mine, and he smiled. "Yes, Nadine. Do you mind running up to my room? I have a cigar box in the bedroom...."

"Yes...

"Baccarat...

"Thank you." He hung up the phone and passed it back to the waiter, who nodded and left, presumably to get our drinks.

"I've never had a Manhattan."

"It's strong. It might be too strong for you, but—"

"When in Rome?"

"Exactly."

The waiter appeared again, holding a silver platter with two martini glasses on it. We took our drinks and chinked them gently. I took a sip.

I couldn't keep the disgust off my face and fought against a cough. It was a searing-hot liquid tasting of straight alcohol. It ripped through my throat. I shook my head and set the drink down, Brad chuckling at my reaction.

"Sorry." I held the back of my hand to my lips, shuddering. "That probably wasn't the most ladylike reaction. You actually like that stuff?"

"It's an acquired taste. Want me to order you something else?"

"No. You made my bed and I'm going to lie in it." I took a baby sip of the cocktail, my second shudder less pronounced than the first. I set it to the side and crossed my legs, putting them dangerously close to Brad's hand, which was resting on his knee. He took notice of my legs and moved his hand to my upper knee, rubbing it gently. A leggy redhead in a black low-cut dress came over with a box of cigars. Bending over, she opened the box to Brad, but he shook his head at her. She nodded and stood, smiled at me and then left. Brad's eyes followed the curve of her ass until she was out of sight. I smacked his arm and he turned to me.

"What?"

"I'm right here! If you're going to check out other women, wait until I'm not around!"

He chuckled. "We're headed to a strip club after this. Are you really going to chastise me for checking out another woman?"

"Good point." I clicked my tongue at him.

He leaned back, laying his arm over the back of the couch, running a finger over my shoulder gently. There was weight in his words when he spoke next, enough to make me look over into his watchful eyes. "Are you one of those women?"

"What women?"

"You know, the jealous type."

"There is a difference between being jealous and being disrespected. You blatantly checking out other women in front of me is disrespectful. I don't care who you check out when you aren't with me."

He tilted his head to the side for a pause, then nodded. "Okay, I get that. But, ignoring that scenario, do you consider yourself a jealous person?"

I thought about the question for a moment, reviewing carefully my past dating experiences and the emotions that went with them. My moment turned into two. Brad sighed dramatically, waiting for my response. I raised my eyebrows at him. "Brutal honesty?"

"Of course."

"I don't know."

He snorted. "*That's* your brutal honesty?"

"Well, smart-ass, give me a minute to explain." I paused again, just to irritate him. "I have never felt jealousy or possessiveness in any relationship. However, in retrospect, I think part of that may have been due to the fact that I didn't really *care* whether or not the relationships ended. I placed no value on if they were faithful or not. I assumed that they were, because I typically place myself in relationships where I have the upper hand. Obviously, my first love left me, so that equation got screwed up somehow. But even when that relationship ended, I wasn't upset at losing him—I was upset at the inconvenience of the breakup. I had planned out a future with him and was going to need a new plan. I was also pissed at the blow to my ego. I wasn't used to being on the receiving end of rejection." I finished in a puff of exhaled air. That might have been too much honesty.

"So, you're saying you *are* jealous…you just haven't found anyone worth being jealous over yet?"

"I guess what I'm trying to say is that I have never been jealous before. I'll leave it at that. Why?" I leaned into his open arm, bumping him slightly. "Why do you care if I *am* jealous?"

"I'm just curious. Relationships with me don't typically last long if the woman is the jealous type."

"A moot point given that we aren't going to be in a relationship. But, since we are both being curious, are you 'one of those men'?"

"The jealous type?"

"Yes."

"I'm always very interested in my partner's activities. *Jealous* isn't really the right word."

"Controlling?"

A smile flitted across his mouth. "Yes, I like to be in control."

"In control and controlling are two different things."

"Spoken like a lawyer."

"I'm learning."

"And at times, I can probably be a little of both."

I didn't have time to contemplate his last sentence because a handsome man of average build, tall, with glasses and a shock of silver hair strode up to our table then. He was dressed in an expensive suit and had a wooden box in his hand—Brad's cigar box, I assumed.

Brad immediately stood up, beaming. "Philipe!" He grasped the man's hand firmly and clapped him on the back. I stood up as Brad turned to me. "This is Julia. Julia, Philipe."

We shook hands and I smiled at him. "Philipe, thank you so much for your help today. I had a wonderful day."

"Glad that you enjoyed yourself. How was Prime?"

"Delicious."

"Julia really enjoyed the seafood tower," Brad said, winking at me. I shot him a glowering look and then smiled again at Philipe. "Sit down with us." Brad gestured to the empty seat next to the love seat.

"No, I won't steal you away from this beautiful woman any longer. I just wanted to bring you your cigars and meet Julia." He passed Brad the box. "I added a few Cubans in there. You looked like you were running low."

"You didn't have to do that."

"I know. You guys skipping *Zumanity?*" he asked, glancing at his watch, a Rolex.

"Yeah. Next trip. We're going to hang out here for a bit and then hit up Saffire."

Philipe glanced briefly at me and then smiled at us both. "Well, I'll let you two get back to it. Julia, it was a pleasure to meet you."

"Likewise. Thank you again." We shook hands and he left. Brad sat down and opened the box, setting it on the table in front of us. The waiter brought us a tray with a tool of some sort and a lighter. He took Brad's empty martini glance and glanced at mine.

"I, umm...am fine."

"Would you like me to bring you something different?"

"No, I'll suffer through this one a little longer." Brad's lips twitched as he selected a cigar, pulled off the wrapping and used the tool to cut the end off the cigar. He passed it to me and then did the same for his cigar. I grasped the cigar tentatively, not sure how to hold it.

"Have you ever smoked before?"

"Uh...weed, once. Not anything else."

"Okay. Pass me your cigar. I'll light it for you."

He flicked the lighter and held the end of the cigar slightly above the flame, rolling it over a few times. He then put it in his mouth, held the flame away from its end and inhaled softly, rotating the cigar a bit. The end lit and glowed red in the dim bar. He passed me the cigar, telling me to hold it between my thumb and forefinger. I held it as he indicated and looked at him expectantly.

"Don't inhale it. Just let the smoke waft in your mouth for a bit, then open up and lightly exhale it out." I listened carefully and did as he said. "Slowly," he cautioned as I exhaled the smoke. "Take your time—I don't want you to get sick." He passed me a glass of water and I took a sip. The ice-cold water felt good going down my throat. He pushed me back on the couch, tilting my chin up, and then moved my cigar hand to the side.

"Avoid the smoke," his sexy voice whispered. I breathed in, the clean air going down easily. I heard him lighting up, and moments later, his head hit the cushion next to me. I turned and was suddenly looking very closely into his eyes. They were so complex, dark brown with reflections of me, hidden fires under the surface. He seemed to be constantly fighting battles in his head and those eyes held all the emotions. I felt like I was being sucked into his vortex, a world so different from my own, a world I wanted no part of, and yet I wanted every part of him. I couldn't pull away, couldn't avert my eyes from his intensity, the sexuality that radiated from him as intoxicating as it was forbidden.

He leaned forward, kissed me softly, then brushed my hair gently away from my face, his eyes following his hand as it tucked a strand behind my ear. I trembled slightly, our eyes still glued to each other, my body clenching uncontrollably in my most private place.

"God, I want to make you bad," he whispered, his hand on my lips, running over them briefly. I laughed softly and closed my eyes, turning my head to face forward and leaning it to the side, resting on Brad's big shoulder.

"Romantic, you are not."

He stiffened slightly, and ran his fingers up and down my bare thigh. "Romance is for relationships, something I don't want. I thought you knew that."

"I did—I do," I corrected myself. "There are just times when it seems you have relationship potential." He didn't respond, and I regretted making the statement.

"Suck on it." The comment shot through me and I glanced up sharply, looking at his eyes. They smiled and looked down at my lit cigar. "You have to suck on it at least once a minute or else it'll go out. Remember, don't inhale, and try not to let the smoke near you."

I smiled, and took a quick puff, trying to emulate every gangster movie I had ever seen.

"I've told you why I don't make a good boyfriend, at least not to girls like you."

"Was I a girl like me when you were between my legs this morning?"

"No, you were all woman then. Trust me…you don't have what it takes to be with me."

I looked at him sharply, sucking on the end of my cigar, and then petulantly blew smoke in his face. He dodged the stream of smoke by ducking down, grabbing my thigh for balance. His hands lingered there, sliding up briefly until they hit my lace panties, and then released. I felt my stomach curl, desire bubbling.

"Julia, it's not an insult. It's a good thing. I date bad girls—

you are wholesome and innocent. You will make a great wife for a tax accountant one day."

I grinned at him mischievously. "Like Bob?"

He grinned back. "Like Bob."

"You shouldn't have run him off so quickly then. Now I'll have to track him down again." I took a puff, then glanced sideways at him, his previous comment gnawing at me. "I'm not exactly innocent, you know."

"You are innocent to my world. And it's not a world I want to bring you into."

The unintended challenge in the statement fed my bad side. *Wholesome* and *innocent* was for Girl Scouts, not the image I had aspired to convey. "What's so dark and dangerous about your world? I know to your ancient self I must seem absolutely childlike, but I can handle whatever it is." I lifted a leg, throwing it over his, the action pushing his hand back to my panties, my crotch exposed to him. I bit my bottom lip, then brought the cigar to my mouth, taking a puff on the thick end, my movements deliberate and sensual. He said nothing, his eyes watching me closely, dark in restraint, though his fingers moved, flicking back and forth over my lace panties. I took a shuddering breath and tried to speak, shoving sex into every syllable. "For a good girl, I assure you, I can be very bad."

He had the nerve to laugh, moving his fingers as he did, a quick motion that plunged one of them past my thong, a quick dip inside. The shock of the touch, his skin against mine, made me jerk forward. He grabbed my hips and slid me up onto his lap. The movement slid my dress up, and my bare ass rested against the feel of his dress pants, my pussy still reeling from the unexpected contact. My face was at his, his eyes on my mouth, and he leaned forward and gently pressed his mouth against mine, before whispering against my parted lips, "And

I assure you, when you do decide to let me fuck your sweet little body, I will make you bad. Very bad."

He took any response I had from me, crushing my lips into his, his tongue electrifying my senses with perfect, delicious tastes of my mouth. When we parted, I was panting, and he had somehow smoothed my dress back into place, looking calm and completely in control.

I ground my teeth in frustration at this game that I was losing by a landslide. Even though he drove me wild, there was a part of me that didn't want to sleep with him just because he was seizing any control I had. I tried to play it cool, leaning back into the velvet couch, and sucking another breath of the cigar. Brad gently pulled it from my hand, setting it on an ashtray.

"Don't smoke any more. I don't want you getting sick on your first time."

I was already a little queasy, but didn't want to admit it. "Fine. You are a control freak."

He looked at me carefully. "Ready to go?"

"What's next on the agenda? Flowers and dancing?"

"Come on, smart-ass." He stood, stuck his cigar in his mouth and pulled out his wallet. Peeling off two hundred-dollar bills, he dropped them onto the table. He held out a hand, helping me to my feet then leading me to the door.

I looked over my shoulder at the cigar box, left on the table. "Brad, the cigars…"

"It's okay. They'll bring them to the room."

We left Baccarat and didn't go far, winding among the tables and stopping at one for blackjack. While many of the other tables were crowded, this one had only two people at it, an obese man with thinning red hair and ruddy cheeks on one end, a lanky man in a suit at the other. Both men had impressive chip stacks. I glanced at the display card and saw that the minimum hand was two hundred dollars. Brad pulled a chair out for me and I sat, giving the men tentative smiles. They nodded back, no smiles or words of welcome.

Alexis decided to wear a hot-pink thong and matching push-up bra, a rip-away tuxedo minidress over it. She dressed carefully, making sure that she and her outfit looked flawless. She was in the big leagues, and wasn't about to piss off Sandra, the house mom, with anything less than perfect attire. She straightened up, did a slow turn in the mirror and then flashed a smile at her reflection. "Time to make some money," she whispered to her reflection.

The dealer's name tag read Xiu. She was an Asian woman who had a quick smile for Brad and a long look for me. "Need to see ID," she announced, staring at me. I glanced at Brad and reached for my purse, pulling out my driver's license and handing it to her. She examined it for four long seconds before nodding and handing it back to me. Brad handed her a card that looked like our room key. She passed it to the pit boss, who had materialized at her side.

"Good evening, Mr. De Luca," the pit boss said, taking the card and walking over to a monitor set up behind the dealer. "Would you like a marker?"

"Yes. Four, please." The pit boss nodded at the dealer, and she began pulling chips and stacking them in front of her. She slid four stacks of black chips toward Brad, each ten chips tall. He placed two of the stacks in front of me and leaned over to speak into my ear. "Are you familiar with the game?"

"Yes, I have an app on my phone."

"That isn't really what I was thinking, but it'll do. Whatever you win is yours. Whatever you lose...I will find a way for you to pay me back." I pulled back, looking at him sharply, and saw the humor in his expression. The dealer cleared her throat and I looked back into her impatient face.

"You in?"

"Yes, please."

"I need your bet!"

Damn, this bitch is feisty. Brad reached over, took two black chips from my stack and placed them on the betting line. He shot the dealer a sharp look. "It's her first time here. Go easy on her."

"Yes, sir, Mr. De Luca." She dealt the cards.

Thirty minutes and two rounds of shots later, our somber tablemates were smiling. Everyone's chip stacks had doubled, and even bitchy Xiu had managed to crack a smile. We had slowly raised our bets, and I was now betting six hundred dollars a hand and starting to sweat. I was dealt two nines against a dealer six. With my heart pounding, I split the nines. I got an ace and a two and doubled down on both. The nine-ace additional card was an eight, the nine-two got a four. Shit. Eighteen and fifteen. Not great hands and I had three thousand dollars at stake. Brad nodded at me and followed suit, doubling down on a twelve and getting lucky, pulling a nine. We high-fived and then watched the dealer expectantly. She flipped over her hidden card, another six. I held my breath and the next card was flipped over—a queen of diamonds. Twenty-two. Dealer bust.

The crowd that had gathered around us burst into cheers, and I stood up with both hands raised, whooping. Brad picked me up with a bear hug and swung me around, setting me gently back down. Xiu counted out a rainbow of chips and slid them to me with a small smile. I tipped her a hundred dollars, my biggest tip ever, and then gathered my chips. "I'm done," I said to Xiu.

Brad looked over, eyebrows raised. "Done?"

"I'm due for a bad turn. Might as well end on a high note."

He shrugged good-naturedly and nodded at Xiu. "All right, count me out also."

I subtracted the two thousand dollars Brad had started me off with and passed them to him. Then I counted my remaining chips. Forty-eight hundred dollars. Holy shit! More than quadruple what I had in my bank account. I couldn't keep the grin off my face and grabbed Brad for another hug.

"Ready to cash out?" he asked.

"Yes!"

I kept an iron grip on my chips as we walked through the casino to the long bank of cashiers' windows. A bored cashier counted out my cash and passed it through to me. I looked up at Brad.

"Can we take it up to the room?"

"If you want. Or we can leave it at VIP reception."

I frowned. "Will it be safe there?"

"Yes, I assure you that your funds will not be disturbed. They're used to high rollers and won't bother your pittance." He grinned down at me.

"Humph. Then VIP reception it is." I left my cash with one of the intimidatingly beautiful girls at the desk, snagged a glass of champagne and two chocolate-covered strawberries and walked out to the limo, my arm looped through Brad's. At some point he had abandoned his cigar, but still smelled faintly of the scent. I felt giddy, my winnings still fresh in my mind, and slightly buzzed from the champagne and rich food.

Leonard was laughing with one of the bellmen when we approached. He slapped the man on the back and hurried over to us. Seeing my big grin, he asked, "Enjoy yourself?"

"The tables were good to us," Brad said, steering me toward the car door Leonard was holding open.

"Where to?"

"Saffire," Brad tossed out, climbing into the car after me.

The man's hands were way too friendly. Alexis straddled his sweaty, overweight, tuxedoed body. His eyes, glazed over in lust, fixed on her breasts, which she kept shaking in front of his face. Every time he started to lean forward, she flipped her hair over, leaning back, out of his reach. But she was having more trouble controlling his hands. They kept wandering, grabbing her hips and ass. She could feel the outline of his small dick pressing insistently against her. His hands moved again, touching her flat stomach. She sighed and spun around, her eyes searching until they met Ricky's, the big black bouncer assigned to her section. She nodded, and he started her way. So much for this tip. She'd been working this guy for fifteen minutes now. Ricky hustled in and grabbed the fat guy's arm.

"Hands off the lady," Ricky said, his deep voice waking the man from his lust-ridden state.

"Whaaatt?"

Oh, please. Like this was this guy's first time at a strip club. Everything about him screamed strip-club stalker. Thankfully, the song chose that moment to wrap up, and she straightened up, stepping away from the man.

"How much?" Ricky's gruff voice asked her.

"Three songs."

Ricky glared at the man, his huge arms crossed over his chest. "That'll be sixty bucks, sir." His "sir" was almost an insult.

A scowl crossed the man's pasty face and he leaned back, pulled out a handful of bills and passed them to Alexis. She counted the bills—seventy dollars—and nodded to Ricky. Leaning forward, she kissed the man's cheek. "Thank you, baby," she said, and sauntered off, swinging her ass. She walked into the back dressing room, dropping a five into Ricky's tip jar, and headed to her locker. She pulled out her cell phone and saw a text alert. One line, from Brad De Luca, sent almost an hour ago.

Heading there tonight. You working?

She texted back, Here now. See you soon BB

Not alone. Am with an innocent. Play nice

She laughed and closed her phone. Brad De Luca with an innocent? She'd believe that when she saw it. He typically avoided the innocent and clingy type. All ass and no commitment, that was Brad's game. Why was he with a newbie, and if she was so fresh faced, why was he bringing her to Saffire? She thought for a moment, then opened her phone and texted back a response.

So should I stay away?

His response was almost immediate.

No. I need you. Get Montana to play with her

Alexis smiled, pleased. She closed the phone and stuck it in her locker, then went in search of Montana.

"So why Saffire? It's the best?"
Brad pursed his lips. "It's not the best, but it's up there."
"I thought you only went to the best."
He laughed softly. "It will be the best—it's getting there.

And I'm loyal to it. It's a relatively new club, but a true gentlemen's club, versus a strip club."

"Oh, really. What makes it so gentlemanly?"

"Well, I'm sure the marketing departments all have different ways of branding it, but for me it comes down to one thing—the girls. Saffire's girls don't do drugs, don't drink at the club or do 'extra favors' in the VIP room."

"You don't like extra favors?"

"I don't like the type of girls who do extra favors. They reek of desperation. The girls at Saffire have more class, more self-respect."

I rolled my eyes. "You are so full of shit."

"Yet, here you are."

I looked out the window at the colorful lights streaming by, the onlookers waving as our limo passed. "Yet, here I am."

Alexis alerted the manager, Janine, as well as the doorman that Brad De Luca was coming. Janine, a forty-year-old former dancer, was cool and smart—always catching the little ways the customers and girls tried to rip them off—but sweet, too. Being a former dancer, she treated them all with respect and knew the different problems they all faced. Other strip clubs worked the girls too hard and treated them like dogs. Saffire gave them health insurance, 401(k)s—not that any of the girls had one—and allowed them to move up in management if they were interested. Alexis was not. She liked the attention she got from dancing, and knew her strengths. Smarts, she didn't have. She would dance until she got too old, and then would probably become a house mom, like Sandra. Alexis was one of the only dancers who did receive a salary. Supposedly it came from her work as a floor supervisor, which she did, technically, but they all knew what it was really for.

Fucking Brad De Luca.

Twenty

The limo pulled up to a long white building with columns in the front and the always-present valet area. A muscular guy in a tight black T-shirt opened my door and offered a hand to help me out. Brad followed close behind and greeted the man with familiarity. They shook hands and conferred briefly, then Brad touched my elbow and we moved to the entrance. Two additional muscular guys opened the large doors, and we moved into a gold hallway with dark carpet. We stopped at a desk, where I was given a red wristband.

"What's this for?" I asked.

"So they know you're with me."

"Why do they need to know I'm with you?"

His eyes slowly traveled down my skimpy dress to my exposed legs. He smirked.

I smacked his arm. "Oh, my God! I do not look like a stripper!"

"I think they prefer 'exotic dancer.'"

I rolled my eyes and we walked forward, down the hall, passing restrooms and a store. *Who'd buy stuff here?* The room we finally entered was huge, with different levels everywhere.

The levels and tables were all focused toward the center of the room, similar to a theater-in-the-round. All over the room, girls were hanging from long ropes that went all the way up to the ceiling. They were wearing glittering straps of sheer fabric carefully wrapped around their bodies, barely covering their privates while they performed aerial acts on the ropes, spinning and hanging in different ways. The tables were discreetly unlit—the lighting focusing everywhere else—so the room seemed well lit despite the pockets of privacy everywhere. The stage had three poles, all with beautiful women dancing on them. Other poles were scattered throughout the room, with more tanned bodies spinning, hanging and twirling on them. Drink girls wandered the room wearing chokers, suit jackets with bare skin underneath, miniskirts and stilettos. They oozed elegance and sex, and were not the stereotypical tattooed, big-haired, bleached-blond strippers of my visions. Maybe there was something to this "gentlemen's club" thing.

Brad led me through the tables till we came to one close to the stage. He pulled out a chair for me and I sat, demurely crossing my legs. I stared at the stage, a symphony of colors, lights and glitter. A trampoline was hidden off the back of the stage and occasionally a dancer would swing down, bounce on the trampoline and swing back to an upper platform. It was like a circus on sex-crack. Most of the girls seemed to be gymnasts, somersaulting and flexing in ways that their bodies seemingly shouldn't bend. Around us, at the tables, the typical strip club activities seemed to be going on—girls sitting on laps, flirting, giving dances. The common theme seemed to be "tanned with big breasts." I looked down at my own chest and felt inadequate.

A drink girl appeared with a bottle of champagne and two glasses. She gave Brad a hug and set down the bottle, popping the cork and pouring two glasses. Brad was fiddling with his phone and slid it into his pocket as she finished.

"Thanks, Jen."

"Of course, Mr. De Luca." She winked at him and walked away.

I looked at him dryly. "I take it you're a regular here?"

"I try to make it by every trip."

I rolled my eyes and sipped the champagne, enjoying the show. The women had beautiful bodies, and I enjoyed the ability to stare. The girl closest to me, a natural blonde crawling on the stage in front of us, met my eyes with a steady stare. She winked at me, and I squirmed a little, unsure how to react. She flashed me a smile and sat up, grabbing her breasts in her hands and pressing them together. I looked away and saw Brad glance up at a girl who had appeared at my side. I turned, seeing a tiny brunette with a slight Asian tilt to her features. She had a tight body with big natural breasts and was wearing a jewel-encrusted bikini. A diamond choker encircled her neck, setting off the diamond studs in her ears. Flanking her was another gorgeous girl, tall and tan with jet-black hair and a hot-pink bra-and-panty set that displayed her assets to perfection.

"Alexis, Montana," Brad said, his face lighting up. "Come, join us. Champagne?"

"Now, Brad, don't you try and test us," the tall girl said with a flirtatious laugh. "You know the rules." She sat down next to him and pressed her body close to his, rubbing his leg. I felt a flicker of irritation, but was distracted by the other girl who had sat down on my other side. "I'm Montana," she said in a girlie, musical lilt.

"Julia," I said, shaking her hand.

"How's your night going so far?"

"Pretty good, I guess. We had good luck at the tables—my first time playing blackjack."

"You don't look old enough to play," she said playfully, hitting my shoulder.

"I'm newly twenty-one," I said sheepishly. "First time in Vegas."

"Been to a strip club before?"

"I thought it was a gentlemen's club?"

She found this hilarious and giggled for about a minute, sitting back on the love seat and holding her tight stomach. "Oh, honey—you will fit right in here. Want the grand tour?"

I glanced over at Brad, who was deep in conversation with the tall girl. He didn't seem as though he would miss me much. "Brad, Montana is going to give me a tour."

He glanced up at Montana and me, and smiled. "Sounds good, baby. Try and behave. Montana can get wild."

"I'll try. You, too," I added as an afterthought. He looked at me strangely, a question in his eyes. I turned and followed Montana, and she held my hand as if we were best friends. We weaved through the crowds and I glanced back, but Brad had already disappeared in the sea of lonely men and beautiful women.

"Finally," Alexis breathed, her finger tracing a path down Brad's neck to the exposed skin between his top buttons. "Want a dance?"

Brad pushed her hands away and grabbed her waist, lifting her in one motion and placing her firmly on his lap, straddling him. His voice was brusque and his eyes feral. "I don't want a dance. I need you, now."

His need was urgent, almost desperate—in a way she had never seen him before. She grabbed his face and kissed him hard on the mouth, then leaned over and whispered in his ear. "Let's go to the office."

The "office" was used mostly by Janine and the accountant who did their books. It was a rectangular space and had floor-to-ceiling windows that faced the club floor. You could see out with perfect clarity, but no one could see in. The minute they were inside, Brad locked the door and turned to face Alexis, breathing hard. His eyes were wild and she knew immediately that this would be different. Normally, Brad focused on her, bringing her incredible pleasure. Tonight she could tell that he just needed release. Spending time with Little Miss Virtuous had clearly taken a toll on him.

Immediately, she knelt at his feet and unzipped his dress pants, his dick already pressing at his underwear. She pulled down and moved the fabric until it popped free. The minute the thick shaft was out, she grabbed it tight and started to suck, her cheeks hollowing from the suction. He exhaled and pressed the back of her head, pulling it onto him. He set up a rhythm and starting rocking back and forth, his slick cock growing until it was rock hard. He groaned gutturally and pulled her to her feet, kissing her roughly, then spinning her around till she was facing the window. She placed her hands on the glass and arched her back, sticking out her ass. He stroked the condom onto his cock and let his gaze travel from her high-heeled feet, up her toned calves, to stop on her full ass. He whispered her name, her real name, and then entered her hard from behind. She winced—his girth always surprised her, but not being ready made it that much more jarring.

"I'm so sorry, Sarah, but I need it so bad."

He took her hard, pounding out a steady rhythm, and she gasped, her body not yet ready for all of him. A few more strokes and the pleasure started, her inner walls lubricated and accepting. She moaned, rubbing her clit with one hand while the other pressed against the glass. He grabbed her breast firmly and squeezed, playing with her tits and nipples through her bra, till finally she shuddered and tightened around his cock, screaming out his name.

Once her orgasm passed, he withdrew and lowered her down to the floor. He knelt over her, spreading her limber legs until they stuck straight out, her body open to him. His fingers pulled down the top of her bra until her breasts hung free, then he gently squeezed them again, running his hands down her body, playing with the outside of her pussy softly until he felt sticky wetness. He dipped one finger in, feeling her grind against him, and their eyes met. She panted, ready for more. He held a leg in each hand and entered her slowly, pulling in and out as she arched against him. The club music thumping, the lights from the dance floor hitting the walls of the office, he fucked her slowly, then faster and faster. He watched her breasts moving from the rough motion, the pink sparkle from her bra glittering in the dim light.

She closed her eyes and her head fell back, her back arching, body open to him. He reached forward, running his hands down her body, wrapping his hands around her small waist. He gave one long thrust, burying himself completely inside her, the depth causing her to gasp in response. Her head snapped down and her eyes flashed open, meeting his fierce gaze. They widened in excitement and he resumed his movement. Using her waist as leverage, he drilled his thick cock deep into her.

Her excitement grew and she met his thrusts, grabbing his hands and stiffening her body. She shouted, "Fuck! Fuck! Fuck! Fuck!" as she came, tightening again around his cock. He kept up the cadence through her orgasm for a minute longer, then pulled out, ripping off the condom. She grabbed his legs and pulled herself upright, reaching for his cock and pumping it with her hand, hard and tight. The first spurt of his cum shot out, a long, thick stream. She watched it hit her breasts. "Come on, baby, give me it. Give me it all." Two more big spurts came and he grunted, his legs twitching.

"Swallow it," he whispered, and she quickly complied, covering his head with her eager mouth, continuing to pump his cock with her hand. His last few spurts were sucked down and she stared into his eyes as his orgasm faded. He gently released her head and stepped back, sinking into one of the rolling chairs in the office, his dress shirt still on, his pants around his ankles. She crawled over and put her head in his lap and he laid a hand on her hair, his eyes closed.

Twenty-One

I followed Montana as we traveled past the big stage, down a side hall and then up some stairs. "We call this HQ," she giggled. "Like headquarters—get it?" I nodded, wondering how she kept her big boobs in the tiny thing she called a bikini top. Her theme seemed to be U.S.A. She had long blue eyelashes, an American flag bikini top and thong bottom and a red cover-up tied around her ass. Her shoes continued the theme—five- or six-inch platform heels, silver-and-blue with red stars at the ankles. We opened a black door and walked into a long, thin room with a wide stretch-window that surveyed the club. Underneath the window were about twenty monitors, all various camera angles. I walked slowly down the bank of monitors, looking at all the camera views. Everything seemed to be monitored, from the valet entrance, to the bathroom lobbies, to the dim tables. More than half the monitors were green, indicating night vision, and high definition. Very high definition. In one screen I could see the outline of a patron's hard-on, in another the cellulite on a dancer's ass. Four employees sat in front of the monitors, all watching raptly, and almost constantly speaking into handheld radios.

"Guy in the bathroom. Red shirt. Just snorted something and placed the rest in his front shirt pocket."

"Kesha at table forty-two just accepted something from a patron. Looks like a roach."

"New dancer—what's her name, Misty, Majesty?—anyway, she's at table three doing shots."

"Patron at bar-top eleven starting to get feely. Watch him."

"Fight starting on top deck, level two."

I could have stayed there all night, but Montana grabbed my hand and pulled me out to the hallway. "They won't let us stay in there," she whispered. "Say we're distracting."

"You guys are watched constantly," I whispered back. "Doesn't it irritate the...dancers?" I avoided the word *strippers,* not sure if I would offend her. She took a few more steps and I followed, her voice returning to normal volume as we moved away from HQ.

"It irritates the dancers that don't belong here. Saffire is kind of the 'good girls' club. Management is superstrict about three things—drinking, drugs and sex. We can't give blow jobs, let guys finger us and definitely no sex. Touching the tits is also supposed to be off-limits, but they let us have some flexibility with that if we want it. A lot of good girls spend a few months working at a club and get pressured into drugs 'cause, like, all the dancers do it. Here, their constant monitoring keeps that off the table." She flipped her hair over her shoulder and pushed on a stairwell door. We entered a no-frills cement stairwell and started going up. I trotted to keep up with her. *How the hell can she do this in those heels?* "I like it, 'cause I don't do drugs. I'm here to earn money, and that's it. I'm waiting to save up a buttload and then move back to Great Falls. That's my hometown."

"In Montana?" I guessed.

"You got it!" She reached the top of the stairs and opened a heavy door, trotting down the hall and into an all-glass cube. A short Korean guy with spiky purple hair and headphones looked up from a turntable at our approach. "Hey, Big M!" he said, holding his arm out for a side hug.

"Hey, Danny," Montana said affectionately. "This is Julia—she's Brad De Luca's date. I'm giving her the grand tour."

"Mr. D's in town?" Danny asked, surprised. *Brad knows the DJ? That's weird.*

"Well, *duh,*" Montana said.

"He throwing an after-party tonight? Nobody said anything to me about staying late," Danny said, looking concerned. Montana turned to me with an expectant look.

"Umm...I don't think so," I said. "We just planned on stopping by, I think. I'm the wrong person to ask."

"Ah, well, that's cool then. It's my girl's birthday and I got to swing by her place after work. Should I do a shout-out to Mr. D?"

"No!" Montana said quickly. "I think he's going low-key tonight. With Julia, you know?" She glanced quickly at me and then at Danny.

Danny looked at me. "All right. You got a song request?"

"Umm...how about some Black Eyed Peas?"

He nodded enthusiastically at me. "You got it, babe. You gonna get up on stage?"

"No, Julia's a good girl," Montana said.

I was getting a little sick of everyone talking around me. I wasn't doing blow in the bathroom, but I didn't exactly consider myself a good girl. And what made Montana think she knew anything about me?

Brad felt Sarah's head move on his lap and opened his eyes. "What?" he said, opening his eyes and staring up at the ceiling.

"What's the deal with the chick?"

He bristled at the mention of Julia. "Nothing."

"You've never brought an innocent here before."

"I tried to take her to *Zumanity*. She wanted to do something different. So here we are. The girl's never been to Vegas."

"You've also never fucked me like that before."

"Sure I have."

"No, not that…hungry. Is it from being around her?"

"I'm horny, Sarah. It's been like…two days, that's all. Don't try to psychoanalyze me."

"And don't use big words I don't know. I'm just saying you seem different. Maybe it has nothing to do with the girl. I'm just asking." She stood, slipping on her heels, and walked over to the desk, pulling out the top drawer and rummaging through it till she found a cigar. She clipped the end and lit it, drawing on it strongly. She walked over to Brad and straddled him in the chair, holding the cigar to the side. "You want to share? I can smell it on you, along with her girlie shit perfume."

He teased one of her nipples. "You sound a little jealous, Sarah."

She slapped his hand away. "First, stop calling me Sarah. It's Alexis, dammit. Second, I don't care about you enough to be jealous. I just don't know why you're wasting your time with that lily-white baby when we both know what you need. And it ain't her."

Brad watched her, the line of her muscles, the length of her hair. She was exactly like most of the women he fucked. And nothing like Julia. He took the cigar from her, puffed on it, then passed it back. Sarah sucked the cigar like she sucked cock, expertly, nothing like the tentative, fumbling puff that Julia had taken. He imagined Julia, on her knees, her sassy mouth on his hard cock, smiling up at him. Just thinking about it was making him hard again.

Sarah tilted her head back and blew a ring into the dark room. "Does she know where you are right now?"

"No. I assume you told Montana to keep her busy." He wondered how she'd react when she found out. Her reaction would be telling of what she'd think of his lifestyle choice. He may have blown the entire weekend with the last fifteen minutes. But being around her for two days, tasting her mouth, touching and licking her beautiful cunt—it had been all he could do not to claim her body as his, to fuck her senseless and feel her tighten around his cock. Abstinence was not a strength of his.

"Montana knows to keep her busy. But she's gonna run out of shit to show her."

"Okay. Get off me. I can't get dressed with your sexy self all over my cock."

She giggled and flipped her leg over, standing up and walking over to her panties, soiled and wet on the floor. "Goddamn you, Brad. My panties are soaked. I'm gonna have to change."

"Go pick something new out from the store. Tell Janine to charge it to me." He pulled up his pants and buckled the belt, walking over to the window and looking out, leaning against the glass with one arm. "How's business?"

She fixed herself in a small mirror hung on the wall. "It's good. Been really busy lately. Lunches are picking up and we're starting to stay busy till at least 5:00 a.m. most nights."

"You working lunches?"

"Only when money's tight. I got a new car—the payments are a bitch, so I've been picking up extra shifts. All the more reason I need you and little Miss Daisy out there to stay away from each other."

"Why are you so worried about her? You've never cared about anyone else I've ever brought here."

"She's different from any other girl you've ever brought here."

She was right about that. Brad folded his arms and looked at her. "You imply that your income is in jeopardy. Your salary isn't paid for you to fuck me."

"I know you don't view it like that. But the only reason Janine promoted me to shift leader is because she wants to keep me here. And I'm not that good of an employee—she wants to keep me here because she knows you like me." She glanced over at him. "Like to…fuck me. And that job security might change if there is a missus in the picture."

He walked over and placed his hands on her shoulders, looking at her in the mirror and nuzzling her neck. "Stop worrying, baby. You know me. I'm a bad egg, and I'll never change. No woman worth her salt will keep me around."

She spun and grabbed his neck, pretending to throttle him with frustration. "Good point. What was I thinking?" She laughed, releasing his neck, and looked down, smoothing his shirt.

He brought a hand up, tilting her face to his, her eyes opening and meeting his, the somber look in them sobering her expression. "I'm serious. This…arrangement we have, when we do meet—I want to make sure it's something you want. Regardless of sex, you will have a job here as long as you want it. Tell me you understand that."

She nodded, meeting his critical eyes. "I know. Just…be careful with her. And with yourself."

He said nothing, grabbing her hand and leading her out of the private space.

Montana led me back into the glitter and glam of the club. We headed to our table, but it was empty. I looked around, unsure, but Montana flopped down without hesitation. "Sit," she yelled over the music, patting the empty seat across from her.

"Where's Brad?" I asked loudly, leaning close so that she could hear me.

She shrugged nonchalantly. "Maybe the bathroom, or talking to Janine."

"Who's Janine?"

"You know, the manager. Brad likes to talk business with her whenever he comes."

I felt neglected, and pissed that I was alone in the club with a stripper named after a state, pissed that I even cared that Brad wasn't sitting there. But I was in Vegas on someone else's dime, had almost five grand in cash back at the hotel and I'd had an amazing trip so far. What did I have to be pissed at?

"Montana?" I leaned forward and put a hand on her shoulder. "I want to get trashed. Think you can help with that?"

Her eyes lit up and she gripped my arm excitedly. "Baby, I can definitely help with that." She looked around a minute, then hopped to her feet. "I'll be right back." She walked over to a tall, suited woman with professional hair and a discreet earpiece. I saw Montana point to me, and then make a bunch of hand gestures, explaining something to the woman. After a moment, the woman nodded and then pointed to her watch. Montana gave her a hug and then bounded back to me. *This girl is femininity on crack.*

"Okay, we are good to go. I had to get permission from Janine."

"For me to drink?"

Montana rolled her eyes dramatically. "Not for *you,* silly— for me! It's no fun to drink alone!" She waved down a drink girl and ordered four tequila shots. My stomach flipped at the thought of multiple tequila shots, but I wasn't about to reinforce her impression of my good girl status. I looked around, but still didn't see Brad, and he obviously wasn't with Janine.

"So where's the VIP room?"

"We don't have one anymore. When the club first started, there was a separate room upstairs, but the guys all seemed to think that you entered the VIP room and anything went. So now there is just an upper layer of tables they call the VIP section. You can't see them from here, but they're above us, on the outside edges of the room. They can see the stage but have a little more privacy."

Our shots arrived and were set on the table between us, along with limes and salt. Montana squealed and clapped her hands together, sliding her butt forward till she was perched on the edge of her seat. She looked at me deviously, and held out the salt. "Body shot?"

I hesitated, only briefly. "Is there any other way to do it?"

She whooped, gave me a high five, then held out the salt. "I'll go first. Where do you want it?" I tentatively pointed to my collarbone and she rolled her eyes. "Come here." She pushed me back till I was lying on the plush chair. She ran her fingers suggestively over the top rim of my strapless mini, gliding her fingers gently underneath, and I sucked in a breath, certain her fingers were going to brush the tops of my nipples. *Oh, my God.* She bit her bottom lip playfully, then pulled the center of my dress down and licked between my breasts, tickling the skin with her pink tongue. She then sat up and sprinkled salt there, patting it with her fingers. Picking up a piece of lime, she placed it in my mouth, running her fingers over my lips gently with a smile. I had never had any type of sexual experience with a woman, but felt that I was getting dangerously close to having one, and I wasn't wanting to stop. I glanced around and saw several interested faces, men's eyes glued to our table. Knowing that I was being watched was a major turn-on, and I began to look forward to the show we were about to put on.

Montana came around till she stood at my head. She reached back and unclipped her bra, pulling it off, her breasts bouncing down and hanging loose. She then leaned forward, her huge tits hanging in my face. I tilted my face up, her breasts lying on my face—the skin incredibly soft. *Why doesn't my skin feel like that?* I felt her tongue lick the salt in the dip between my breasts. She straightened abruptly, flipping her hair back, grabbing the shot and downing it quickly. She then bent back over, putting her mouth on mine and pulling on the lime gently till she had it in her mouth. She sucked it hard, dropped it into the empty shot glass, and bent over again. Catching me off guard, she kissed me, tasting of lime, salt and my sophomore spring break in Cancún. I kissed her back, our tongues meeting softly, then with more confidence. It was the first time I had kissed a girl, and to quote Katy Perry, "I liked it." She climbed off me and offered her hand, pulling me upright. Her eyes danced with fun, and I caught her excitement.

"My turn," I said. "Where do you want it?"

Brad walked alone through the club. Dancers nodded and squeezed his arm as he passed, but he didn't stop, his eyes scanning the crowd for Montana and Julia. He had taken longer with Alexis then he had intended, and didn't want Julia alone and pissed at the table. His eyes searched the crowd and finally stopped on the table where they had originally sat. His lips set, he strode forward.

He had to push himself through the crowd that had gathered, a mixture of drunk executives and Abercrombie-attired college boys. Julia was kneeling on the round table that had previously held their champagne flutes and ice bucket. Her strapless dress had been pulled down; her breasts were exposed and alert. Montana had an ice cube in her mouth and was running her mouth over Julia's breasts, making her nipples stiff and pink. As he watched, Julia leaned forward and placed her hands on Montana's breasts, pushing them together and kissing her deeply. *Jesus Christ.*

The girls separated. Montana sprinkled Julia's nipples with the salt and then licked and sucked one of them, kissing Julia long and hard, both their hands roaming. Julia and Montana then grabbed shots of tequila and downed them, holding up the glasses in celebration.

The crowd cheered and started chanting. "Another! Another!" Their energy swelled, and Brad was jostled by a push of bodies behind him.

Where the fuck is Janine? He looked around but didn't see her. Montana shouldn't be drinking, though he could probably see how this had happened, and cursed himself for taking too long with Alexis. Finding a black-shirted security guard, he yelled into his ear, trying to make himself heard over the crowd. "Did Montana get approval to drink?"

"Yeah. Janine gave her an hour of drinking, then said she'd need to go home—no working afterward."

"All right. Make sure the crowd stays under control and doesn't mess with the girls."

"You got it, boss. Ricky's keeping an eye from the other side. Right now everyone's behaving."

Brad looked back to the two girls. Montana was pulling Julia's dress over her head, exposing her tanned, toned stomach and a lace thong that left nothing to the imagination. He groaned, the image pulling at his recently restored composure.

"Want me to get you in there, boss? I can move these guys outta the way."

It was tempting, but… "No. Let them play. I'll watch from the upper level. Montana knows the rules." He turned and moved quietly through the crowd and climbed a flight of stairs to what they considered the VIP level. He walked about halfway down and then sat in a chair. The tables up there were in private alcoves, and he felt as alone as he could in the packed club at 1:00 a.m. He pulled out his cell and called the line for HQ.

"Yes, Mr. D." A calm, nasally voice came over the line.

Brad smiled to himself. Saffire's HQ. Where horny nerds came to die.

"Yes, I'm in VIP section…" He craned around to see the number discreetly painted on the wall, high up, out of normal view. "Section eight. I'm gonna kill power to this cam. Didn't want you to be alarmed."

"Understood, Mr. D. We can kill power from here if you want?"

"No, I'll do it. That way you'll know when I'm done."

"Sounds good, Mr. D. Is there a party planned for later?"

"Not tonight. Make sure everyone knows."

"Will do. Thanks, boss."

Brad stood, moved the chair over to the wall and stood on it. He reached in his pocket for his key ring, shuffled through till he found the security master and stuck it into the wall, turning the cam switch to the off position. He sat back down and watched the action below. Julia was now straddling Montana. They were kissing passionately, their hands traveling everywhere.

Montana lifted her mouth off my neck, her eyes flashing. I grinned down at her, my hands on her large breasts. I had never held another woman's boobs before. Mine were small, barely B cups, but Montana's were huge—and natural, I assumed. The skin on them was so incredibly soft, and the weight of them was heavy in my hands. Her nipples were light pink, like mine, and I touched them the way I liked mine touched—softly.

The cries of the men surrounding us energized me. That, and the three—or was it four?—shots of tequila we had taken, on top of all the drinks I'd had earlier in the evening. Everywhere I looked, I saw aroused faces, eyes watching us. It was the feeling of power I got from teasing, but multiplied times ten, turning me on to a degree I had never reached. My eyes danced over the crowd, then to the spinning dancers, then up, passing and then focusing on a man. *Brad.*

He stood on an upper balcony, his eyes locked on mine. Even with the expanse of the room between us, I could feel his hunger, his heat, and it poured gasoline on the fire that was my arousal. I wanted to show him everything in that moment. That I could be bad. That I wasn't the good girl that he kept painting me out to be. The room spun, and I focused on Montana's face to bring it still. I reached for her, our lips meeting, tongues dipping together, hands traveling. I fought the urge to look up at him, knowing he was watching, that all of them were watching. She was like a beautiful exotic flower—all the best things about a girl—soft skin, long hair and yummy scents. I could understand why men went to strip clubs. It was as if the most popular girl at school was your best friend for an hour.

Montana stood, climbing up on the chair, and I sat back on the round table, my face now close to being between her legs. She reached down and grabbed the bottle of Cristal that had been chilling next to us. Pulling the cork out with her teeth, she cheered, holding the bottle high in the air. The crowd and I instantly responded, throwing hands up into the air in celebration. Then she told me to lean back. I did, resting on my arms and arching my back, my breasts held up to the sky and in full glory of the fifty-some men who were surrounding us, some standing on chairs in order to see better. Montana let the champagne rain and it hit me, cool and sweet, splattering my neck, hitting the swell of my breasts, running down my stomach. My nipples instantly responded to the cold liquid bubbles, puckering and standing at attention. Montana laid me back and began to lick it off, her tongue making magic happen on my skin.

Twenty-Two

Rule 4: Her pleasure is the most important objective.

I woke up in a strange bed. I lay there, the room dark, and tried to figure out where I was. I reached out: sheets covered in a heavy down comforter, feather pillows underneath my head. I felt skin—a hand, big. Brad.

I sat up, the quick movement causing a sharp pain in my temple. "Ohhh," I groaned. Brad's hand twitched under mine, and I moved my hand off his, slowly pulling the covers back and sliding out. My mouth was like dry cotton, and I felt my way quietly through the suite to the bathroom, where I reluctantly turned on the light, wincing against the searing brightness. Fumbling through my toiletries bag, I found the small aspirin bottle I had packed, and shook out two pills. I stuffed them in my mouth and took a big swig of water from a glass I filled at the tap, then turned out the light. Padding back to the bedroom, my eyes adjusting to the dark, I saw the outline of Brad sitting up in bed.

"That you?" I whispered stupidly.

"Yeah. You feeling okay?"

"Not really."

He chuckled and patted the bed next to him. "Lie back down." I chugged the rest of the water, ignored the water that missed my mouth, and shakily set the glass down on the nightstand. I crawled into bed and turned away from him, curling into a pitiful ball. He reached his hand out and cupped my waist, dragging me until I was flush against his hard body. He kissed the back of my neck. "Go to sleep," he whispered.

"I hate alcohol," I mumbled.

"Shhh…" he said. I didn't hear anything else after that.

I woke up hot and sticky to an annoyingly high-pitched screaming sound. I looked around groggily, the only light coming from the TV, which was on. A yellow square cartoon was screaming incessantly, a loud feminine sound interrupted by short pauses. The video seemed to be stuck on some sort of repeat. The sound went on and on until another character finally interrupted the screams. I flopped over and tried to go back to sleep. Then the same annoying cartoon started laughing, a continual braying laugh that scraped at my subconscious. I scrambled through the covers and grabbed the remote, pressing buttons until the screen, and the room, thankfully went dark. Ugh. I did a self-analysis and found that I wasn't that badly off. I was hot, but that was easily fixed; sticky—where did that come from?—and my head was pounding, but not at an intolerable level.

I found Brad, eight short steps later, in the dining room, the phone to his ear and the paper spread out in front of him. I gave him a halfhearted wave and collapsed in the closest dining room chair. He stood, still on the phone, and poured me a glass of orange juice, which I grabbed and gulped with glee. Fresh squeezed and ice-cold.

He looked shower-fresh and gorgeous, and not at all suffering. *Damn man*. He wrapped up his phone call with a few more "uh-huhs" and "okays," and then hung up. He tapped his fingers on the table and looked at me. I swung my legs and looked everywhere but at him. I felt like I had done something wrong, but wasn't sure what.

"So…" he said, drawing it out. "Are you hungry?"

I frowned, pondering the question. I felt thirsty, but not necessarily hungry. "Depends."

"On what, pray tell?"

"What the plan for today is."

"Well—" He consulted his watch, a Patek Philippe. "It's 10:00 a.m. now. I have an errand to run off the Strip that will probably take a few hours. I thought maybe we could grab breakfast, then I could do my stuff and you could do whatever you want to do, and then we could meet back up around two-thirty. Our flight leaves at six. We should probably start heading to the airport around 4:00 p.m."

"What kind of errand?"

He fixed me with a steady look. "A personal one."

"Can I come?"

He tilted his head, thinking. "I guess so. It won't be all that exciting. Let's eat and then you can decide."

"Not exciting" was starting to sound pretty good to me. I felt as if I had been in Vegas a month with all that had happened. I stood up and headed to the bathroom. "I'll take a shower and get dressed."

I walked into the bathroom and turned on all the jets in the shower. I was wearing a pair of worn pajama pants and a T-shirt—the most modest of the nightwear I had packed. I frowned, looking down at it. I didn't even remember putting it on last night. I undressed, turned off all the lights and stepped into the shower. Sometimes I loved showering in the dark. One reason, it helped my hangover headache to not have a blaring light shining down on me. But it also left me alone with my thoughts. I stepped forward, under the rain head, and let the hot water hit my face, the tiny streams feeling like heaven. I tried to let the tension and stress flow out of my body with the water, to focus on my thoughts and try to remember the night before, but I could only think of one thing: Brad. *Him in the next room. Me naked in here. Yesterday, his mouth waking me up, the incredible pleasure created by his tongue, the waves of pleasure...*

I tapped my fingers on the wall and tried to think rationally. I was horny, a feeling that had rarely, if ever, occurred. I think it took the act of having an orgasm for me to recognize sex for what it was supposed to be. Carnal pleasure. Need fulfillment. Not just a power play, or an expected obligation. Fuck. My epiphany was coming at an inopportune time. I thought for a moment, ridiculous justifications filling my head. The truth lay out there, stark and unavoidable. *I wanted him.* So badly that my fingers were finding their way downward on their own accord, fantasies pushing uninvited into my mind. All of Brad's words from the other night, his argument for casual, unattached sex bombarded my weak resolve. *Damn.* I opened the door, a wave of steam blowing out, cool air hitting my naked skin as I left the shower. I walked, soaking wet, to the entrance to the living room. *Maybe this is a mistake.* I took a deep breath and stepped out.

Brad was on the phone again, trying to explain custodial rights regarding relocation to one of his paralegals, when Julia appeared from the bedroom. Dripping wet, her skin tanned, her body flushed and perky from the shower's heat, she looked like every wet dream he'd ever had as a teenager. Her hair slicked back and her face makeup-free, she also looked very young and innocent. His dick twitched in his pants, and he felt it start to harden.

"Debbie, I have to go."

"But—"

"Later. I'll call you back." He ended the call and stood up abruptly. Julia's eyes shifted to his crotch, and he moved to cover his erection, but it was too late. Her mouth curved into a knowing smile and confidence grew in her eyes. She knew she had him.

Hesitantly, I stood in the doorway, my confidence wavering as I waited for Brad to look up from his call. I was losing my nerve when he saw me and started to stand, ending his call. He stood erect and I saw the firm outline of his dick in his dress pants. *He wants me.* I gave him a saucy smile and slowly spun, running my wet hands down the curve of my back, and walked back to the shower, willing him to follow me.

Brad breathed hard, trying to decide what to do. Every bone in his body, especially that one, wanted to follow her. Wanted to be selfish, to own her with his body. But at what price? What stock would she put in the act? She had never had casual sex, may not be able to separate emotion from the act. He couldn't afford another love-struck intern, another office scandal, more judgment from Broward and Clarke. Plus, he didn't want to destroy her vacation and purity in one moment of weakness. He should be stronger than that, should have the willpower to resist one sexy-as-hell woman. But the image of her waiting, wanting, her body ready for him, barricaded his senses, twisted his morals and demolished any sensibility left in his head. He finally cursed under his breath and set his phone down. He'd face the music if he had to—it would be worth it to have her, if even just once. And he would just have to hope and pray she took it for what it was—carnal pleasure, and nothing else.

I flipped the switch, bathing the bathroom in soft indirect light. I met him outside the shower door, grabbing his shirt collar the moment he walked over the threshold. I pressed my wet body against him and he cursed. His mouth was quickly on mine, taking me by force, as if by desperation, his large hands everywhere—on my slick ass, around my tiny waist, cupping my tender breasts and squeezing. I had a huge and growing need in between my legs, pounding so hard I could hardly think of anything else, any thoughts of stopping fleeing my mind. I ripped hard at his dress shirt, popping buttons and tearing it open so that I could see his tanned chest, thinly covered in dark hair, huge muscles under my palms. My hands ran down his stomach and grabbed hard at his pants and belt, pulling them away from his body, trying to reach down into his pants. He kept me at bay, unbuckling his belt and dropping his pants to the ground, his athletic briefs the only thing covering his cock. It now stuck almost straight out. I scrambled, need overtaking me, and grabbed the top of his briefs and pulled down, his cock popping out, and I gasped, amazed at the size and shape of it. It was the biggest cock I had ever seen, thick and tan colored, meaty. The head was swollen, but not too big, in perfect proportion to his shaft. I worried, seeing its girth, that I wouldn't be able to take it, that it would break me in half, ruin me forever.

He grabbed my waist hard, and lifted me up. Automatically, I wrapped my legs tight around him, my ass resting on the length of his stiff dick. He held me by the cheeks of my ass and carried me into the shower, his tongue fighting in perfect harmony with mine. We couldn't get enough of each other, and I felt rabid for him.

He closed the shower door. We were in the spray of the water; it ran hot down my back. I let my feet hang and he set me down gently. Our mouths separated and we panted, breathing at each other. He cupped my face with both hands, pressing against me until my back hit the cold shower wall, and he ran one hand down my neck and body, grabbing and squeezing every part he hit, from my breasts to my stomach, to the cheek of my ass, to the cup of my sex. I panted, wanting him, but he held me back, pressed against the wall as his eyes unapologetically devoured me.

"I don't know what to do with you," he finally gasped, his voice gruff. He moved forward, pressing his hard body to me, and I felt his dick twitch against my leg, his mouth on my neck, sucking then biting, his need as obvious as my own.

"What do you mean? I want you. I need you to fuck me," I gasped, my voice jagged with need, my hand reaching down, wrapping around his hard thickness, my eyes closing in overwhelming desire

"I can't," he ground out. "You're too...you'll be too attached. I'm not a boyfriend, Julia."

"I don't want a damn boyfriend. I want a cock. Your cock right now. Put it in me and fuck me." I had steely determination in my voice and glared at him hotly.

His eyes grew dark with want. He kept one hand on the back of my neck and moved the other down to my cunt, brushing over the lips with his fingers, his gaze on mine, responding to my gasps with perfect precision. He seemed to know exactly where, when and how hard to touch me. It was ridiculously unfair, and I suddenly realized that there was no way I would ever to be able to say no to this man. Once this happened, once he took me, I would be his, in body at least. No man could possibly ever compare to this.

He put two fingers in me, bending them in such a way that

almost brought me to my knees, a surge of pleasure debili-tating me. He smiled at my gasp and I struggled to keep my stance, my pussy grinding uncontrollably against his fingers. My eyes shut in silent ecstasy and I bit my bottom lip.

"I thought you were a good girl," he whispered in my ear. "Didn't fuck unless you're in love."

I shook my head quickly, back and forth. "I changed my mind. I want you. I need you." My voice now pleading.

"I can't be what you want. You know that? This will be sex, and that's it." His voice rasped in my ear, his fingers mov-ing faster and faster in my wet pussy, building my need, slid-ing over and over again on that incredible, wonderful place.

"I don't want anything from you. I just need your cock. In me. Now." My voice was coming in gasps now, my legs shaking with the intensity building between them. My eyes rolled back and I started to sink, my legs Jell-O. He pulled out his fingers, and my eyes flew open. "No—don't stop, I was just about to—"

He spun me around so that I was facing the body jets, and turned them all on full force. I gasped, the initial water cold, but then it turned hot, three separate jets spraying my tits, stomach and pussy. Brad turned the bottom jet until it sprayed strong, the highest intensity. "Not yet. Spread your legs," he said gruffly. I obeyed, placing my legs the way he wanted, then arching my body when the water hit me in just the right spot. Oh my God. The strong stream felt amazing, vibrating my clit and spreading pleasure throughout my body. Brad groaned behind me, and ran his hands underneath my body, brushing my nipples, then traveling down and making sure that the spray was hitting me where it should. I wasn't expecting his dick when the huge girth pressed insistently on my wet pussy. He forced it in, fast and quick, and I called out in pain and surprise.

"I'm sorry, I'm sorry," he whispered, holding my body against him and grabbing my breast, his voice thick in my ear.

"I'm not," I gasped, my body beginning to adjust to his size. He was so hard, so thick, so…everywhere inside me. For the first time in my life I felt full—felt him in every wall, muscle and nerve in my pussy. He moved slowly, in and out, then faster, the movement shaking me, my inner walls tightening around every inch of him. Squeezing my breast, he drilled himself into me, and I arched, fucking him back. The water spray continued on my clit, and I could feel myself getting close to the edge, the crescendo in my head and body growing. I started letting out every pent-up emotion I had, telling him to fuck me harder, and longer, telling him how much I loved his big cock. I heard the words leaving my mouth, some other person's declarations, some untamable slut running out of control. My words ran together until finally I exploded, a scream leaving my throat, my legs shaking and pussy pulsing, pleasure bursting over and over again in sweet, blinding, earth-shattering release. He kept up the incredible rhythm, stretching out my orgasm until it slowly subsided. As it left me, so did any remaining strength in my legs. He caught me when I collapsed against him, and he turned me, his cock falling out, and held me to him.

My eyes focused and I frowned at him. "Did you…?"

He smiled and kissed me. "No."

"Then why are we…?"

"I wasn't fucking you for me. Besides, I was stupid. I shouldn't have been inside of you without a condom. I got caught up in the moment and wasn't prepared." He let out a long breath, looking down into my face, a wary look in his eyes that seemed to convey more than just remorse about the condom.

I shifted, finding the strength again in my legs, and bumped into his cock in the process. It responded, twitching, and I looked up quickly, catching him in an unguarded moment, his face tight, eyes closed. *He was struggling.* I realized it instantly, his desire to resist me conflicting with his male need. And I was the source of it all. The knowledge was power, and I reached down, catching him in my hand, gripping the shaft firmly, closing my own eyes at the utter bliss of having his huge organ rock hard in my hand. The first stroke of my hand elicited a quick intake of breath, his eyes flying open and his face frowning down at me.

"Stop," he whispered, his eyes searching mine.

A playful smile filled my face. "You want to make this about me?"

"Of course." He gritted the words out, pulling my slick body to his again, and rocking gently forward in time with my strokes.

"Then finish the job. I'm not leaving this shower until I have your cum in my mouth." I spoke the words deliberately, a challenge behind them, and was pleased at the reaction in his face, the blatant arousal that he allowed to break through.

He groaned, both of his hands instantly on my ass, gripping the muscles there and lifting me easily into the air again, spinning until I was up against the wall. My legs automatically wrapped around him. He held me there, the cold tile against my back, lifting me up until my breasts were in his face, his mouth urgently on them, gentle nips with his teeth followed by soothing swipes of his tongue. I felt a finger on my ass, rubbing the tight pucker of skin, gentle pressure that caused a delicious clench in my cunt. I moaned, throwing my head back, his mouth moving to my neck, driving me wild, his finger taking me deeper, a second one now inside my wetness, teasing me mercilessly. His mouth was suddenly at my ear, his deep voice so feral and masculine, taking me, owning me with the words he whispered. "God, I've wanted this so bad, wanted inside you, to feel your sweet cunt tightening around my cock. You drive me wild, Julia. I just…I don't know what to do with you."

I tightened around his fingers, gasps coming from my mouth, his words taking me to the edge. "I need it, please." I squeezed my legs, digging my heels into the firm muscles of his ass, my hands grabbing his neck, gripping it tightly. All I could think about was filling the giant need my body had for his cock, the need that was being fueled by the orgasm building inside of me. "Please."

His mouth claimed me at the same time that his cock did, both of them taking my body by storm, assaulting my senses in sensual perfection. He drove into me in long, sure strokes, pinning my body to the wall with his strength, and moving only his pelvis in deep, penetrating movement. I took my mouth off his, too overwhelmed by sensation to be able to do anything but moan. My head dropped back against the wall, eyes shut tight. His lips moved to my neck, devouring it as his finger pressed incessantly on the pucker of my ass. I fought the crest of pleasure, the wave of ecstasy, but lost the battle, his strokes quickening when he felt me tighten, his body knowing the moment my orgasm came. It was unending, a full-body spasm that seemed to last forever, waves strengthened with every jackhammer thrust he gave.

I collapsed against him when it finally ended, sagging in his strong arms, my breaths coming out in gasps, my fingers tight in his hair, wanting every part of him touching me. He lowered me, setting me on my feet, his cock sliding out of me, slick with my juices.

I slid down his body and knelt on the hard stone floor, sitting on my heels, looking up at him. He stood like a dark shadow above me, his torso silhouetted by the light, the water spraying off his back, creating a halo of liquid heat. It fell like a curtain around me, my body protected by his. His face was shrouded in darkness but I heard his voice over the water, gruff: "Now. Please." His hand pressed on the back of my head and I focused on the new center of my existence, the rock-hard masterpiece in front of me.

I took it deep on my first taste, angling my neck and squeezing the girth of it down my throat, past the curve and to a place that was intended only for this. I gagged, my eyes tearing at the effort, my saliva coating his shaft and causing it to slide easier into my mouth. I sucked hard as I withdrew, feeling it tighten in my mouth, swell to its full width. I went to town, working the shaft with my hand and mouth, focusing only on the feel and taste of him, pure masculinity that was, at the moment, all mine.

He moaned, tugging my hair as he rocked into me, saying my name over and over as he dominated my mouth. My gags excited him, and I felt it the moment he hit the edge, a loud groan emitting from his mouth, the moment his cock twitched in my hand, liquid sex pouring through it, and I sucked it down, greedily, wanting proof of his arousal, proof of my new ownership. My mouth was filled with his load, the mass of it spilling out on my hand, lubricating the strokes I continued with gusto.

He finally shuddered, pushing me back gently, sliding his cock from my lips, watching closely, his eyes dark with wonder. He bent, grabbing me under my arms, pulling me to my feet as I wiped my mouth. I turned, stepping under the hot spray, rinsing my face and allowing the heat to run over my body, to massage my spent muscles. I felt him behind me, his hard body flush against mine, his hands wrapping around me, cupping my small breasts from behind. He kissed the back of my neck. "Thank you," he whispered.

I turned, snaking my arms around his neck. "Thank you. For letting me pay you back. I needed it as much as you did."

He grinned down at me. "I doubt that." His eyes turned serious and he ran his big hands down my arms. "Are you okay?"

I frowned at him. "Why wouldn't I be okay?"

"I didn't know if you regretted it."

I blew a wet strand away from my face, closing my eyes in spent bliss. "I'm not one of those girls, Brad. I needed you just now more than I've ever needed anyone. I wanted you to fuck me. Which you did—very well, by the way." I smiled but his hands didn't leave my body; his eyes remained watchful.

I avoided his examination and stood on my toes, kissing him, his cock still hard against my leg. I reached down, wrapping my hand around it, squeezing tight, loving the feel of stiff rod beneath tight skin. I moved my hand, jacking its length, and his breath caught in my mouth, his hand pushing mine away.

"Stop," he whispered against my lips, his tongue taking ownership of me before I could respond. When he pulled back, his eyes glinted merrily as I pouted.

"Fine." I turned, grabbing the body scrub, squeezing a generous amount onto my palms and working it into a foam. He came up behind me, the closeness causing my breath to hitch. *I have got to get myself under control.* He kissed me once, gently, on the back of my neck, then I heard the shower door open and close, and I was alone in there once again.

For breakfast, we decided to go to the buffet downstairs. I dressed casually in ripped jeans, a white tank and leather flip-flops. The buffet was huge, and I unintentionally piled my plate high just by grabbing a little bit of everything. We sat in a plastic booth and I grinned through a mouthful of pancakes at Brad.

"Whaart?" he said, his mouth full as well.

"It's just funny. You and me at an all-you-can-eat buffet in Vegas, stuffing our faces after you just boned me in the shower. You know Broward would have a heart attack right now if he knew what we were doing."

"I don't think pancakes are outlawed in the corporate handbook."

I stuck my tongue out at him and grinned. "So," I said, spearing a lone strawberry and dipping it in yogurt, "can I go on your supersecret mission, or what?"

"You just want to go to find out what it is. It's really not that exciting."

"Then tell me what the errand is. Then I'll decide if I want to go."

"I'm going to visit an old friend of mine. She lives in Boulder City, about a half-hour drive east of Las Vegas."

"An ex-girlfriend?"

"No… I do have female friends that I don't sleep with."

I snorted. "Likely."

"Do you want to come or not?"

"Will the…friend mind if I come?"

He smiled. "I think she can hold her jealousy in check for your visit."

"Do you mind if I come? I feel like I'm forcing myself on you."

"No. If you come, I have a side trip we can take. Though you are a pain in the ass, I wouldn't mind your company for just a bit longer."

"Fine. Then I'm coming. I'm getting a little sick of the…" I waved my hand to encompass all that Bellagio was.

"Luxury?" he asked with a grin.

"Yeah. Luxury. Thanks for the help."

"No problem."

Twenty-Three

One hour later, we were standing next to a brand-new Dodge Viper at some type of a Hertz on crack. The rental dealership had a collection of Vipers, Ferraris and Lambos, as well as the more-refined Bentleys and Rolls. I guess Tiffany had gone with the lower price point and set Brad up with the Viper. It was bright blue, a convertible and as ostentatious and sexy as they got.

"You're driving this? I was thinking we'd be in, you know, a four-door Mercedes or something. Is this even street legal?"

"I'm driving this. You're driving that." He pointed over my shoulder and I spun, seeing an identical red clone. "It's stick shift. Will that be a problem?"

I turned and looked back at him coolly—at least with my best impression of coolly. "Not unless you can't keep up."

He laughed and banged the top of the car with his hand, eliciting something close to a gasp from the salesman. "You're on, baby."

An employee showed me the basic schematics of the car. There wasn't much to show. The car was built for one thing— speed. Other than basic A/C and what looked like an impressive sound system, all he really had to show me was how to operate the top. We went ahead and left it down. It seemed way too complicated to operate, and I didn't want to break anything in the next four hours.

"Any last questions?" the man asked, handing me the keys.

"Does it have a radar detector?" I asked innocently.

The pain in his eyes answered my question.

I pulled up next to Brad, my eyes flashing in excitement.

"You sure you want to miss out on riding with me? You look a little glum," he said sarcastically.

I sighed dramatically. "It's going to be really tough, but I'm going to try and suffer through."

"All right then. Follow me out of the city. If we get separated, stay on 515 till we get to Boulder City. There's a Taco Bell right in the city limits. Meet me there."

"Got it." I gave him a thumbs-up and revved my engine. He shook his head at me and pulled out.

We took a left out of the dealership and came to an almost-immediate stop at a light. The engine roared, even at a standstill. I massaged the pedals and prepared myself. My start was a little rough. I gave it too much gas and the engine revved high. *Better than a stall.* I worked my way through the gears as we drove through the city, getting used to the feel of the car. Finally, Brad got in the turn lane for the highway and we merged into the fast-moving traffic. Opening up the car felt similar to taking off. I cranked up the radio and was doing eighty before I could blink, and was still in third gear! I upshifted and felt the car comfortably cruise. We behaved, never crossing over a hundred, but zigzagging past cars as if they were sitting still. Three songs later, we were slowing and pulling over to a Taco Bell. I frowned, not ready to be at the destination yet. I pulled up next to Brad and turned down the radio.

"You want to ride with me from here?" he yelled, over the drone of the engines.

"Nah. I'll follow."

"Whatever you want. Stay close."

He pulled a tight U-turn in the small parking lot, and I followed suit, the rear-wheel drive throwing me off a bit. The back end spun out a little and I came close to plowing into an older-model minivan and a mother walking with two kids. I made an apologetic grimace and tried to call out an apology, but Brad was pulling out and I didn't want to get left behind. She shot me a glare and pulled her kids *way* over onto the curb. *A little overdramatic.* One of the kids, a preteen boy with thick glasses, tripped over the curb, staring and pointing at my car. The girl, a little older, with a bored look on her face, whipped out an iPhone and took a picture. I rolled into traffic behind Brad.

Boulder City seemed to be a typical small town. It had a few of the tourist booths advertising Hoover Dam and Lake Mead excursions, but also had all the standard trappings of normalcy. Our cars had seemed normal on the Strip, but in suburbia they stuck out like sore thumbs. Ambidextrous, jeweled thumbs, but still sore ones. I loved seeing kids' reactions in passing sedans and SUVs, and felt as though every guy in a three-mile radius craned his neck to look as we passed. We left the highway and turned down one side street after another, Brad seeming to know the route well. The engine was beginning to get hot beneath me by the time we finally stopped, pulling up to a small house at the end of a cul-de-sac. The yard was tiny but well tended, and there were fresh flowers planted by the mailbox. A midlevel Mercedes was parked in the driveway, the only sign of wealth.

I turned off the car, letting it work its way to silence, and then stepped out, trying to smooth my windswept hair and

brush the road dirt from my face. *I should have brought a brush.*
Knowing Brad, this woman would be dressed to the nines
with her breasts on full display while I looked like a bedrag-
gled homeless girl. I gave up on my appearance and joined
Brad on the front porch. He rang the bell and we listened to
its chimes ring through the home.

Thirty seconds later, the door opened.

I found myself staring at Betty Crocker. Or, at least, her
identical twin. I expected this old woman's twentysomething
daughter to pop out from behind a ceramic rooster, but Brad
greeted the woman heartily enough that I understood her to
be the "old friend" that we were visiting. I didn't realize that
the man literally meant "old."

I stood quietly on the front stoop, waiting for the woman
to stop gushing over Brad. Finally, her eyes turned to me. Behind her delicate gold glasses sat razor-sharp blue eyes, and I
understood immediately that this woman was neither senile
nor unintelligent. "Brad, introduce me to your friend," she
chided, placing a slightly shaky hand on his shoulder.

Brad turned to me with a smile. "Evelyn, this is Julia. She's a
friend of mine from home, and came along with me this trip."

Evelyn sniffed disapprovingly. "She looks awfully young."

Irritated, I stepped forward onto the threshold. "I am young,
and he's practically ancient. But he has managed to make this
trip so far without his walker, and I am still fresh-faced and
virtuous, so there is hope for us yet." I kept my face blank
and eyes innocent and hoped she wouldn't smack me with a
spare oxygen tank.

She burst out laughing, her face a sea of delighted wrinkles.
"Now, where are my manners? Come in!" She held open the
door and a burst of wonderfully cool air hit my skin. I walked
through the doorway; she shook my hand energetically as I
passed. She scurried around us and told us to go to the liv-

ing room, which had plain cream sofas and lots and lots of afghans lying around. The woman clearly crocheted in her spare time, and apparently had lots of spare time. The huge TV, an impressive flat screen that made mine at home seem pathetic, was turned to a cooking show. She picked up a gigantic remote and turned it off.

"Brad, I have Coke for you. Julia, what can I get you to drink? I have tea, water and Coke."

"Water will be fine, thank you."

She turned and entered the kitchen, a lemon-yellow room with grayish-green linoleum just off the living area. I looked at Brad. He had settled into the only recliner in the room, already had the leg rest up, and was easing into the soft leather. He looked at me and grinned, a boyish look on his face.

"Who is she?" I whispered, not wanting to piss off Mother Hubbard.

"An old friend. Don't worry, she doesn't bite." At the sound of Brad's voice, a series of high-pitched yelps came from a back room.

Evelyn called from her place at the counter, "Brad, will you let out Mitzi and Richie?" Brad swung the recliner shut and heaved to his feet, a loud sigh escaping his lips.

Evelyn carefully walked into the room, balancing a plastic tray on which she'd painstakingly placed three glasses, baby white napkins and a collection of lemon squares, sprinkled with powdered sugar. "Now, don't you give me that! They've been waiting all morning to see you!"

"Thanks, Evie," Brad said, snagging a lemon square and heading down a side hall. She set the tray down on the coffee table and looked at the recliner, still rocking slightly, embroidered pillows squashed in the seat. "That boy! Creates a mess everywhere he goes...." She gave an exasperated sigh and grabbed the pillows, fluffing them and setting them aside, a small smile on her lined face.

"Have you lived here long?" I asked, leaning forward and picking up my ice water and a napkin.

She settled into the love seat kitty-corner to me, and looked upward, her face furrowed in concentration. "Why, about eleven years I guess. Moved in here when this was the only house on this street. Now look at it, all grown up and crammed together." Her reflection was cut off by a stampede of tiny clicks. Two dachshunds burst into view, fighting each other around the corner and jumping on me as if I was a new toy.

"Richie! Mitzi! Get down!" scolded Evelyn, reaching forward and smacking their butts. "That is no way to greet a guest!" Brad came in and collapsed again on the recliner, which creaked a bit in protest. The dogs seemed intent on covering me with kisses, and I moved to the floor so that they could have easier access to play. The girl dog immediately ran off and brought me a pink chew toy, and I began to play tug-of-war with her. Silence fell.

"Now, Bradley, business first. What is going on with the club?"

Brad closed the recliner and leaned forward, his elbows on his knees, gaze level on Evelyn. "The club is strong. Covers are increasing due to cross-promotion with area casinos. We have a new marketing program geared at bachelor parties and have had a twenty percent increase in group events since last year. The—"

"How much is the marketing program costing? The bachelor one, I mean."

"About three percent. So the twenty percent increase is more than covering it."

"And the girls? Why did Vicky leave?"

"She's pregnant."

"Are we covering her health expenses through the birth?"

"If she returns within two months."

"Make it three. Brad, you don't know what it's like for a new mother."

He grinned. "No, I don't. Neither do you."

She waved that off. "What about Harmony—she left, too."

"Heather was into drugs—we caught her twice at the club. Told her to leave them or us. She chose them, and she's at Painted Horse now."

The old woman harrumphed and sat back. "Okay, then, I guess it's under control."

"Janine is supposed to be having weekly calls with you regarding all this. Has she not been calling you?"

"You know me—I don't like the phone. I like this better, face-to-face. Besides, I'm not crazy about Janine. Too stiff and numbers-oriented."

"Which is exactly why I hired her. Those girls will walk all over someone if they don't keep a distance. And I don't recall you complaining about the numbers last quarter."

She grinned and patted his leg. "I know, Brad. I just have to keep tabs—you know that. It makes me feel useful. Gives me something to think about."

I played with the dogs in silence, eavesdropping, my mind digesting the new information and what it meant—Brad owned Saffire. Why was I not surprised? Richie, the male dachshund, started humping my bare foot. Ewww. I moved it away from him but he followed, his tongue hanging out and his eyes buggy. I sat cross-legged and tried waving the rubber toy in his face.

"You been getting the deposits?"

"Yes, honey. Like clockwork on the first."

"Why don't you get out of this place, move to one of those active senior living places?"

"You say that every visit, and my answer hasn't changed. I like it here. This is home. I'll stay here till they carry me away in a coffin. You know that."

"Julia."

I looked up, caught off guard by Evelyn's beckon.

"Yes?"

"We've been awfully rude, dear, talking business. Tell me about yourself. How did you and Bradley meet?"

Brad answered the question for me. "Julia is an intern at my office."

"Oh."

Her "oh" said volumes and I arched my brow at Brad.

"It's not like that, Evie. Julia and I are friends, nothing more. She is Broward's intern, not mine." *Kind of not like that. Sort of exactly like that.*

"I wasn't judging you, dear."

Sure she wasn't. "How did you two meet?" I said, trying to steer the conversation anywhere but where it was currently headed.

"Oh, Bradley helped me with my first divorce."

"And your second," Brad reminded her.

"Hush now, Brad! No need to air all my dirty laundry! I just met this nice girl."

"Are you married now?" I had looked around for evidence of a man, children or grandchildren, but couldn't find evidence of anyone but her and the dogs.

"Oh, no, dear. I learned after the second one that men and me don't mix. I can only see the good, and they can only see the bad."

"I didn't think you practiced law in Nevada," I said to Brad.

"I am licensed here, but don't make a habit of taking on cases. In Evie's case, I'd represented her sister in a big suit back home. Once Evie's marriage took a bad turn, her sister asked if I would represent Evelyn."

"And no one can say no to Ruth," Evelyn sniffed.

"And that was, what, eleven years ago?" Brad asked.

"Yes, thank you for making me feel old. Eleven years ago. And Julia, this man has been driving me crazy ever since! Why I let him come by and visit me is a mystery." Brad grinned at me and I fought against the urge to smile back. The man was so damn charming it was criminal.

"Evelyn, when are you visiting Ruth next?"

"Thanksgiving, I suppose. Haven't heard from her yet, but she came here last year, so I'll probably go there. Will you join us for supper?"

"I would never pass up your turkey and dressing. As long as I'm not a burden, I'll be there."

"Julia, do you live with your family?"

"Ah—no. My family is in Georgia. I live with roommates—other college students." Brad listened closely. I realized this was the most he had heard about my background.

"What do your parents do?" This seemed to be of high importance to her.

"My mother is a nurse. My father is retired. He was a science professor at UGA—the University of Georgia."

"A bulldog."

I grinned. "Yes. You don't want to see our home. The only theme Mom decorated in is red, white and black."

"Well, my first husband, scoundrel that he was, was an Alabama fan. Now I root for anyone else in the SEC."

"You didn't win his season tickets in the divorce?" I said with a straight face.

"Honey, what can I say? I guess my attorney wasn't as good as his."

We looked at each other, and at Brad, and laughed.

After two helpings of lemon squares and three rounds of ice water, we rose to leave. Richie had finally abandoned my foot and I had finally endeared myself to Evelyn, and her to me. We all hugged in the foyer. Evelyn, clasping Brad with both hands, seemed on the verge of tearing up.

"I'll be back in about six weeks. Will you come and stay at Bellagio? I can send Leonard with the car."

She waved her hand irritably. "I guess. You know I hate going to that godforsaken city. And don't send Leonard in that big car! A normal town car is all I need."

"Deal. I'll take you to see *Mystère*."

"I don't want to see those double-jointed Cirque freaks. Celine Dion?"

"Only for you, Evie."

"You know they say this year is her last!"

"I've been hearing that from you for four years now. I'll believe it when I see it."

"Well, behave yourself. And drive carefully in that death trap!"

She gave him another quick hug and turned to me. "Oh, wait!" she cried, throwing up her hands and running to the kitchen as fast as her old lady hips would take her. "I almost forgot. I packed you some sandwiches and drinks." She returned carrying a small blue cooler with "Taylor" printed on the side of it. "There are some other snacks in there, too. Don't you worry about that cooler—you keep it or throw it away. I've got plenty." She passed Brad the cooler and kissed him on the cheek.

"Thank you, Evie."

"Can't let you kids get hungry. Julia, will I see you again?"

I hesitated. *Chances of me and Brad making another run to Vegas? I hadn't even figured out what would happen when we returned home. Whether I would be smart or foolish. Follow my head or my libido.* I realized an awkward silence was imminent and spoke quickly. "No, Evelyn, I think this is it. This was a one-time trip."

She surveyed me wisely, her brows set. She leaned forward and hugged me tightly. Whispering, so soft I almost didn't hear, she said, "You be careful. That man is a big hole to fall into." *Don't I know it.* She pulled back and squeezed my shoulders merrily. "Now, you guys leave! I got a lot of stuff to do today and can't be watching after you two all day long!"

I got in my red beast, Brad in his blue one. He set the cooler on the seat next to him. He pulled out first and I followed, both of us waving and honking our horns at the tiny blue-haired lady on the little front porch of the house at the end of the cul-de-sac.

Twenty-Four

The day had gotten hot. I blasted the air on high and cursed the Dodge designers who'd put black leather in the car, the hot material burning my ass and legs. I couldn't even imagine being in shorts; my jeans were barely protecting me as it was. The highway was flat and narrow, just two lanes. Beautiful and quiet scenery flew by, mountains on one side and valleys with water on the other. "Back in Black" by AC/DC blared and I put on my sunglasses and let my hair flip in the wind, feeling like the ultimate badass. Barely out of the city limits, we came to a sign for the Hoover Dam and followed a long, curving road up. The Viper's engine roared and the car felt glued to the road as we whipped up the curves. I loved shifting high and low and feeling the vibration and the power beneath me.

We finally arrived at the dam. We avoided the parking garage and continued up the road, driving until we came to an overlook point. Every bad "dam" joke crossed my mind as we parked and walked to the railing. There was a mist coming up from the water, and I felt it hit my face as I leaned over the rail. Brad leaned over also, then stopped as the railing shifted a bit under his weight. We laughed and he stepped back a few steps before moving behind me and putting his hands on my waist, squeezing me. "Want to go on the tour?" he asked.

"No…unless you want to. I'm not really a tour-type girl."

"Sounds good to me. Want to eat lunch out here?"

"Depends…. How good is Evelyn's cooking?"

"It's hit-or-miss. Let's see what she packed."

We opened the cooler. It was jammed full. If we got stranded out here, we'd be set. She had chicken and egg salad sandwiches, raw carrots, sliced apples, three bags of chips, baby brownie bites and grapes. She had also packed three bottled lemonades.

"Good—chicken salad she does well. Let's eat here."

We sat on the warm hood of Brad's car, the cooler in between us, and ate looking out on the view. That high up, there was a nice breeze, and it felt just about perfect.

"So," I said, munching on a raw carrot, "tell me the full scoop on Evelyn. You guys are, like, business partners in Saffire?"

He finished chewing a bite of sandwich and set it down on the car. "Evelyn's first husband was a surgeon. They lived in a big house, up in the Hills. When they divorced, she got a substantial amount of cash, enough to buy the house you saw today, plus had a bit left over."

"What's a bit?" I couldn't help it. I was nosy.

He raised an eyebrow at me, then shrugged. "Two hundred grand, maybe a little more. Around that time I was looking at opening a club in Vegas. I approached Evelyn, asked if she wanted to go in as a minority partner. She had been looking at different investments at that time, CDs, bonds, et cetera. I convinced her that her money would be better served at Saffire."

"A strip club? You convinced that little old lady that she should put her life savings in a strip club? What if it went belly-up?"

He stared at me. "I'm not out to swindle old ladies out of their pensions. If the club had flopped, I would have covered her loss. We own the building—there are actual assets tied to her money. Plus, I don't see anyone complaining about the return Saffire has done. That 'little old lady' has more than ten times her original investment now sitting in the bank."

"And she owns what percentage?"

"Thirty."

"You own seventy?"

"Sixty. I gave Janine ten percent."

"Why?"

"You'll learn in business that no one runs the company like the owner does. That ten percent ensures she stays honest and doesn't look for another job. Janine is strong. The dancers like her, the clients like her and I like her."

"You ever slept with her?"

"Why do you seem to ask me that with every woman we meet?"

"I didn't ask you that with Evelyn."

"Maybe you should have."

I recoiled and wrinkled my nose, scooting a little farther away from him on the hood. He laughed through his sip of lemonade.

"No, I haven't slept with Janine. She's too hard for me. I don't go for the muscular look."

"So that's why you haven't slept with her—because her body type isn't for you, *not* because you think that it'd be a bad idea to screw your business partner."

He fixed his dark brown eyes on me and reached forward, gently wiping some mayonnaise from my lip. I pushed his hand away in irritation, trying to ignore the full-body tingle that occurred whenever he touched me.

"I wouldn't have chosen a business partner or manager that I was attracted to. I know my strengths. Staying away from good-looking women isn't one of them." He shot me a sly look. "But then again, you seem to suffer from the same problem."

I shot him a puzzled look. "What do you mean?"

He leaned back on his hands and stretched his neck, looking at me through thick lashes. "You know…last night—you and Montana."

I sat there for a moment, trying to sort through the drunken haze of memories. I vividly remembered the tour of the club with Montana. Then us getting to the table and Brad being gone. Then… I frowned, trying to remember. We were going to do shots, tequila shots. She had to ask permission. Then… *Oh my God.* My eyes widened as I had a brief memory of Montana's mouth on my bare breasts—us kissing, and guys, lots of guys, their faces surrounding us, staring. Brad's included. I slumped down on the hood, lying back, my hand covering my face. "Oh, God," I moaned, mortified. "It's, what—one o'clock? And you're just now mentioning this to me?"

He laughed and leaned over me, pulling my fingers back, exposing my pained eyes. "You don't need to be embarrassed. Trust me—Saffire has seen a lot crazier, though we typically try to keep that behavior out of the club."

I groaned miserably, closing my eyes. "What was I thinking?"

"You weren't—the tequila was." His hand moved from my face down, sweeping over my breast, playing with the exposed skin between my shirt and the top of my jeans. "Besides, I liked watching you."

"With Montana?"

"Yes. You, in your element, having fun and being turned on by her touch. It drove me crazy watching you, surrounded by that crowd, the men watching." He pulled gently at my skin, gripping me. "You are very sexy, Julia."

I blushed and moved his hand, sitting up and tossing my hair dramatically. "I am quite sexy, it's true."

He laughed and looked skyward, rolling his eyes. "Oh… the ego."

"Where were you before that? You weren't at our table when we got back."

He looked away, out over the dam. "I was with Alexis."

"Getting a dance?"

"Sort of."

I tossed my half-eaten carrot at him, which he blocked easily. "God, you are a pig. No wonder you've been such a 'gentleman.'"

He looked at me carefully, taking a small sip of lemonade. "You mad?"

"No. Just understand that my drunken playtime with Montana was due to me being left unattended. When the cat's away…" I grinned mischievously at him and took another bite of carrot.

"So, not jealous?"

I chewed on my lip, reaching into the cooler. "You what, had sex with her?"

He nodded, watching me closely. "In the office. Upstairs. We—"

"Stop. I don't want the details. Let me think for a minute." I knew I wanted more. Didn't want to end whatever this tryst between us was. But I also knew what we were right now. Absolutely nothing. He'd never promised me anything, other than that he wasn't the boyfriend type, which was clear. The thought of him and Alexis, his hands on her body, his lips on hers…. I *was* jealous, but it was jealousy in the true sense of the word—I wanted what she had. I yearned for that missed opportunity, hated that I missed a chance to have him inside me, that she got to experience it instead of me, especially when I was right there for the taking…even though I guess I hadn't made that clear until this morning. But I knew what he was really asking—if I was insecure about it. I searched my subconscious, examining all the nooks and crannies where insecurities and hidden emotions like to hide. I was shocked to find nothing there.

I shook my head. "Not jealous, at least not in the sense that you're asking. But, we just met. I think, as I mentioned earlier, that a certain depth of feeling is necessary for jealousy." I met his eyes. "Guess that means I don't care, huh?"

"Guess so, Julia." He looked back over the dam. "Guess so."

We munched along in silence, Brad opening up a bag of salt-and-vinegar chips and diving in, the bag making a loud sound in the quiet landscape. I wrinkled my nose and looked at him. "Those chips are going to give you vampire breath."

"Vampire breath? Is that the cool term right now?"

"No, but it's true. I'm not kissing you after this. Probably all part of Evelyn's plan—separate us with the power of bad breath."

"I think Evelyn liked you."

"I don't know…. She's a hard read. I take it you two are close?"

"Yes. I'm not close with my family—they weren't exactly nurturing. Evelyn takes good care of me, and she needs someone checking in on her, making her feel important. That's one of the reasons I brought the club proposal to her. I could have easily covered that nut alone, but the club makes her feel important, gives her something to think about. I get her down there every once in a while. She loves being backstage, taking over as house mom for the evening."

"So you're basically a saint. That's what you're saying? Saint Bradley?"

"God, you are a pain in my ass."

"No, I just call you on your crap."

He leaned over and placed a soft kiss on my lips. "You are a mess, you know that?"

I pushed him off. "No kisses! I told you—vampire breath!"

Beaming at me, he grabbed an extralarge chip and chomped down, chewing noisily. I looked at my watch and started to pack up the cooler.

On the way back to Vegas, Brad insisted we stop back by Evelyn's to return the cooler.

"She said we could keep it!"

"Yeah, she also said we could throw it away. She can say whatever, but she wants that cooler back. Trust me."

So return it we did, winding our Vipers through the suburban streets once more until we were crammed into her tiny cul-de-sac again. I waited in my car as Brad took it up to the front and rang the bell. I watched a gushing Evelyn hug Brad about five times before he finally detached from her grip and walked back down the drive. Stopping by my open window, he leaned in.

"I was gonna take the scenic way back. Ready to open them up?"

I revved my engine in response. At the sound, at least two curtains moved in the homes surrounding us. We exited the cul-de-sac carefully and respectfully, and began to head back to the open road. We reached it in two and a half songs, and I raised both hands and cheered into the wind as we hit the highway. I amped up the radio and pressed my foot on the pedal. The car instantly responded, literally jumping forward and throwing my head against the seat. I upshifted and began to fly. Brad and I leapfrogged each other and flew past cars as we traveled through the desert. I felt alive, liberated, and as the car drove, all thoughts of anything rational left my mind.

Twenty-Five

Rule 5: No socializing or communication out of the experience.

"So tell me about the intern you slept with."

"Which one?"

I coughed on a sip of Dr Pepper and shot him a look of disgust. We sat in Rick's Roadhouse, a chain restaurant located off Terminal D. We had about forty-five minutes before our flight, and were killing time there instead of the overcrowded concourse.

"I'm kidding! There was only one. Blonde, with a tight body. She was my intern, a colossal mistake by HR. Second week she started wearing short little skirts and revealing tops." He dipped a fry in some ketchup and popped it in his mouth. "You know me, keeping my eyes to myself isn't my strong point. I started looking...she started bending over more. I lasted another two weeks before we went for drinks after work. Drinks led to sex, which she loved and I didn't."

"Why not?"

He shifted uncomfortably. "I don't like to kiss and tell."

"Oh, please. I think we passed the polite conversation stage a week ago. We have moved into full disclosure and then some."

"Still…"

"Okay, answer my questions and I'll open the door wide for any questions about my past lovers."

"So, you do kiss and tell?"

"You seem trustworthy. Plus, it doesn't appear like you have any friends, so there's no one for you to giggle and share this with."

His brows rose amusedly and he stood for a moment, surprising me.

"Where are you going?"

"Just a minute." He strode away from the table and went up to the bar, where he was drooled over by a bleached-blonde forty-year-old waitress who, by the look of her skin, should have worn sunscreen and stopped smoking about twenty years earlier. He returned to the table a few minutes later with two shots of a golden liquid. He set them down, one in front of me. I crossed my arms and narrowed my eyes at him.

"Come on. It's the last day of our fun." The lizard-skin waitress from behind the bar appeared with a glass of lime wedges and set them down, hovering a moment too long, smiling at Brad, before heading back to the bar. "Tequila," he said.

"Trying to get me to hook up with your bartender?"

"Ha. Ha. I'll answer your question if you take the shot with me."

"Sounds like coercion."

"Guilty as charged. I'll let you figure out my punishment later." He held up his shot and I met his with mine. "Toast?"

"To guilty men." I clinked my glass to his and we downed the yellow fire. I winced and grabbed a lime, biting down on the tart fruit. I followed that with a sip of tea, and pointed at Brad, indicating for him to answer the original question.

"Fine. It was bad for me because she was too loud—moaning and wailing the entire time. She acted like she was constantly either orgasming or on the verge of orgasming. Supposedly, she had about twelve during the twenty minutes we had sex. I finally stopped and told her I was done."

I thought of our experience together and blushed. Best I could recall, I had been pretty vocal.

He caught my look. "What?"

"Nothing."

"Come on. What?"

"I was pretty vocal with you also. Maybe it's an intern thing."

"Julia." He reached forward and grabbed my hand. "You are an intriguing, beautiful woman. You are incredibly sexual and I love how you are during sex. Being vocal is a great thing. She took it to the extreme and made me think she was overembellishing. That was the turnoff. I want a real, genuine reaction, not an imitation of a porn star."

I sighed and licked some ketchup off my finger. "I was just stating an observation. I'm not worried about my bedroom prowess."

"And I was just explaining the difference between you two."

"So, that was it. You guys never did it again?"

"Oh, no, we did. I just gagged her the next time."

"What?! You did not!"

He shrugged. "She was kinky and into that type of stuff anyway—kept wanting me to hold her down, spank her ass, that kind of thing. I worked it into the foreplay and she was hot for it. Kept her quiet and the sex was better that time."

"So you kept seeing her?"

"No. Like I said, her outfits were beyond inappropriate, and her behavior at the office made it obvious what was going on. I told her we had to stop. It wasn't worth the headache I got from Broward and Clarke. They moved her to another attorney and then ranted and raved at me for at least two weeks—sent me down to HR for a chat like I was a junior associate."

"Yet, here you sit with me."

"Well, I've got to misbehave every once in a while just to keep them on their toes."

"Plus, no one's ever going to find out about this trip," I reminded him.

"Right. Plus no one's ever going to find out about this trip," he monotoned.

"I'm serious!"

"Hey," he said, raising his hands. "I don't have a problem keeping my indiscretions secret. It's the girls who always talk. I can't help it that I make such an impression."

"Oh, lordy. Is there enough room for your ego at this table, or should we pull up an extra chair?"

He laughed. "In all seriousness, it would make my life at the office easier if you kept this to yourself."

"First of all, you're not that great, so I have nothing to tell anyone about. Second, no worries. Our secret is safe with me. Plus, once we're back home, we're steering clear of each other, right?"

"Definitely. And you're okay with that, right? No dates, no nightly phone calls, no gushy emails?"

"You got it." The words left my lips confidently, my tone flippant. Nothing in my response communicated the wrestle of emotions that I felt, the dread I felt at parting ways. The idea of staying away from him seemed impossible, his charm and sexuality too magnetic to resist.

"God, you are the perfect woman." He leaned in and I kissed him briefly. Leaning back, he looked at me with a sly grin. "Now, do we have time for a quickie before our flight?"

I tossed my napkin at him and quickly stood, speaking before my mind had a chance to even consider the temptation. "You are impossible! Get the damn check. We need to head to our gate anyway, or else we'll be staying here another night."

Twenty-Six

I woke up Monday morning in my old bed, looking up at my popcorn ceiling with the one suspicious water stain that our landlord insisted was from an old patched spot. The alarm was rudely blaring and I reached over and smacked it until it shut off. *Back to the real world.* I yawned and rolled out of bed, rubbing my eyes.

I had gotten home at eleven-forty the night before. I hadn't bothered unpacking; my bags were sitting in the middle of my room, and I stubbed my toe on one as I tried to get into the hall and to the toilet. One benefit of having slacker roommates was that I didn't have to fight anyone for the shower in the morning. I stood under the pathetically gentle spray, already missing the body jets and rain head at Bellagio.

Brad, huge inside of me, his wet hands slick on my bare skin. The water spray, pure ecstasy on my clit, bringing me close to the edge of oblivion.

Jesus. I will never be able to take a normal shower again. I despondently turned off the shower and stepped out, wrapping my body and head in towels. Seven hours earlier Brad had dropped me off, giving me a quick kiss and helping me with my bags. I hadn't invited him in, and we'd had only a quick goodbye on the front stoop.

Back to Home Sweet Home, I thought grimly.

I scanned my closet, settling on a boring brown pantsuit and low heels. I didn't bother with contacts, just brushed my wet hair into a low bun and put on light makeup. Brad and I had agreed to stay away from each other, which I figured would be easy, seeing as Broward had strict rules for me in that regard anyway. I would just actually follow them this time around. I tried not to let that thought depress me.

The week passed quickly. Miraculously, Broward gave me a lunch break on Thursday, so I met with Becca and Olivia at Panera. Over chicken-and-rice soup I gave them most of the scoop on the weekend. I left out the shower sex and my girl-on-girl action, but included pretty much everything else. The girls, as expected, had strong opinions on everything. Olivia was adamant that I keep my distance from Brad, her opinion of him only slightly higher than that of a pedophile. Becca thought I should be his travel ho, and wanted to know if there was room for her on the trips. I navigated through their endless questions and finally begged off, telling them I had to get back to work.

By Friday I was watching the clock, and when Broward finally knocked on my door at 8:30 p.m., I was more than ready to leave. I shut down my computer and hurried after him. He held the elevator for me and we rode down together. As the elevator clicked and hummed, I leaned against the wall.

"Big plans for the weekend?" Broward asked.

"No. Sleep." I smiled at him. "You?"

"Kids got soccer games on Saturday. I'm thinking Sunday I'll do some work around the house. The wife wants me to build a bookcase in our media room."

I nodded politely, Brad's opinion of Broward's life coming to me unbidden. *Boring. Dull.* I don't know that Broward saw it like that. A lot of people were perfectly happy with their lives being ordinary. Not everyone needed fast cars, excitement and sex. *Did I?*

The elevator dinged and I nodded to Broward and walked out into the garage, headed to my Camry.

I spent the weekend in bed with a giant roll of chocolate chip cookie dough and a carton of milk, trying to do anything but think of Brad. I went old-school, watching the first season of *Desperate Housewives,* enjoying the drama underneath a big, comfy blanket. Sunday, I started getting a little bored, and decided on a bubble bath and a book. I only soaked for fifteen minutes before Alex, roommate number two, started banging on the door. I sighed and pulled the plug, watching the bubbles circle the drain and disappear. Hearing my cell ring in my bedroom, I pulled my naked body quickly up and out of the tub. I barely made it to my phone before it was sent to voice mail.

"Hello, Becca."

"*Hola, chica!* What'cha doing?"

"Something superexciting. Too exciting to go into now."

"Yeah, right. This is you we're talking about." She giggled into the phone.

"Hello? Do I get no credit for being superexciting and impulsive last weekend? I am a wild child, and don't you forget it."

"*Riiiigggghhhhtt.* So sorry, Miss Thang. Anyway, the new Tom Cruise movie is playing at 4:00 p.m., and I know how much you like older men…so what do you say?"

"It was one older man, Becca. Don't brand me with this forever. And I say that I'll forgo the superexciting thing that

I'm in the middle of just so I can spend quality time with you. Is Olivia coming?"

She growled into the phone. "No. Says she has to *study.* How lame is that?"

I smiled into the phone. "Superlame. Gosh, her sense of responsibility is absolutely ridiculous."

Becca completely missed my sarcasm. "I know, right? I'll pick you up in twenty. We can shop a bit first, 'kay?"

"Sounds good." I hung up, a smile on my face. For the first time in years, I had money to burn. Time to go shopping.

I took extra time getting dressed. Becca was a tough critic and I wanted to look reasonably fashionable. When she blared the horn outside twenty minutes later, I was still pulling on heels and it took a minute for me to walk out. Becca had the top of her Mercedes convertible down, Gwen Stefani blasting. Designer shades on, she strongly resembled Malibu Barbie.

"Looking good, sistah," she said, pushing her glasses up, approving of my skinny jeans, wedge heels and silk tank. I had put curl enhancer in my hair and had it down, hoping it would air-dry with some semblance of style. I opened the door and got in, reaching over to hug her.

"Got the goods?" she asked.

"You know it," I said, opening up my biggest purse and showing her the candy stash inside. I used to smuggle cans of Coke and bags of ice into the theater, but Becca put the brakes on that, saying that was going too far. So now I stick to just candy. That day I had packed Skittles, Peanut M&M's, Sour Patch Kids and Milk Duds. A mix of sour, sweet and chocolate. I shut the door and she burned rubber, leaving skid marks in front of my mailbox. I laughed, turned up the radio, and we sang and danced all the way to the mall.

Hanging out with Becca was an experience. In some ways, it was similar to being with a toddler in that you had to watch her constantly or she would get into trouble. For Becca, the trouble was normally with *M-E-N*. She liked all the wrong ones, which, when I came to think of it, was yet another reason I should stay away from Brad. Becca thought he was great.

"I mean, it seems pretty stupid if you ask me," she lamented, flipping through dresses on a rack in Bloomingdale's. "You and him had a great time in Vegas, you get along well, the sex—" she looked sideways at me "—was fantastic. Why would you agree to never hang out again?"

I stopped my rack rifling and faced her. "I never said we had sex."

"Well, I know you never *said* it, but *puh-lease!* You have sex countless times with two losers—sorry, Jules, but in retrospect you can admit it—losers—and never orgasmed. This guy makes you come in the first four minutes that he gets you in bed! You're telling me you just said 'thanks, but no thanks' on seconds?" She shoved the dress hangers shut and glared at me. "I may be stupid when it comes to microbiology or the ancient history of Mayans, but I know sex."

I bit the side of my cheek to keep from laughing. She pointed a finger at me, her face dead serious. "You tell me right now, Julia Campbell, or I will not tell you what part of your outfit looks hideously tacky."

"What!" I looked down at my…flawless…outfit in shock. She snapped her fingers at me and continued pointing, looking ridiculously somber considering she was wearing hot-pink capris with matching fingernails.

I huffed. "Okay, okay, but only so you stop pointing. Geez!"

"So you admit that you, Julia Campbell, prude of all prudes, had *sex*—" she whispered the word as though it was revered "—with that man?"

"Yes, I did! And it was wonderful, and hot, and I had another orgasm. Happy?"

She sank to her knees in dramatic fashion. "Ecstatically. Welcome to my world of slutdom. It is an amazing place to be."

I stepped over her kneeling form and moved to the next rack. "Wait. What—"

"The leopard-print belt," she muttered, getting to her feet and wiping her pants off. "Who pairs that with cork wedges?"

Three bags filled with amazing clothes later, we sat at a minuscule table in the food court, devouring a cookie-cake slice and two Cokes. I had splurged on one item—a pair of suede Manolo Blahniks. It was the most I had ever spent on a pair of shoes, but I had wanted to spend part of my Vegas windfall on something exorbitant.

"So, seriously, Jules. Why stay away from each other if you both had fun?"

I toyed with a piece of icing that had broken off the cookie crust. "I don't know—a few things, really. One is my internship."

"Attorneys aren't allowed to date interns," she said, nodding. "Seems like a logical rule."

"Right, but it's a little more complicated than that. Brad isn't just an attorney—he's a senior partner. And Broward, my boss, specifically forbade me to even speak to Brad, much less do all of the...other stuff...that we've done. So it's really important that I keep this a secret, which so far I've done. If we keep seeing each other, the likelihood of it coming out grows. And the last thing I need blocking my acceptance to law school is a bad rec."

"Yeah, but you could get around that. My dad could give you a recommendation."

"That's beside the point. CDB is one of the top firms in

the city. It's on record that my internship is with them. I don't want to mar that opportunity."

"Okay, so that's one reason. But your internship is over in, what—six weeks?"

"Yeah."

"Okay. So lay low and don't see each other until then."

"But what's the point? Yes, we had fun, but there are plenty of guys out there that I can have fun with. I don't see why I should waste my time with someone when 'the one' could be out there waiting."

"Oh my God. You and your freaking 'the one' theory. Was Dickhead One or Luke 'the one'?"

"Dickhead One has a name."

"Are you really defending him? Anyway, moving on, you wasted time with both of them to figure out if they were 'the one.' Why not do the same thing with Brad?"

"To start with, they were both interested in dating me. Brad isn't. I don't think he does girlfriends, or if he does, they have some type of agreement worked out where they're okay with him sleeping with other people. I don't need to tell you that that isn't something I am interested in."

"So you would have an issue with him fucking other people?"

My mind alighted on his screw of the stripper, and how surprisingly unjealous I was over that. "If we were dating...yes. Obviously, I would not be okay with him cheating on me."

"It's not really cheating if everyone is okay with it happening."

I blew out a frustrated burst of air. "Then obviously *you* are the type of woman he's been dating—women who are okay with him sticking his dick everywhere he wants to. Again, I am *not*. So no point in discussing *that* any further."

"Geez, Jules, you don't have to get all bitchy on me. I'm just playing devil's advocate."

I took a big, bitchy bite out of the cookie and let my emotions simmer. Becca's big, mascaraed eyes looked away and she scratched her neck.

I glared at her through a mouthful of cookie. "And nothing is wrong with my fucking belt! Leopard and cork go fine together! The straps on these shoes are dark brown!"

She started giggling uncontrollably and clamped a hand over her mouth to try and cover the sound. Coke spurted from her nose and she waved a hand rapidly in front of her, trying to calm her giggles and find a napkin. I handed her one, my face softening. Then I was laughing, too, seeing the Coke dripping down her beautifully made-up, bright red face.

That night, after the movie and a quick bite at Zaxby's, I lay in my bed and stared at the ceiling. Through the thin wall I could hear Metallica or Death Grip or some other heavy metal band playing on Zack's stereo. The room was hot and I flung off my comforter and kicked my legs a bit to free the sheet. I tossed and turned, but couldn't get to sleep. Finally, I plugged my iPhone into the stereo beside my bed. Turning up the volume just enough to drown out Death Cab, I put it on Katy Perry and set the sleep timer for fifteen minutes. I selected "I Kissed a Girl" and lay back down, staring at the ceiling. As the words floated through the air, I remembered lobster claws, sequined bras, champagne and the flow of desert wind through my hair. Finally, I fell asleep, to the memory of Brad's eyes, staring down at me, dark, complex voids of mystery.

The next week and a half flew by. Broward had a business acquisition closing, and preparing for it meant extra-late nights and jam-packed days. The closing finally occurred on Wednesday at 2:00 p.m., and Broward gave our whole wing permission to leave at five. I'd never been so excited about a normal workday in my life. I was merrily stapling briefs together when Todd Appleton stuck his head in the door. "Can I come in?"

Feeling extragenerous, I waved him in with a smile. "Of course, Todd. How's everything going?"

"Great. Really great. We heard in the East Wing that you guys were getting an early night off. Want to come out with us?"

"Where you guys going?"

"Cantina del Mar. Drinks are half-off till six."

"Ohhh…tempting."

He grinned at me. "Hey, don't act highbrow. You may be putting in the long hours, but you're getting paid the same as me—nothing."

"Yeah, don't I know it." My desk phone rang, interrupting us. "Julia Campbell," I answered.

"What are you doing?"

It was Brad. My heart skipped briefly, his deep voice causing a shot of heat through me.

"Just sitting here." I tried to sound casual, feeling anything but.

"With who?"

I narrowed my eyes, leaning back in my seat and spinning it slightly, gesturing with one finger for Todd to wait. "I assume you know or you wouldn't be calling."

"Meaning?"

"I'm talking to Todd," I said sweetly, through my teeth.

"Let me talk to him."

"Why?" I didn't bother to sensor the irritation that seeped into my voice.

"Because I need to, and he left his cell phone here."

"Just tell me the message, and I'll pass it on."

He growled into the phone, the guttural sound taking me back to his hands on my body, the forceful way he gripped my skin. *How he fucked like he couldn't get enough of me.* His words came out clipped and measured. "Stop being difficult."

I tried to breathe normally, tried to stop the flush I felt hitting my cheeks, tried to block the image of him from my mind. My words behaved, coming out stern. "I just feel like we're back in the Bob scenario—the only thing missing is your intimidating self darkening my doorstep."

"Just tell him to get his ass back here." He ended the call.

I raised my eyebrows at the phone and hung it up. Todd was trying to look as if he hadn't been eavesdropping on my half of the conversation. "So…will you come?"

I grinned at him, wishing that his hair was darker, his build was larger and that he oozed sex from every pore. "Wouldn't miss it. I'll see you guys there around five-thirty."

"Awesome!" He smacked his hand on the desk and stood, bouncing on his toes a bit and looking around, searching for something to say.

I turned back to my briefs, stapling and sorting them, and he took the cue and started to leave. I waited until he had just passed through my door.

"Oh, and Todd?"

"Yeah?" He was back in an instant, standing in my doorway.

"De Luca wants you. Right away."

At 5:00 p.m. I swung by the bathroom and used my emergency makeup stash to amp up my look a bit. I had worn a black suit that day with a light blue lace cami underneath, so I removed the jacket and let my hair down. I had a pair of dangly earrings in the car from some event weeks ago, and swapped my pearl studs for them. I looked good—not sexy, but a big step up from the frumpy intern that had strode into work nine hours earlier.

Trying to find a spot to park downtown was typically hell, but at five-thirty a lot of spots had opened up and I was able to snag one just a block and a half away from the restaurant.

I saw Jennifer, Renfield's intern, parking her Jeep on a side street, and I waved at her and waited. She jogged up, giving me a bright smile and a quick hug. "Girl, haven't seen you since orientation!" she said. "What do they do—lock you guys up in the West Wing?"

I laughed. "No, just work us to the bone. The Broward rumors are all true. What about at Renfield's? Is she as big of a bitch as everyone says?"

"Depends on the day. Most days she's okay—just every once in a while it's like *whoa*—watch out!" She held the door open for me and we entered the restaurant. Todd was already there, along with Anton Wu and Trevor. They all had beers, and I ordered a Michelob Ultra from the waitress as soon as she passed.

"We got *queso* and chips coming," Trevor said, pulling out stools for both of us.

"Awesome," I said. Todd seemed to be avoiding my gaze, and I shot him a quizzical look. He gave a quick smile and then started asking Trevor something. I shrugged and turned to Jennifer. "You take the LSATs yet?"

"Once. I did okay, but I'm taking a review course this summer. You?"

"I took one my sophomore year. Did well enough then, but I'm gonna try an online course first, see how that helps me."

We chatted about menial crap, and kept ordering beers and eating chips. Pretty soon I was well buzzed and needing real food. I flagged down our waitress and ordered a chicken quesadilla, then made my way over to Todd's side of the table. He gave me a quick smile, then started studying the salt-shakers on the table. I moved in front of him, standing where he couldn't avoid me.

"What's wrong? Why are you acting so weird?"

"Nothing. I'm not acting weird."

"Yes, you are. You're avoiding me like the plague. You invited me here. If you didn't want me to come, you shouldn't have asked."

"I did want you to come. Then... But..."

"But what?"

"De Luca told me to stay away from you."

I stumbled back, staring at him in surprise. "What?"

He chewed at his bottom lip nervously. "When I got back to the wing today, after talking to you, he called me into his office and told me to stay away from you."

"Did he say why?"

"He didn't allow me to ask any questions. Just told me that fraternizing with coworkers was bad news, and he expected more of me. Told me to stay in our wing and stay away from the other interns."

"What did you say?" I sputtered.

He looked down. "I asked him if I could still hang out with Trevor after work. We've been best friends for three years and I told him that. He said Trevor was okay." He shoved the salt-shakers away. "I really have to go. I shouldn't even be here." He rose despondently and went over to Trevor, placing a hand on his shoulder and whispering something in his ear.

I held up my hand. "Todd." He didn't hear me, so I repeated it louder. "Todd!" That got his attention. He looked up at me quickly, a beaten look on his face.

"You stay. I'm leaving."

"What? No, I'll just—"

"Stop. It's done. I'm leaving." I reached in my purse, rifled through the side pocket until I found forty dollars and laid it on the table. "Give that to the waitress, and you guys can have my damn quesadilla." I stomped out of the restaurant, leaving them stunned and staring after me.

I stood outside in the warm breeze, seething mad. That prick. I whipped out my phone and tried Olivia, then Becca. No answer from either. Damn. I was too buzzed to drive and didn't know where I was going. I saw a cab approaching and I waved frantically till it turned on its light and pulled over. I got in the back and slammed the door. "Just head north, please. I'll give you an address in a minute."

I assumed that Brad lived in the north side of town. Mansions and manicured lawns seemed to be his thing. I pulled up WhitePages on my iPhone, but there was no listing for a Brad De Luca. Next I checked the property appraiser's site. That did it: 1244 Olive Line Trail belonged to Bradley De Luca. So did three or four apartments, but I figured the Olive Line Trail address was his home. According to the tax collector, he'd paid $1.8 million for it three years earlier. The beauty of the internet, a stalker's fucking dream.

I gave the taxi driver the address and quietly steamed in the backseat. *Fucking De Luca. Thinks he can decide who I hang out with? The man who doesn't want me, but doesn't want anyone else to have me? Thought he wasn't the jealous type. I will wring his ridiculously large neck with my own two hands.* I ignored my grumbling stomach and flexed my hands in anticipation.

Olive Line Trail was on the north side of downtown, but just barely. We were there within ten minutes and I paid the cabdriver before thinking. He sped off into the darkness and I stood there on an oak-lined residential street wondering what exactly my plan was. I checked my watch: 7:00 p.m. The man might not even be home, though he definitely wasn't still at work. I walked up a paved drive and climbed steps to a set of double doors. I started to reach for the doorbell, but decided that dramatic was a better approach so I reached forward and pounded the shit out of the door. No one answered. I pounded again, then turned, looking at the empty street, taxi gone. *Shit.* I heard something from around the side of the house, so I teetered down the front steps and went around.

In the back of the house was a large pool, hot tub—big surprise—and deep covered porch. Brad was sitting on the back porch in a chair turned to face the house. He had a tennis ball in his hand and was throwing it against the house, letting it bounce back and catching it. A phone to his ear—I could hear him talking. I cleared my throat and stood on the steps behind him, my hands on my hips. He tilted his chair and looked over his shoulder. His eyes hardened, then softened when they saw me. "Rick, I'm gonna have to call you back." He hung up and stood, turning to face me, wearing a white V-neck T-shirt and workout shorts, tennis shoes on his feet. His neck and back were wet from sweat, and he looked as though he had just gotten back from a run. "What are you doing here?" He sounded irritated.

"What am I doing here? What are you doing!"

"I'm at my house."

"I'm not talking about here, you idiot! I'm talking about with Todd—with work—with us!"

"There is no us." His voice sounded raspy as he said it.

"Exactly! You made it very clear that you didn't want a relationship. Yet *you* ran off Bob. *You* told Todd to stay away from me. You are not my father, you are not my boyfriend, you are not my boss. You don't have the right to fuck with my life!"

He looked around the empty yard, then stepped forward,

into my personal space, his scent invading me, his essence weakening my body. He lowered his voice, his eyes locked on mine, staring into my soul. "Why are you yelling?"

I stepped back, keeping the anger in my voice but lowering the volume to a more reasonable level. "Because nothing seems to be getting through your skull!"

"Do you like Todd this much? Is that what this is about?" His eyes watched me closely, and I suddenly realized he was very interested in the response, a crack showing in his armor, faint vulnerability in his stare.

I hesitated, wanting to hurt him, wanting some reaction other than stoic perfection, but going for honesty instead. "I don't like Todd at all. That's not the point. The point is if I *did* really like Todd, or someone else, I don't need you walking around telling people they can't date me. That's not your place. It's like you don't want me, and you don't want anyone else to have me. That's bullshit, especially because you're Mr. Polyamorous!"

"Who says I don't want you?" He stepped forward again, and I looked away, finding nothing but tan skin, gorgeous features and ripped muscles to look at. His hand found my chin, forcing my face in place, his eyes again arresting mine. There they were, those carnal depths of sin, dark brown pools of irresistible temptation that I had tried to forget.

I rolled my eyes and inserted an extra layer of bitch into my tone, determined to save face in a situation I was destined to lose. "Okay, I misspoke. It's like you don't want to date me *exclusively*. God, I forgot I was talking to an attorney and had to clarify everything."

"Let's go to dinner." He moved his hand from my chin, dropping it to his side, and my skin wept at the absence.

"I already ate." As I spoke, my stomach growled. I ignored it.

"Then tomorrow night."

"I already have plans." At that sentence, his eyebrows rose. I was bluffing my ass off, but wasn't about to give him dinner so easily.

"*Oh-kay,* when is your packed social schedule free?"

"Umm...maybe Tuesday? Wait—" I shook my head, trying to think clearly. Trying to hold on to my anger. "Why are we going to dinner?"

"To talk. About this."

"About what? And I came all the way over here to talk about this. Why can't we talk now?"

He sighed and put his hands on his hips, looking absolutely, ridiculously sexy. I fought to keep my hands by my side and the enraged look on my face. "We can't talk now because you're drunk."

"I am not drunk!" I sputtered, though either I was now swaying or the sidewalk was.

"Okay, then you're impaired. Either way, I'm not having this conversation with you right now. Where is your car?"

"At the bar. I took a taxi."

"Where is the taxi now?"

"I don't know. He left."

Brad turned and looked at the house, and for the first time it occurred to me that he might not be alone. "I'll take you home. Come on."

"No!" I held up my hand and he folded his arms, looking at me with irritation. "I'll have one of my friends pick me up." I fumbled in my purse and pulled out my phone.

"Julia..." He reached for me, grabbed my arm, pulled me into his strong embrace. I pushed back, holding a finger up at him, and dialed Olivia's number. *Please pick up, please pick up....*

"Hello?" *Thank God.*

"O, it's me. I need a ride."

"I'm kind of in the middle of some—"

"O, I *need* a ride."

A sigh. "Okay, where are you?"

"Twelve forty-four Olive Line Trail. It's just north of down-town."

"I'll put it in GPS."

"Thank you. I'll be out front." I ended the call and looked up at Brad. "My friend's picking me up."

"A guy or a girlfriend?"

I threw my phone at him, a long, perfect heave that easily could have taken out one of his eyes if he hadn't ducked with an athlete's reflexes. He laughed, looking at my phone now lying harmlessly on the grass. *Good thing he wasn't standing in front of pavement.* I stalked over and picked up the phone, then marched over to the driveway and started heading back to the front of the house. My defiant stomp was marred slightly by the fact that I was wearing heels and the damn man had a cobblestone driveway, but I forged on, stumbling twice, him there beside me, catching me both times.

"Julia…" Brad hurried ahead of me, grabbing my arms and holding me in place. I ripped them free, pushing him aside, seeing a quick flash of his face, frustration in his eyes, and rounded the curve of the house. I plowed through a bed of recently planted tulips—*what bachelor has tulips?*—stomping up the first two steps to the front porch and dramatically flopping down on the step, hugging my purse to my body and staring stonily out at the street.

He moved in front of me, my stubborn gaze now locked on his crotch, clad in loose athletic shorts that, despite their best effort, did nothing to hide the bulge of his cock.

"Look, I'm sorry I said anything to Todd. That wasn't my place." His apology was scratchy and stilted. He was probably out of practice admitting he was wrong.

"And to Bob."

"*And* to Bob. Though I didn't really say anything to Bob."

I grumbled through my purse. "No, you just sucked all the air out of my office and stared him down like he was a rogue agent."

Brad sighed and sat down next to me on the step. I fought the urge to lean against him. He was just so damn…everything: strong, protective, sexy—and smelled ridiculously good, even with dried sweat all over him. He started to put an arm around me and I stiffened. "Don't." He dropped his arm and leaned back, gazing out at the street. It was warm, and in the distance we could hear the sounds of the neighborhood. Somewhere a basketball thumped; garage doors opened and closed. We sat in silence and I tried to calculate how long it would take Olivia to get here from campus. Assuming she had been at her apartment, which was about a fifty-fifty chance, I figured about seven minutes, and probably—

Brad's voice interrupted my calculations. "What are you thinking about?"

"What a dick you are."

"Wow. Not the first time I've heard that."

"I bet."

"Again, I'm sorry about Todd. Tomorrow, I'll talk to him." I snorted. "Like *that* won't be awkward."

He let out a deep breath of air. "It's all I can do."

"Well, thank you for the apology. The good news is there aren't any other good-looking interns, so you can't really do any more damage." I turned and looked at Brad, his strong profile gently lit by the recessed step lights. "I don't get you, Brad. This has jealousy written all over it."

He clasped his hands and looked at them, then at me, his gaze direct. "I don't know what to tell you, Julia. It was just a reflex action. I heard Todd talking on his cell about meeting you for drinks and it just popped out. I know it was out of place. I just didn't want him getting you drunk and taking advantage of you."

"This coming from you—the man who whisked me off to Vegas and poured drinks down my throat at every opportunity? The man who had me naked on his bed the first morning of our trip?"

He frowned at me. "Don't try to twist that trip into something it wasn't. I didn't take you to Vegas to woo you into sex. I took you to Vegas because you had never been, and it was an opportunity for us to get to know each other without fear of running into someone from the office. I don't think I was pressuring you when you walked naked and dripping into the living room and invited me into the shower."

I blushed and gritted my teeth. The man had a point. I changed the scope of my attack. "And you told Todd that fraternizing with coworkers was bad business? What about fucking clients? Did you include that in your business advice? And you can't even talk about fraternizing with coworkers! Seriously, did you choke on your own bullshit?"

"Okay, Julia, you've made your point—I'm an asshole. I was out of line. I have apologized. I'm not going to sit here and have you chastise me like I'm a child. I'm not used to not getting what I want. I'm not used to being told I can't have something. I'm sorry if it pissed me off to see someone else getting you so easily." He swore angrily and stood up. I quickly followed suit, grabbing his arm when he started to step away.

"I'm not a fucking object! I'm not something that you can choose to have, or choose to toss away. Does it even matter to you what I want?"

He looked down, at my hand, which still gripped his strong biceps, my fingers not even reaching halfway around it. Then he looked at my eyes, his face unreadable.

"What is it you want?" he asked. "What do you want from

me? You want me to spend a weekend with you, have you naked against me, your smile, your laugh, and then just cut you off? Kiss you goodbye and then let anyone else have you? You want me to sit in my office and watch Todd ask you out? I'm not engineered that way. Maybe I am polyamorous, as you put it, on one hand and territorial on the other. That might seem fucked up, but it's how I am. I take what I want, and I own what I have. I'm just trying to figure out what you want."

I stared at him, my jaw tight, my eyes unable to pull from his. "I don't want a fuck buddy, much less to be owned by one." I released his arm, crossing mine over my chest.

Thankfully, Olivia chose that moment to arrive, pulling up and waving at me. Brad stood, hands on his hips, and watched me as I walked past him to the car. I didn't look back, and he didn't say anything, didn't chase after me.

I got in the car and looked at Olivia. "Is he looking over here?"

"Yep. He's looking and shaking his head, like he's confused."

"Okay. Stop looking at him and drive away."

"Is that De Luca?"

"Drive away. Then you can grill me."

She obediently put the car in Drive and pulled off, waiting until she hit the first light before turning to me with an expectant look.

"Yes, that was De Luca. No, I don't want to talk about it."

"Damn, Jules, the man is a god! Those shoulders—"

I held up my hand, stopping her gush. "I really don't want to hear about it. I spend at least half of each day trying *not* to think about his body. Can you just take me home?"

"Sure. Just so I know, where's your car at?"

I groaned. "A metered spot by Cantina del Mar. I'll have a taxi take me by it in the morning." I leaned against the cool window, watching the streets zoom by. She pulled up at my house just when I was beginning to doze. I gave her a grateful hug, and dragged myself inside to my bed. Crawling under the sheets, still in my work clothes and makeup, I barely remembered to set the alarm before I fell asleep.

My alarm rang at 5:45 a.m.—forty-five minutes early so I would have time to figure out my car situation. I hit the alarm, stumbled to the bathroom to pee, then wandered back into my room. I grabbed my phone to look up a taxi company's number when I saw a text sent from Olivia at eleven-twenty the night before.

Becca and I picked up your car. It's in the driveway. Your extra key is back in the hidden magnet

God bless friends who know every aspect of your life. I crawled over my bed to the window, looked outside to verify that my car was, in fact, in the driveway, and then crawled back under the covers, resetting the alarm for 6:30 a.m.

7:35 a.m.

Jogging into the CDB lobby, I called Olivia's phone. It rang once and then went to voice mail. I left her a short but sweet message thanking her profusely for both rescuing my ass the night before and for returning my car. I decided to wait to call Becca; she was undoubtedly still asleep. I made coffee in record time, a feat I had now mastered, and my butt was firmly in my seat by 7:45 a.m. I nodded a good-morning to Broward as he passed, then rose to pour him a cup.

"Morning, Julia," he said as I set the coffee mug in front of him.

I smiled at him pleasantly. "Good morning. Anything special on the agenda today?"

"Not really," he said, flipping through some papers on his desk. "Except that I have that mediation next week that I have to fly to Dallas for, so I'll be gone from Tuesday through Thursday." He looked up at me expectantly.

Yes! Three days without Broward. I tried not to let my exuberance show and nodded calmly at him. "Anything I can do to help you prepare, sir?"

"Yes, I'll need all of the files related to the Bandor Construction suit. Also, it will be informative for you to sit through the mediation prep calls with me. Check my calendar and invite yourself to any events that are related to that case between now and Tuesday. When I get back, we'll have a lot of mediation paperwork, and hopefully a settlement offer to work on."

I nodded mutely and turned to leave.

"Oh, Julia?"

Oh, no. I turned demurely and smiled at him, my eyebrows raised. "Yes, sir?"

He stood, now at eye level with me. "Last time I was out of town, I heard from Sheila that De Luca had been…bothering… you. I was worried, but it appears that he has backed off. Is my leaving town again going to cause a problem?"

I kept my voice light and my eyes perplexed. "I don't see why it would, sir. I've only spoken to Mr. De Luca a few times, and always regarding work items. He hasn't bothered me."

He looked relieved and sank back to his seat. "Great. That's great. Just checking, Julia. You have a bright future ahead of you, and I didn't want it being tarnished. I know I don't need to tell you again, but please stay in the West Wing, and as far as you can from Brad De Luca."

★ ★ ★

Back at my desk, I held my head in my hands. Halfway through my internship and I was lying to my boss and breaking the only rule he had given me. Combine that with the fact that Brad was a headcase, and the right thing to do seemed obvious—stay away from him and hope that no one ever found out. Stick to the plan, and maybe salvage the ridiculous internship that I was already regretting taking. My phone rang.

"Julia Campbell."

"It's me." *Brad.*

I hung up the phone.

Twenty-Seven

Thursday morning, 10:45 a.m.

Todd Appleton knocked on my door and stuck his head inside. "You busy?"

"Nothing I can't pause. Come on in." I smiled at him hesitantly, with him doing the same to me. Neither one of us spoke for a minute.

"Look, Julia, De Luca came and talked to me this morning. He said I could talk to you, or hang out, or whatever. It's cool."

"So he gave you permission?"

"I guess. He just let me know that he shouldn't have said anything, and I can hang out with whoever I want."

"How swell of him."

He sat down in the chair across from me and played with a lone paper clip that was lying there. "What's the deal with you two?"

"What do you mean?" I said. I swore silently to myself. I should have realized that this would all seem really weird to Todd.

"I mean, you act so pissed at him…and the way he warned me about you—are you seeing him or something?"

I laughed harshly. My laugh sounded weird, not casual the way I had meant it to come out. "Todd, I've never even met the guy. Maybe once, in passing. I just hear all the stories and he sounds like an asshole."

"De Luca? No, he's like the coolest guy ever!"

"Well, he sounds like a jerk. I just don't like anyone telling you what to do. Last night I was drunk, and overreacted. I'm sorry."

"Yeah, you like…wigged out. We were all wondering where you were headed—you had this death stare going."

"I was just pissed about something else. I'm sorry. I swear I'll be normal and sane next time."

"Yeah, heard Broward's going to be out of town next week some." He looked down at the paper clip, which he had now twisted into something resembling a fortune cookie. "Maybe next week you'd like to hang out or something?"

Just what I need right now, more workplace drama. "I don't know, Todd. I've heard they take interoffice dating really seriously."

"Dating! No, I didn't mean dating." He laughed nervously. "I just meant, like hanging out. Watching a movie or something."

"Sure, Todd. Something like that sounds good." I smiled at him and his whole face lit up.

"Awesome! Really awesome. Okay, I'm, ah, gonna get back to the East Wing. We got a lot going on today."

"Thanks for stopping by." I waved at him and he reciprocated, turning so fast he bumped into the door frame. He blushed and ducked out, closing the door softly behind him. I groaned and returned to the brief I was proofreading. I don't know why, but it seemed my good-girl days were gone, and all I knew how to do now was break the rules.

★ ★ ★

I didn't hear from Brad again after I hung up on him. The weekend passed uneventfully, with me spending Saturday cleaning my room—*oh, joy*—and Sunday working on photo scrapbooks with Olivia. I wasn't really sure if Brad was mad at me, or if I was still supposed to be mad at him. It had been a little childish of me to hang up on him, but I was fresh off Broward's admonishment, and it had seemed like the easiest thing to do. Tuesday was coming up, and I wondered if he still planned to take me to dinner. I didn't know if I wanted to go. Well, I knew I wanted to go, but didn't know if I should.

I could only screw with my mind for so long before it would just up and quit on me, walking out the door holding its middle finger up. I think I was close to that point. I knew what I should do in the Brad department. It was so freaking obvious and easy. *Stay away from him.* Old Julia would not have hesitated. She would have walked away, never looking back. But New Julia really, really wanted to tell Old Julia to go to hell.

Monday, I listened for my office phone to ring, hoping for De Luca's call. It didn't come, and I worked fervently in my silent and lonely office, trying to distract myself with case prep. I hated the fact that I even *noticed* the absence of a call, hated that I glanced at the phone every ten minutes, as if the voice mail button would magically light up, indicating a heartfelt message waiting from him. I wondered if he knew about my date with Todd. Now, in the absence of possessiveness, I wanted him to care, to warn Todd away. *Talk about being fucked-up.* I was as guilty of it as him.

As night fell, and everyone trickled out, only Broward and I were left. We worked in and out of the conference room, all the mediation prep files laid out on the big table, us passing each other silently in the halls. At seven-thirty, I stuck my head into his office and asked if he wanted me to order dinner.

"Yeah," he said, distracted by the document he was high-lighting. "Have one of the couriers go get us something. Subs, if possible."

"What kind do you want?"

Silence, then, "What?"

"What kind of sub do you want?"

"Oh. Uh, meatball on wheat. With provolone." I withdrew my head from his office and walked back to mine. I got on the phone and tracked down Jerome, our night security guard, the only person we had resembling a courier at that point in the night. I told him I'd call it in if he'd pick it up. I went ahead and got his order also, then called the local Jimmy John's.

At 8:00 p.m., I heard the elevator ding and walked out to the lobby to meet Jerome. From behind the East Wing doors, I could hear voices and see lights. My brow furrowed. It was odd for anyone on their staff to work past six or six-thirty. I helped Jerome by grabbing one of the bags, and he followed me to the conference room, where I had cleared off a section of the table. "Want to eat here with us?" I asked.

"No, I appreciate the offer, but I need to be back at my post." Jerome gave me a quick smile and held up one of the bags. "Thanks for the sandwich."

"Sure. Thanks for picking it up." I hesitated, wanting to ask what was going on in the East Wing, and who was still there. I refrained, and just sat down instead. I laid out the sandwiches and went to the kitchen to get drinks. "Food's here!" I called out to Broward, who nodded and held up a finger.

I sat down in the conference room and unrolled my Philly cheesesteak. Cracking open a Dr Pepper, I ate, enjoying the chance to relax. My neck was killing me, and I rolled it a few times, trying to get the kinks out. I heard Broward come in behind me, and I lifted my chin in greeting and pointed to his sub, which I had laid out on a plate with a napkin.

"Thanks, Julia," he said, settling down and unwrapping the sub. I slid a Coke down the table to him.

"What do you normally do for dinner?" The words popped out before I thought them through. He looked up at me quizzically, sub in his mouth. "I mean, you always work so late—till at least eight, and it doesn't seem like you pack a dinner...."

He shrugged and wiped his mouth. "Claire, my wife, she makes a plate for me—keeps it in the fridge. I eat it when I get home. We've been married twelve years. She's used to my schedule."

"Do you always plan on working such long hours?"

He stared at me for a moment. I'm not sure if he was thinking or just staring, but finally he responded. "At the moment, I work to live. We are very cautious with our spending, and set aside ample amounts for retirement. In nine or ten years I plan on retiring, to either North Maine or the outskirts of Chicago."

I nodded, trying to think of something to say other than *Boring.* "Sounds nice."

"We're excited about it. Claire is a stay-at-home mom, and when the kids graduate we're really looking forward to some one-on-one time, a chance to get to know each other more." *Something I would think you would have done during the first twelve years of your marriage, but I'm not really the person who should be giving relationship advice.*

"How long have you worked here?"

"Let's see, now...eleven years...been a partner for nine. I worked at another firm, Daly and Fountain, before here. Perhaps you've heard of them?"

I nodded, even though their name drew a blank in my mind.

"I thought so. They're a big firm, though not as big as us."

"Why did you choose to come here?"

"Well, at the time it was just Clarke Law Firm, and I knew that a partnership opportunity was in the cards." I ate my sub quietly. The absolute last thing I wanted to do was have the conversation turn to Brad. Which, of course, it did next.

"I became partner after two years and considerable effort. Back then, it took more than large billings to gain partner status." His contemptuous tone just asked for a response, but I stayed far away from the low-hanging fruit and took another bite of cheesesteak.

The silence grew, and he finally continued unaided. "I mean, when Brad came on, for example, he was with us for only six months before Clarke approached him about partner status. I was vehemently against the idea, but Clarke's shares overrode my opinion. Brad is just cut from a different cloth than us. He doesn't understand the hard work behind law." Bitterness laced his voice and my rebellious side spoke up before I had a chance to rein it in.

"Is that why you told me to stay away?"

"What?"

"You've told me a few times now to stay away from the East Wing, and from De Luca specifically. Why?" He shot me a perturbed look, as if irritated that I would question his authority. I held my gaze steady, despite the battle that raged inside me.

He avoided my gaze, and suddenly seemed very interested in the remaining piece of his meatball sub. Finally, he set it down and looked at me. "I don't like De Luca, Julia. Some in this office would say I hate him, but that isn't the case. I dislike Brad for two reasons. First, I don't think he displays the work ethic or ethical standards that I would like upheld by our office. But second, six years ago—and I apologize for the language—Brad fucked my wife."

I gasped and stared at him, my half-eaten piece of sandwich hanging limply in my mouth. Somehow, ridiculously, I felt tears welling up somewhere behind my corneas, and I blinked them off. I didn't know what to say and I stumbled over the next sentence.

"I'm so sorry."

He stared off in the distance, pursed his lips, then shook his head. "I shouldn't have told you that. I'm sorry. It's too personal. I just wanted to give you an honest reason. You are a beautiful, innocent young woman, and it was very inappropriate for me to assume anything, but I didn't want you to fall into his trap like other interns have. You seem too intelligent for that, but I wanted to give you a warning anyway."

I blinked at him, not really knowing what to say. Then I nodded, my eyes grim. "Trust me, that's one thing you don't have to worry about."

We ate the rest of our meal in silence, with me having so many questions that were way too personal to ask, and he seeming to prefer brooding over chatter. Once we finished, I cleared our plates and we continued working, the bustle of papers shuffling and keys clicking the only sounds in our deserted wing.

I drove home with the radio off and the windows down, trying to think. I don't know what I even had to think about. Any confusion I'd had about Brad should have been answered by this new information. Brad had slept with his business partner's wife. Enough said. So what did I have to think about? Nothing. I rolled up my windows and tried to think about anything other than De Luca.

Twenty-Eight

Tuesday at 1:00 p.m., my office line finally rang with De Luca's extension showing. I ignored it, letting voice mail pick up. He didn't leave a message. He called again at 3:00 p.m. Again, I ignored the phone. With Broward in Dallas the workday was light, and at 4:45 p.m. I started packing up, preparing to leave. I wandered by Sheila's desk and spent the last fifteen minutes of the day chatting up the older woman. She had warmed to me considerably over the past few weeks, and now bordered on almost friendly. I was intent on cracking her shell before my internship ended.

I pressed the down button on the elevator and waited in the lobby for it to arrive. Todd came through the East Wing doors and gave me a big smile. We waited, the doors opened and we got on together. When the doors shut, we both started talking at once. I stopped, and Todd hesitated.

"Go ahead," I said with a laugh.

"I was just going to ask if you were free tomorrow to, ah, hang out."

"Sure. Do you have my number?"

"Yeah. It's on the intern roster Dr. Ennis distributed the first day."

"Great." I looked at my feet as the elevator doors opened to the parking garage. He stepped out and we kind of shuffled around.

"So, tomorrow night?" he asked.

"Yeah, tomorrow night. See you then."

"I'll call you. Maybe around eight?"

"Sounds good, Todd. Night."

He gave a quick wave and spun on his heel, sauntering to his truck, a late-model Ford F-150. I headed to my car and stopped short. There was a note tucked into the window. I opened it cautiously. It was a hand-scribbled note on thick, embossed paper. It had only one word, and initials scribbled underneath.

Dinner?
BDL

I crumpled the note as tight as possible, then I had an idea. I uncrumpled the paper, ripped it in half and then recrumpled the two pieces. I looked around for the car I had passed in Brad's driveway. I saw it parked by the elevators in one of the three reserved spots, a new BMW 750Li, white, with a personalized tag: B D BEST. Nauseating. I strode over and dropped the crumpled pieces in Brad's open sunroof, and they fell onto the driver's seat. What was really shocking was that the man was still at work at 5:15 p.m.

I felt that I had accomplished something by the time I got into my car. I cranked up the radio, backed up and pulled out of the garage. I had plenty to smile about. I was currently flush with cash, had made a decision on the Brad debacle and had a date the next night with a smoking-hot guy.

★ ★ ★

Todd and I decided to stay in and watch a movie at his place. He let me pick, so I tried to pick something guy-friendly and went with *Old School*. It was a typical college date, a barely disguised excuse to hook up, minimal expense and effort required from the guy. But I didn't really care. I was pissed at the Brad situation and wanted a rebound. Todd was available and hot. I didn't need much more than that right then.

After another day passed with zero contact from Brad, I'd gotten home from work around 5:45 p.m., showered, shaved and dressed in tight jeans and a spaghetti-strap tank that showed a little of my stomach. I wore sexy panties and a shelf bra in case the evening led to anything other than kissing. Old Julia would never have considered anything more than kissing on a first date, but I seemed to be throwing caution to the wind these days. Brad had been a little too persuasive regarding casual sex, and I figured if I took his teachings outside our nonexistent relationship, tough shit.

Todd had offered to pick me up, but I wanted to have control over when I left, so I told him I'd meet him at his house.

He lived in a townhome complex, located in an area at least two steps up in price from mine. Todd yanked open the door with a huge smile and a giant Great Dane. The dog launched himself at me and I found myself in a sort of dance with the pooch, holding both his front paws and trying to dodge his huge tongue.

"Walker!" Todd yelled, grabbing his collar and pulling him off me. He herded the large dog down a side hall and through a doorway, shutting it firmly behind the dog. There was some whining and scratching, and Todd shot me an apologetic smile. "We have about five minutes till he goes bat crazy, so I'll give you a quick tour before we let him out."

"Sounds good." I set my purse on the counter and looked

around. The living room was small, but with nice furniture— a leather couch and granite coffee table. *Todd must have rich parents.* A large *Godfather* movie poster hung over the couch, and the small room was dominated by a big plasma TV. The smell of Febreze hung suspiciously in the air and a candle was lit on the kitchen counter. The house looked tidy, but not necessarily clean, as though everything had been picked up or hidden just moments before, and nothing had been wiped down or vacuumed. I looked at Todd. He appeared to be clean. Really clean. He had on soft sweatpants and a short-sleeved Under Armour shirt. His hair was wet from a recent shower, and I could smell the soap he had used, some type of "ocean breeze" scent. He didn't have the manly, developed body of Brad, but his thin frame was what I was used to, and his Abercrombie looks were what I had spent the past ten years of my life pining after.

"So, the kitchen and the living room. Very impressive," I drawled, leaning back against the counter and letting the action slide my tank slightly up, exposing my stomach. Todd's eyes instantly focused there. "Anything else to show me?"

"Um…yeah," he stammered. "My bedroom is back here." He went down the hall and opened a well-stickered door, revealing a king bed and white dresser set. He got points for no dirty clothes, at least none in sight. I grabbed him and threw him on the bed. His eyes widened and he scooted back, but I pressed him down with my hand and straddled his hips, grinning down at him. "Oh my God, this is so hot," he whispered.

I was back in my element. Not like being with Brad when I'd felt like a bumbling, inexperienced geek.

I pulled my tank off, revealing my lace bra and tanned stomach. I leaned forward, brushing my breasts against him, kissing him, starting at his neck and moving up to his ear. He squirmed beneath me, his hands grabbing my waist and my back. Our lips met, a battle of tongues. He was a hard, forceful kisser, and I tried to match the tongue thrusts and soften his firm play, but it didn't quite work. I finally pulled my mouth off his, moving forward until my breasts fell in his face and he gobbled at them, using his hands to free my nipples; his rough mouth found them and sucked.

It was hard, a little too aggressive, his tongue jerking over my skin, teeth scraping. I winced and pulled my tender nipples away, putting his mouth at my neck instead. My hands grabbed and teased his hair, and I traveled back down his body until our faces were together again. I reached down and slid my hand over the ripped abs of his stomach, under the waist of his pants and met boxers. *Who still wears boxers?* I fought with his hands as they reached for the zipper of my jeans, forceful and rushed. *This is so not what I expected.*

A series of loud barks and bangs erupted from the hall, and I figured that Walker's five minutes of patience had been reached. I climbed off Todd and rolled over, lying flat on my back. Todd rose on an elbow and looked at me yearningly—a look I used to get off on. The barking increased, punctuated by howling every four or five barks. I sat up, grabbing my top. "Maybe you should get him before he breaks something."

Todd groaned and sat up, hopping off the bed and walking out. I heard a door open and him scolding Walker, apparently ineffectively, because the dog came bounding into the bedroom ten seconds later. I had my shirt on by then and was planning my exit strategy. I was feeling zero spark and starting to fantasize about my warm bed and a good book.

Todd chased Walker into the room and grabbed his collar, pulling him off the bed. "Maybe we should move to the living room," I suggested.

His face fell, but he shrugged it off. "Sure. Walker will leave us alone in there."

I walked back to the living room, snagging my purse on the way. "Hey, is there a bathroom I could use?"

"Sure. It's back in my bedroom, the door by the closet."

I walked to the bathroom, locked the door and leaned against the sink. Pulling out my phone, I searched through my apps. Some computer nerd, circa 2010, had invented an ingenious app called Fake-A-Call. I opened the app and scheduled it to send a fake call to my phone in five minutes, from Broward. I set a second call in six minutes, also from Broward. I then set my ringer to extraloud and put it back in my purse. I flushed the toilet, washed my hands and primped for a minute. No point in looking bad on my way out.

I exited the bathroom and wandered back to the living room, where Todd was standing awkwardly with a Coke and a bottled water. "I thought you might be thirsty," he said, thrusting both out to me.

I set my purse down on the coffee table, grabbed the water and grinned at him. "Thanks. You want me to put in the movie? We can watch it out here on the couch."

"Uh...yeah. Sure."

"You got any popcorn?"

"Naw. I got beef jerky. Want some of that?"

"Umm, maybe in a little bit." Like, never. "You sit. I'll put the movie in." I fumbled around with the DVD case and his TV, changing the channels and inputs until the correct screen popped up. Right about then, like clockwork, my phone rang. "Todd?" I asked, facing the TV on my knees. "Will you look in my purse and see who that is?"

He instantly obliged, unzipping my purse and digging around as if he was looking for gold. He pulled out my phone and looked up at me quickly.

"It's Broward."

"Broward?" I frowned, making a show of looking at my

watch. "That's weird. Don't answer—let's see if he leaves a message."

"He's in Dallas, right?"

"Yeah. Maybe it's a pocket call." I shrugged nonchalantly, turned back to the TV, grabbed the DVD remote and hit Play. I shoved to my feet and sat on the couch next to Todd, snuggling close to him. My phone rang again and we both looked at it lying upright on the table. "Broward" was clearly displayed. I moved uneasily. "Todd, I'd better answer."

He nodded quickly. "Yeah, get it."

I answered, and spoke to the inert phone. "Hello?" I paused for a beat. "No, I've already left...."

"Which statute...?"

"On your... Wait, let me get a pen."

I turned to Todd and covered the phone. "Do you have a pen?" He hopped off the couch and ran to the kitchen, opening and closing drawers until he came back with a pen and paper. I held the phone close to my ear and scribbled some crap down on the pad. "Okay, fourth file cabinet to the left, Henderson file... And you have to have this tonight...?

"No, I don't mind...."

"Yes, sir...."

"I'll call you when I have it in hand...."

"Bye."

I hung up the fake call and frowned regretfully at Todd. "I have to go to the office."

"Now?"

"Yeah. Broward needs something for court tomorrow and he wants me to send it to him now. ASAP, in fact." I ripped off the page and stuffed it in my purse. I handed the pen and paper to him and leaned forward, kissing him briefly on the cheek.

"Thanks for the invite, Todd. Sorry I couldn't stay for the movie."

"Want me to come with you?"

God, no! "Aww, that's sweet, but no. I don't know how long it'll take, or if Broward will want me to do other stuff there."

I leaned down and patted Walker's head, silently thanking him with my eyes for being so damn noisy during our uncomfortable make-out session. The dog lolled his tongue to the side, smiling at me. I left while Todd was still sitting there, pen in hand, trying to process the sudden change. I gave him a bright wave and firmly shut the door behind me, jogging down the front steps and hopping into my car before he could think of something to say.

Holy crap. I'm getting too old for this stuff.

I swore at that moment to stay away from men and become a spinster, collecting cats and eating raw cookie dough till I got old, fat and happy.

Twenty-Nine

Rule 6: Brad is always in control.

Thursday, my brand-new Manolos on, I started running out of things to do, a welcome problem. I got only one email from Broward all day. He gave me an off-network email account and its log-in information and asked me to print and fax some attachments for him. Five minutes later, with that task complete, I wandered over to Sheila to see if she had any items I could help with. I was determined to keep busy, and keep my mind off anything related to Brad. Sheila happily handed over a few projects and I locked myself in my office and busily worked away till the end of the day. Twice, my phone rang with Brad's extension showing; both times I ignored the call and pushed him out of my mind.

At 5:45 p.m., I wrapped up my last email, shut down my computer and organized the files on my desk. *Time to go home.* I waved to Sheila and Beverly and walked through the West Wing's double doors to the elevator lobby. Brad stood there, his hands in his pockets, the elevator button unilluminated; he saw me and hit it. *Crap. Was he waiting for me?* My steps faltered, but I couldn't turn back without looking as if I was running. I gave Brad a stiff nod and stood a few steps behind him, waiting for the elevator. I prayed for someone else to come out, but luck wasn't on my side, and the elevator opened for just the two of us.

We got in and Brad pressed the *G* button for the garage level. As soon as the doors closed, he turned to me. Before a word could come out, I held my hand up. "I'm not saying anything to you," I said tightly.

"Julia—"

"No, Brad. I mean it."

He gripped his fists tightly, then slammed one hand on the wall and punched the red emergency stop button with the other.

In movies, when the elevator's stop button is pressed, the car comes to a gentle halt and the people have their tryst, or argument, or bank robbery, or whatever it is they stopped the car for. That is *not* what happened here.

The car shrieked, a painful squeal of metal on metal ten times worse than any nails on a chalkboard, and we slammed to an immediate halt. My legs buckled underneath me and I had to grab the arm rails for support. Pressing the stop button also triggered the emergency sprinklers built into the ceiling, and caused a loud, blaring alarm to sound. The overhead light stayed on, but an emergency light, now illuminated, blinked on and off, casting the car into alternating modes of red-and-white light. Whoever had created the system had not taken occupant hysteria into account at any point in the design process.

"WHAT ARE YOU DOING?!" I shrieked at Brad over the sound of the blaring alarm.

"WHY WON'T YOU TALK TO ME?" he yelled, his eyes blazing, fists at his side.

"BECAUSE I DON'T WANT TO TALK TO YOU.

WE AGREED TO STAY AWAY FROM EACH OTHER, REMEMBER?"

"WHAT IF I WANT TO RENEGOTIATE THE CONTRACT?"

"THE CONTRACT IS NOT UP FOR RENEGOTIATION!"

The water fell heavy on our heads, not a gentle mist, but buckets of liquid, cold and probably unfiltered. I couldn't hear myself think over the blaring sound of the alarm, and I glared at Brad through the spray of the water. Somewhere inside the car a phone rang.

"IS THIS ABOUT TODD?" he yelled over the sound of the alarm and phone.

"NO! THIS IS ABOUT YOU BEING A DICK, AND A SLUT, AND SOMEONE I HAVE NO BUSINESS HANGING OUT WITH!" Our faces were now inches apart, close enough for me to see the hurt in his eyes.

So the monster bleeds.

The phone continued ringing, insistently, and Brad broke the seal of our stare and fumbled at the side of the car, finally finding a panel, opening it and grabbing a phone.

"HELLO," he yelled, holding one hand over his free ear, trying to hear the person on the other end.

"IT'S DE LUCA…."

"NO. NO EMERGENCY. CAN YOU TURN OFF THE FUCKING LIGHTS AND WATER?" At that sentence the alarm died, though the lights continued, as did the unrelenting downpour of water.

"Yeah. And take the car down to the service level. I'm not walking through the damn lobby like this."

He hung up and turned, looking at me through the spray, his handsome face turning red-and-white with the changing lights.

"What's this really about, Julia?" He said the words quietly, almost inaudibly, when combined with the sound of rushing water.

I sank against the wall of the car, chilled to the bone. "Broward told me."

He stilled. "Told you what?"

"What do you think? About you, his wife. Six years ago."

His shoulders sank. "How much did he tell you?"

"I didn't ask for details, Brad. I didn't need any. There's no excuse for that."

The emergency lights finally died and the downpour began to diminish until it was just dripping from the overhead spigot. My last sentence hung in the silence. The elevator began to move, lurching at first, then resuming its normal, smooth ride. The car came to a stop and the doors opened to a level I had never seen, full of large machines and pipes. Water gushed out the open doors, and two maintenance workers in blue coveralls stood there waiting for us. The first guy stepped forward with a smile until he saw the somber look on both of our faces. I ran a hand through my drenched hair and accepted his outstretched hand, stepping out of the elevator. "Thanks," I said.

I approached the second man and asked him how to get to the garage level. He pointed to a stairwell and I banged through the door and headed up the stairs. Brad called out to me, but I didn't stop, trying to keep from getting emotional and just wanting to be dry at home, in my bed. I heard his heavy steps on the concrete stairs behind me, and increased my speed, taking steps as quickly as possible in my soggy heels. *Just keep moving.* Hitting the garage level, I reached for the handle and pulled. The door was stopped by Brad's big hand, pressing it closed. I gritted my teeth and looked up into his face, now above me, his eyes frustrated and his jaw set.

"What?" I ground out.

"I don't know what to say, Julia, except that it was a mistake I made a long time ago. One I've spent the last six years trying to make up for."

"I did the math, Brad. You were *married* then. If it wasn't bad enough."

"I told you I had been unfaith—"

"Stop it, Brad. Please. I know I'm young, but I'm not out fucking around for a good time. I know you see sex as a cavalier passer of time, but I don't. I'm looking for him—the one—someone I can marry and have kids with, and not worry that he's out fucking half the town while I'm washing his fucking laundry. He's not you. I haven't seen a more clear-cut case of *not the one* in a long time. So I realize that me ignoring you is a black mark on your fucking conquest record, but I don't really give a damn. Because I am looking out for me. And you are nothing but a time bomb ticking on my well-being. Plus—" I felt tears welling and my voice cracking as I fought to keep my composure "—these are *brand-new* Manolo Blahniks, which I spent a lot of fucking money on, and you and your stupid dramatic elevator act ruined them! They're suede and now they are fucking ruined!" I sagged against the steel stairwell door and sobbed, my tear ducts fully open now, my beautiful new shoes the final straw.

Brad caught me and lifted me easily, setting me down gently on the top step. He sat next to me, looking out, thinking. He pulled off his soaking-wet suit jacket and folded it over his lap.

"You're right, Julia. I'm not any good for you, and you're smart to stay away. I'm sorry. I wasn't thinking. I just can't seem to help myself…there's just something about you that I'm drawn to."

My sobs subsided a bit and turned into sniffles as I tried to get my emotions under reasonable control.

"I guess the issue is," he continued, "I want happily-ever-after, too. I don't want to be living alone in my big house, eating lunch with a housekeeper that doesn't have more than fifteen English words in her vocabulary. The parties and trips are to keep me distracted, to keep me from realizing that I have nothing, nobody. I don't ever want to live a dull life. But I need some stability—I want a partner who can enjoy this lifestyle with me."

"So marry. I'm sure you have a waiting list a mile long. Just go through your client list." I fought to keep a smile off my face at the subtle dig.

He laughed briefly. "It's complicated. The trophy wives waiting in the wings don't get my sexual needs. And the girls that do aren't ones I want to grow old with, or spend a Saturday afternoon at the house with."

"Your sexual needs being the need to go and sleep around— to cheat?" I huffed into my hands, trying to dry at least one part of my body.

"No. I don't want to get into it with you."

We sat for a minute, not speaking.

"So many of the divorces I deal with are for superficial marriages. The couple marries out of loneliness, or fear of being alone, or for convenience, or for status or money. Then they end up as two people living separate lives in the same house until one of them cheats, or one of them decides they want something more fulfilling."

I looked at my ruined shoes and sighed. "I think that's what my parents' marriage is like. They never fight, and they've been together forever, but they just seem...I don't know... apart, I guess. Mom has her work, and when she's not there she's doing stuff with friends. Dad spends all his time out at our lake house fishing, or fixing stuff in the garage. That's what I grew up knowing, and I don't want that for my life. I want someone I can't stay away from, who I love spending every free moment with." I hugged my knees and rested my chin on them. "Maybe it's an unrealistic expectation."

He groaned and reached over, fingering a piece of my wet hair. I flinched, but didn't push his hand away. Having him there, so near to me, was difficult. His presence alone weakened my resolve, his essence pulled at me. I wanted nothing more than to have his arms around me, his lips on mine. I hated myself for my weakness, for the crack in my common sense. A crack that would break me open if I didn't stay strong.

"What if what we're looking for is each other?" he asked quietly.

That was unexpected. I turned and stared at him. "You've got to be kidding me." In his eyes I saw a flicker of vulnerability, but that disappeared before I could grab hold of it.

"Look, we're both looking for a soul mate, right? And I know you want your prince to come riding up, all perfect and unmarred, but this is real life. Typically the best things come from the most screwed-up circumstances. How do we know we aren't the person we both are searching for?"

I began to fluster, spitting out words in quick succession, but he held up a hand, quieting me. I glared at him.

"Build a case," he said with a challenging look. "Give me supporting evidence."

"Fine. Next time, don't give me such a cakewalk for my first assignment."

He raised an eyebrow at me. "Don't underestimate your opponent, Ms. Campbell."

I rolled my eyes and started. "First off, don't get offended by anything I'm about to say. I'm stating the facts, and if you don't like them, tough shit."

He grinned at me. "My skin is very tough, Julia. I promise to not get my feelings hurt."

"*Oh-kay,* there are multiple reasons why you would never

be my soul mate." I faltered slightly as I tried to organize my thoughts, tried not to think about his hand so close to my leg. "One, you have a proven history of being unfaithful. Two, you are deceitful. Three, you have control issues. Four, you seem to have some mysterious sexual ailment that you refuse to discuss." I folded my arms and looked at him, waiting for his response.

"You're right—I have been unfaithful in my past. In that marriage I unknowingly set myself up for failure by marrying the wrong woman and expecting myself to be content in that situation. There are ways for me to be faithful, to stay loyal to my spouse. But I would need the right woman, the right situation. As far as temptation, there are ways for me to curb that, ways for me to fill that need without cheating."

I snorted in response to that load of crap.

"In response to your earlier statement that I am deceitful, that is absolutely incorrect. I have never misled you or lied to you. I have been nothing but honest with you, regardless of whether it caused your opinion of me to be diminished."

He paused, waiting for an argument from me, but I shrugged. He had me there. He was a pig, but he was an honest, or rather unapologetic, pig.

"We are compatible. We get along well, enjoy each other's company, have incredible chemistry and desire a similar life-style. I believe in living life to the fullest, and as my partner you wouldn't have to worry about me burying myself in work."

"I don't think anyone in this building is worried about that happening."

"Plus, I believe that sex is crucial to a relationship, and have never met a more gorgeous, sexual woman."

I punched him in the arm. "Oh my God, how many women have you said *that* to?"

He turned and looked me dead in the eye. "I'm serious. You

have every single physical trait I look for in a woman. Most women I pick apart in my mind, wishing that this part or that part of them was different. But I don't do that when I'm with you. Even your imperfections I find attractive."

"I don't have any imperfections."

He leaned over, his lips hovering over mine. "No, you don't." He closed his eyes and waited, asking my permission. I froze, his face inches from mine, his breath warm on my lips, his magnetism reaching straight into my core. What if he was right? What if this is the real-life compatibility I'm meant for? *I want to fight it. Want to be strong enough.* But despite my better judgment, I leaned forward, closing the gap, and pressed my lips to his.

They were soft and salty. He opened his mouth and grabbed me with his free hand, sliding me until my wet body was sandwiched into his burning-hot one. His tongue met mine in perfect harmony, and there was nothing to think about, no moves to make with the kiss. It just happened, perfect and hot, and passion grew with every second that our kiss lasted. I pulled away, gasping, and looked into his eyes, dark and full of fire. I felt like Alice falling into the rabbit hole, getting sucked farther and farther down. I looked away quickly and tried to scoot back, but his strong arm kept me there, kept me still.

"Okay," I said quickly. "We have established that you find me attractive."

He shook his head, and tried to find the track he had been on. "What else—oh, the control issues. I like to be in control. If we were dating exclusively, I am sure that I would have to occasionally tell guys to back off of you. I'm not naive enough to think that that's something I can control. It's hardwired into my body. I am an aggressive person. If that's a deal breaker for you, then I understand that. But don't take my control habits as jealousy. Jealousy can be an evil, two-headed snake, and

I've seen the harm it can do. If you knew more about me, you would understand that I am anything but jealous." He pulled at the back of his soaked dress shirt, and looked over at me. "Anything I missed?"

"Yeah, the gigantic elephant in the room—your secret sexual need that no normal woman can fulfill. What, you need it like eight times a day?"

He laughed softly and removed his arm from around me, placing his palms together and thinking. Then he turned and faced me head-on. "Before we go into this, if I didn't have any sexual hang-ups—would you date me? Would you be my girlfriend?"

"I don't know. I don't really want to answer that question yet."

He didn't respond to that, just seemed to be quietly mulling something over. Then he turned to me, his eyes burning with intensity. "I know that I have what many people would consider a fucked-up view of relationships. But for me it just comes down to being honest with myself and with my partner about what turns me on." He thought for a second, then continued. "I thrive on competition. I want to know that I am pleasing a woman better than any other man. The idea of my wife having sex with only me for the rest of my life doesn't feed that competitive streak." He paused before throwing me the ultimate curveball. "I love to watch. What you did with Montana—at Saffire—but typically the game goes a lot further than that. It would turn me on to see you with women and other men, to share you sexually."

I didn't say anything, but all my mind could think was: *what the fuck?*

He refolded his jacket. His voice was deep and measured. "Other than it being what turns me on, I also don't think humans are engineered to be monogamous. It's against our basic instinct to be tied to one person for the rest of our lives. It is a losing concept that we fight hard to keep because it is what society expects. I believe, for a couple to value their partner and learn their sexual needs, they need to occasionally sample sex with other people."

I spoke for the first time, my words careful and measured. "So you'd want me to let you go around fucking other people every once in a while?" *And he wonders why he can't find a good wife.*

"Not just me—you, too. But not alone, it would be something we do together, as a couple."

"I don't get it."

"I'm part of a group that meets occasionally. You and I would attend, and if you were attracted to any of the guys there, you could fuck them. The same with me and women at the party. Or, if you wanted to hook up with me and another woman, or with two guys...anything that turns you on is available. But we fuck together, either in the same room or in a threesome scenario."

I put my head in my cold hands and groaned. "Oh my God. I can't believe I had sex with you without a condom."

"That's your response to this?" He shook his head and pressed his hands together, looking at them and then at me. "Don't worry about that. Everyone wears condoms at the parties. Safe sex is a nonnegotiable."

"So that's the big thing. You're a swinger."

He winced, making a face, then nodded. "Yes, though I'm not crazy about the word. And my girlfriend, or soul mate, or wife, would need to be part of that lifestyle, as well. It is the only way I know that I will stay committed."

"So it's a nonnegotiable?"

"Yes."

He grabbed my chin, tilting it to him so that he could see

in my eyes. I tried to pull away, but he held strong, forcing me to meet his gaze. His eyes looked turbulent, tortured. I wondered what he saw in mine.

"Julia, nothing would turn me on more than to watch you fuck. A guy, a girl, it doesn't matter. Just to watch you cut loose and succumb to your deepest fantasies, for me to be a part of making that happen. Whether you know it or not, you are an incredibly sexual person. You drive men crazy and I would love to watch you with a group of them."

My mouth dropped open. Of all the things I had imagined, whatever it was that I thought he was into, group sex hadn't been considered. My head spun from the assault of concepts on my brain. I shivered.

"I'm wet." The minute it came out, and the grin spread over his face, I realized what it sounded like. "From the sprinklers. Wet and cold. I need to get home and shower."

"Come home with me. It's closer, and you can shower there." I was too overwhelmed by everything to argue. I just nodded, and he stood, offering me his hand and pulling me to my feet.

I drove my own car, planning on leaving Brad's after I had a chance to shower and to talk. Though I wasn't sure talking would solve anything. I didn't know what to think, what to do, but I wasn't interested in the prospect of orgies.

A memory shoved its way into my mind. Me surrounded by men, their eyes on me and Montana. Brad, watching me, his eyes hungry. The reaction it had caused in my body. I tried to push the memory away, tried to not relate it to this new fucked-up relationship possibility.

Within five minutes of pulling out of CDB's parking garage, we were driving down Brad's oak-lined street. The last time I had been there I hadn't been able to see much in the dark, but in the daylight the grand homes set back from the road gave quite an impression. Brad had a big plantation-style home with white columns in front and an ivy-covered privacy fence enclosing the sides. His driveway ran down the side of the house, and I rolled in slowly after him. He had a three-car garage set back on the lot. As we pulled up, one of the doors opened and he drove in. I parked my car to the side and left my keys in it. I'd be lucky if it got stolen in this neighborhood. Brad's homeowner's insurance would probably replace it with a Mercedes.

Brad emerged from the garage and we walked up the back steps. I glumly carried my shoes in my hands, my wet, bare feet leaving prints on his stone floor. He unlocked the door and held it for me. "Thanks," I mumbled, entering the house, which was freezing cold. *Geez. And I came here to warm up?* I rubbed my arms with my hands. "Where's the shower?"

He paused in the wide hall. "You want to use mine or the guest shower?"

"Whichever one's nicer. And no, you won't be joining me in it—in case that makes a difference."

He scoffed playfully. "Julia, give me credit. I am a gentleman!"

"Sure you are. Where's the shower? I'm about to turn into a Popsicle."

"Upstairs. The master is on the left. I'm pretty sure you'll be able to find the shower once you get there." I moved past him, trotting up the wide staircase, leaving wet footprints behind me. When I hit the top of the stairs, my wet feet felt plush carpet and I wiped them just for spite. It was marginally warmer up there and I paused on the landing, my eyes locking on the thermostat mounted on the wall. I stood on my tiptoes and looked at the display. Whoever had installed the thing had put it ridiculously high up. Sixty-eight degrees. *Good lord. And this level is warmer than the bottom floor?* I reached up and pressed the up arrow until it read seventy-four. I then went exploring.

The second floor had a master, second bedroom, office and media room. The whole floor had the impersonal, perfect style of an interior designer stamped all over it. I stood still, trying to get a feel for the house. It just didn't seem like Brad. I went into the huge master bedroom with blackout shades that put the room in darkness. I flipped on some lights and looked around. This room had a more masculine feel—a heavy California king bed with lots of pillows, and a cream duvet. Some incredible landscapes were framed and illuminated with small lights. I wandered over and looked at them closely, marveling at their beauty. "Peter Lik" was signed on the corners of the photos, a name I didn't recognize. But the real focal point of the room was above the bed: a nude woman, photographed on her side, her eyes looking directly at the camera, her mouth in a sexy pout. She had large breasts, big nipples, a flat stomach and a small patch of hair between her legs. She radiated confidence and sex. I wandered into the master bath and stared at my drenched appearance in the large framed mirror above the double sinks. My hair hung damp and stringy, and my face was pale. I had big black splotches under my eyes from my mascara; any other makeup had washed off. My white cardigan looked dingy, and the silk blend, dry-clean-only, Banana Republic sheath dress underneath was wrinkly, sticking to me in weird places. *Ugh. Remind me not to look at the vixen back in Brad's room.*

I shut the bathroom door, thought for a moment and then locked the handle. I stripped, not even bothering to lay my clothes flat, and opened the shower door. Brad's shower rivaled the one at Bellagio, a huge steam shower with two rows of body jets, a rain head and an adjustable handheld. I figured he'd probably be showering somewhere else in the house, so

I resisted turning on every nozzle and instead stuck with just the rain head, turning it on full force and giving it a minute to heat up. While I waited, I looked around, my nosy tendencies in full force. The bathroom had marble and granite covering every surface, and was decorated in navy blue and cream. He had a large, jetted tub and a toilet room. I wandered into the toilet room to pee and stopped short. A gun of some sort was sitting on a windowsill in the room. I approached it gingerly, picking it up, feeling the heft of it. I set it back down, peed quickly, then left the room. *Who needs a damn gun in the bathroom?* Leaving the toilet room, I saw about forty towels, all plush-white, rolled into neat coils and stacked in a large shelving unit set into one wall. I pulled two towels out and, seeing a towel warmer installed in the lower half of the unit, opened it up and set both towels inside. Turning the dial to fifteen minutes, I pressed Start, then got in the shower.

I stayed under the hot spray for ten minutes, my head pressed against the cool marble, the water massaging my back and head. Finally, I quit wasting time and opened Brad's giant jug of man soap, squirting a big blob on my hand and soaping up my body. I looked through the three lonely bottles in his rack and chose the only option for shampoo, some Italian-sounding brand that looked expensive. The man didn't have conditioner, so I settled for clean hair and turned off the shower. I opened the door and grabbed a hot towel out of the warmer. Wrapping my body in it, I turned, headed to the sink and almost ran into Brad.

His big arms caught mine as I started to scream. Seeing it was him, my screams died down, and I instead reached out, punching him in the stomach, aiming for the solar plexus. I must have missed, because he didn't flinch and instead smiled down at me.

"Seriously?" I asked, moving past his body and making my

way to the sink. "Did you notice that the door was locked? Ever heard of privacy?"

"Sorry, babe," he said, shrugging out of his dress shirt and unzipping his suit pants, the sound of the zipper causing my cunt to involuntarily contract. "I should have mentioned that the lock is broken."

"Or…you could have knocked—novel idea, I know." I started washing my face and avoided looking at him, knowing he was now naked, standing at the shower door. My hands shook and I tried not to think of his body exposed, less than ten feet away, and the things it was capable of doing to me. I heard the door open and close, and I relaxed, rinsing my face and patting it dry. "Who's Lady Godiva in your bedroom?"

"Who? Oh, that's Stephanie. A girl I used to date."

I didn't say anything.

"I should have taken it down by now, but I haven't found anything to replace it with, or taken the time to think about it."

"How long did you date her?"

"About a year. Off and on."

"Did she, ah…you know…" I trailed off, not sure what the proper lingo was.

"Yeah." Brad's tone was casual. "We had a few threesomes, two with girls, one with a buddy of mine."

"And she liked it?"

There was a long pause. "Julia, the entire point of the threesome is the woman's pleasure. That's what gets me off. I wouldn't have done them with Stef if she didn't like it."

"So why did you break up?"

"We enjoyed sex, but not much else. We were too different." There was a squeak as he turned the nozzles and the sound of water stopped. He cracked the door and hot steam billowed out. I opened the warmer and grabbed the extra towel that I had put in there, holding it out for him. He stepped out, pausing and looking at the outstretched towel. Then he flashed me a gorgeous grin and took it from me, flicking it out and wrapping it around his waist. I tried not to, but caught a glimpse of thick meat hanging between muscular legs and inhaled sharply. I couldn't help myself, the man did things to me that I couldn't even try to control. Could I really turn away from this? From him? *Holy shit, I am in trouble.*

"Okay," I said.

He tilted his head at me, confused. "Okay?"

"Okay. I thought about it. I'll try it one time. Then I'll decide about us."

Thirty

A giant grin broke out on his face—a grin tinged with a hint of relief. "Really?"

"Yes. But if I want to back out at any time, I can. And if I have a billion stupid questions, you have to answer them all. And—"

He silenced me with a firm kiss, grabbing my waist and lifting me up to him, moving his hands to my ass so that I was forced to wrap my legs around his waist, our wet skin touching. "Yes. Whatever you want, yes. You make the rules."

He gave me another kiss and set me down gently, trying to bust a move by pushing me toward his bed and pulling on my towel, but I spun out of his reach and ran toward the closet. Halfway there, he tackled me. We went to the floor and he pinned me, resting his weight on his elbows on either side and giving me a long, deep kiss, his skin hot and slippery against mine. The deep kiss turned into more, our hands moving in rapid unison, both of us unable to resist. He reached down, lifting his pelvis off me, and with one quick yank, his towel was gone and he pressed bare skin against me.

There was a frenzied force behind our kisses, a desperation

to have anything and everything we could capture in that moment. He rolled me over, our mouths never leaving each other, and I was suddenly on top, my towel bunched and irritatingly present between us. I yanked off of his lips, jerking the soft terry cloth, panicked in my desire to have my flesh against his, nothing between us but the unknown future. I finally freed my body and launched back downward, his body coming up to meet mine, his hands gripping my hair, his want as present as my own. He said something against my mouth, his words lost in the kiss and I pulled off him, panting.

"What?"

"Condom. To your left. Bottom drawer."

I fumbled, stretching to my left, yanking open the bottom drawer of a dresser, fumbling with the only item there, a large box of gold-foil condoms. I felt his hands, stroking down my breasts, following the dips of my stomach, his fingers and palms everywhere, slow teasing strokes that made my breasts ache with need. My fingers finally found a condom and I shoved back into place, holding the packet out to him, a triumphant smile on my face. He ripped open the foil with his teeth, his eyes on me, dark and dangerous, desire dominantly present in them. I leaned back, resting my hands on his knees, watching as he rolled the condom down his shaft, his cock tight and ready, a pole ready for impaling. I scooted up, straddling it, and leaned forward, kissing Brad's neck while I clasped it in my hand and pressed it against my wet slit.

It didn't fit, an impossibility seeing as how he had rocked my world with it just a few days prior. I winced, pressed down onto it again, the pain of his girth in my tight pussy making me gasp.

"Wait," he said, pulling me down to his chest. I lay there, his heartbeat loud against my ear, his hands busy. Two fingers slid in and out of me, spreading my wetness over my lips and taint, his perfect strokes lubricating me more, my walls tightening around his fingers and then loosening as he opened me up. There was a pause, and then the head of his cock was back, pushing in, so much bigger than his fingers, but so impossibly perfect now that I was ready. I moved, resting my weight on my arms, sliding up and down his shaft, the thickness stretching my lips, creating a delicious friction with every stroke.

I took in the sight of him beneath me. His arousal was so evident in his eyes, dark against his tanned skin, locked on mine at first then tugging downward, drinking in my movements, the joining of our bodies. "You are so fucking hot," he said. "Watching my cock take you. I can't wait to see someone else inside you, how you react when they fuck you."

The statement made my jaw drop, and he grinned at my face, his expression turning quickly hungry, and he grabbed me suddenly, his strong arms wrapping around my back, bringing me down to his hard chest, the smell of masculine clean hitting my nose. I moaned as he took over, my slow strokes disappearing into his furious drives from underneath me, my body fighting to stay in place as his battered it, a staccato of perfectly timed thrusts. He moved with restrained passion, the chorus of fucks amazing in their relentless assault, his hands keeping me in place, gripping my ass, tightening on my waist, squeezing my breasts. His words, delicious and deep in my ear, whispering of dark buried fantasies of twisted depraved actions, images flooding me that I had never allowed in, his words making them possible, probable, *holyfuckIwantitrightnow* desirable.

My orgasm came quickly, barreling down like a runaway train, out of control and unstoppable. I could think of nothing, knew of no one, but the animalistic fucking that I was enjoying. It was raw, untamed and hot as ever-living hell. I couldn't move, couldn't speak when the waves ripped through me, delicious spasms that rocked every muscle in me for what felt like a full earth-shattering lifetime. I dug my nails into his skin, clenched myself tight around his body and said good-bye to my soul. In that moment, he was my god and I was his servant.

Forty-five insatiable minutes later, I collapsed on his floor, his body above me, sweat glistening on his skin. He rolled off, groaning. "You are going to be the death of me."

I smiled in exhausted bliss. "And to think I didn't want to fuck you today. Or ever again for that matter."

He stood, modesty never entering his mind as he stretched, muscles popping everywhere. He rolled off the condom, grinning at me. I propped myself up on my elbows and smirked up at him. "I'm going to need to borrow some clothes. Mine are still soaked."

"Hmm… Everything I have is my size. How about a big V-neck tee?"

"As long as it's clean, I'll take it." I frowned, rethinking that. "Actually, do you have a sweatshirt, too? Your house is freezing."

He offered me his hand and hefted me to my feet. "Sorry, I like to keep it cold. Though you don't seem uncomfortable now." He grinned at me, his eyes sweeping my body, the thin sheen of sweat covering my skin. He turned on the light in his closet, illuminating rows of Italian suits, pressed shirts and polished shoes. The back half of the closet held his casual clothes, and he grabbed a Gold's Gym sweatshirt and plain white tee, tossing them to me. He pulled a shirt over his head and put on gym shorts.

"You seriously don't have a stitch of women's clothing in this house? No niece, ex-girlfriend or friend has left any clothes here?"

"If they did, Helga or Martha put them somewhere. I'll have to ask them where in the morning."

"They're your maids?"

He paused in the middle of flipping through some shorts. "Helga is, part-time. Martha more runs the house. If you call her a maid, she'll bite your head off and I'll be eating burned food for a week."

The walk-in closet had a granite counter and I hoisted myself up onto it, pulling the shirt and sweatshirt on once I was seated. "What time does Martha get in each day?"

"Typically around six-thirty, really whenever she gets out and about. She lives above the garage in the carriage house apartment."

I stopped swinging my legs. "She lives here? Why don't we just borrow some clothes from her? It's only like seven o'clock."

He raised his eyebrows and looked at me. "I'll wait for you to meet Martha. She's not someone you want to borrow clothes from on her time off. She commits forty hours a week to me and has made it very clear that living on property does not make her available to me after hours. I have to respect that."

I raised my hands. "Okay, it was just an idea. Obviously not a good one."

He had taken a set of shorts out of the stack, and handed them to me. "These are the smallest I've got. They have a drawstring, so you can probably tighten them to a point where they won't slide off. They'll look ridiculous, but I won't tell anyone."

I pulled the shorts on and jumped off the counter, yanking them the rest of the way up. I cinched the string as tight as I could and tied it.

"So, you gonna feed me, or should I pick up fast food on my way home?"

He grabbed me in response, lifting me over his shoulder like a sack of potatoes, and I giggled as he jogged down the stairs and into the frigid lower level. He deposited me on the kitchen counter and headed to the fridge.

His kitchen was built with three materials—stone, granite and stainless steel. It was commercial grade, though I was pretty sure cooking wasn't in his skill set. As if he was reading my mind, he spoke from behind the open refrigerator door.

"I don't cook, but Martha always leaves more than enough food. Let's see…we got chicken and rice, vegetable soup and meat loaf. Any of those sound good to you?"

"They all sound great. I'll take some chicken and rice if there's enough."

He pulled an armful of Tupperware containers out, stacking them on the counter. I could see the meals he mentioned, plus a few vegetables and a salad. One container looked like it held banana pudding. My stomach growled.

We ate at a huge teak table in the kitchen, on paper plates and with disposable silverware.

"You and Martha typically eat together?"

"No. She likes her space."

I raised a brow. "Antisocial?"

"Sort of. She's like the grouchy neighbor everyone stays away from. We have an understanding. I stay away from her, and she keeps the house running and the fridge full. She respects my privacy, and I respect hers."

"Sounds a little cold."

He looked up at me while waiting on his soup to cool. "A lot of people are overly interested in my activities. It's nice to have someone who keeps their distance."

I toyed with a piece of broccoli. "So, about your activities… I have some questions."

"Shoot."

"What would happen? I mean, explain the scenario that would occur."

"That would all depend on you. The purpose of the meeting is for your pleasure. What are some things that turn you on?"

"You know, normal stuff."

"Normal stuff?"

"Yeah."

He sighed, taking my hand. "Julia, we're kind of doing this backward from a normal flow. Typically, we would grow in our relationship until we are at the point where you would be comfortable sharing your fantasies with me, no matter how sick or slutty or dirty you may think they are. Then we would find a way to play out those fantasies, together. I want you to know that you don't have to do any…activities…right now. We can have a normal, typical relationship until we build the level of intimacy where you can share those fantasies. Then we can act on them. I went ahead and told you about my participation in this lifestyle, about my need for you to be involved, because I didn't want to sideswipe you with it later on in the relationship. I wanted to bring it up now, in case it was a deal breaker for you. I don't want to waste your time, or mine. But we don't have to do this now. We can try it later, when you're ready."

"And I want to find out *now* if this is something that I would not be okay with. So I won't waste my time or yours if it is something that I can't handle."

"Understood."

"So, going off of the understanding that I am turned on by basic vanilla stuff, how would the scenario play out?"

He spoke carefully, not taking his eyes off me, as if walking through a minefield. "There are a few ways this can play out. We can either go to a club and pick a partner, or you can describe to me what you want, and I can give you a selection to choose from—their applications, if you will. Then I would bring that person to you."

"What would happen once they were here?"

He shrugged. "Whatever you're comfortable with. I would suggest we stick with heavy petting or oral as an expectation. If you want to take it further than that, you can take it as far as you want. I would expect, given how sexual you are, that you would get into the experience once it begins. I would also suggest we set a time limit for your first time, like fifteen minutes. After fifteen minutes, I would get us alone and ask you if you want to stop. The goal is to make sure that you're comfortable with the entire experience, that nothing occurs that you don't want. You would be in control until you're ready to turn that over to me."

I had tilted my head to the side, listening to his words and trying to envision the meeting. It sounded...fine. Given the slutty thoughts that had just partied relentlessly in my head, more than fine. Not anything I couldn't handle. I looked up into his expectant eyes and nodded. "Okay. I'm okay with that."

We cleared the table and did the few dishes in comfortable silence. Apparently Martha had trained Brad well. He seemed diligent about following her rules, a fact I found funny since he seemed to break every other rule. As I dried a glass, a sudden thought popped in my head, and I started to laugh.

"What?"

"What was up with that elevator? The alarm, lights, sprinklers?"

"Sorry—I had a hand in the building's renovation a few years back. I pretty much used the philosophy 'go big or go home' with most of the building's overhaul, including the new elevator system."

"You knew that would happen?!"

"No!" He started laughing. "I didn't read the damn manual. I just told them to get every option available. In retrospect, it might have been a slight waste of corporate dollars."

"Well, at least I know never to pull a fire alarm in the building."

He grinned and handed me a bowl to dry.

At 10:00 p.m., Brad walked me to my car. The moon was out; frogs were everywhere and croaking. Other than that, the road was silent, lights off in the surrounding homes. He'd invited me to stay the night, but I'd declined. I needed my own bed and some alone time to think.

We stood by my car, his hands in his pockets. I was still wearing his gym shorts and enormous T-shirt, my dress clothes in a plastic bag hanging from my hand. I started to unlock the door and stopped, turning to him.

"What happened with Broward's wife?" *I need to know.*

He sighed heavily, looking contrite. "I don't have any big, fancy excuse. There is absolutely no justification for what happened. We were on a corporate retreat in Aspen. I was down at the bar, drinking, and Claire showed up. She and Broward had had a fight about something, and she was pissed, downing drinks faster than me. As time passed, she got less pissed at Kent, and more friendly to me. I should have said no, or called Kent, or done anything other than what I did."

"Had sex."

"Yeah. Had sex. We went to my room. It was over fast. I didn't even finish. We both knew it was a mistake and stopped. She went back to her room, immediately told Kent."

"I didn't know you guys had corporate retreats."

"We don't anymore."

Right. Of course. "What happened after that?"

"The next morning, Broward had a meeting with Clarke. Told him what happened. Said he wanted me gone. Clarke disagreed, told Broward if he wanted me gone, he'd have to buy me out himself. Broward didn't have the capital."

"So you stayed."

He nodded, his face grim. "So I stayed. I know Broward hates me, and I don't blame him for that, but the firm is my home, too. I'm not leaving unless I'm pushed out, and I don't respond well to being pushed."

"Shocker."

"Hey, go easy on me. It's been a long day." He moved close to me, pinning me against the car. He bent down and gave me a long, deep kiss, squeezing my waist. I threw my hands around his neck, kissing back and tugging on his coarse hair gently.

"It has been a long day, Mr. De Luca." I pushed him off me gently and opened my car door, getting in. He stepped away and watched me, waiting until I backed out before he turned and headed into the house.

God, I am a glutton for punishment.

Thirty-One

I knew the girls would judge my decision harshly, but I needed to talk to someone, so I invited Alex, one of my roommates, to a late fast-food run. Alex had grown up the son of hippies; his parents had taken the concept of free love to heart. Alex often wandered naked through the house, and I saw him date men and women, young and old. I knew I could freely discuss just about anything short of bestiality with him and wouldn't be judged. I called him on my way home. At the first mention of a free Whopper combo, he was game, and he was standing outside by the time I pulled up.

"Nice outfit, Jules," he said, crawling into my passenger seat. Alex was a six-foot-tall blond who probably would have been attractive if it weren't for the shoulder-length dreads piled high atop his head.

"Thanks," I said, not bothering to explain the attire. I pulled out of our driveway and headed for Burger King. We rode in companionable silence as I tried to organize my thoughts.

"How's your new job?" Alex asked, scrolling through my radio stations.

"It's good. Complicated. How's Julian?" Julian was Alex's

current hookup partner, a tattooed pothead who didn't believe in bathing regularly or shaving.

"She's good. I don't know how long we're gonna last. She's starting to get all bitchy on me, nagging me about stuff." I tried to look interested, but I was shocked they had lasted as long as they had.

He finally found a station and leaned back in his seat. "How's your love life? Luke still being all stalker on your ass?"

"I haven't heard from him in a while. I changed my cell and he still hasn't found out where I live, so I think I'm in the clear."

"Who you dating now? You went to Vegas with some guy, right?"

"Yeah. I wanted to get your advice on that, actually. The guy I'm kinda seeing…he's into like, threesomes and stuff."

"And you're not…."

"I don't know. He's asking me to try it and I told him I would. One time." The words were out of my mouth and I cringed, suddenly wishing I could take them back.

"Good." Alex nodded. "Good for you, Jules."

"Really?" I risked a glance at him, putting my turn signal on and preparing to turn into BK. He was tapping his knee with a finger and looking out the window, his face unreadable.

"Shit, yeah. Why wouldn't you? You want to have plain, boring sex the rest of your life? Everything gets old after a while, Jules, everything. You need to try stuff like this now while you're young and unattached. Experience everything, just to see what you like. You've got the rest of your life to be boring."

"I guess. It just seems so…wrong."

"That's because society says we should all be monogamous and have missionary sex three times a week," Alex drawled in a monotone voice. "You got to say 'F you' to society, Jules, and do what floats your boat."

The car in front of us in the drive-through moved up and I ordered a Whopper combo with a Coke for Alex. I added a medium strawberry shake for myself.

"Have you ever had a threesome?" I asked. We were now parked in the restaurant's parking lot. Alex had his food, and was noisily sucking on the straw in his Coke.

"Yeah. A couple." He stuffed a few ketchup-laden fries into his mouth.

"Did you like it?"

"One experience was really hot—one wasn't. A lot depends on who you do it with—kind of like sex. You know, like how you can have missionary sex with two girls and one is fucking hot and you come in two minutes, and the other one you fall asleep during?"

"Well, I've never fucked a girl missionary-style, but yes, I understand your point."

"So when are you doing it?"

"I don't know. Anytime, I guess. I don't really have any reason to wait. I'm kind of using this experience to decide if I want to date the guy."

"Like a test?"

"Like a qualifier."

Alex shook his head. "Man, I don't understand women."

This coming from the guy who was eating postnooky breakfast with a sixty-year-old woman last Monday.

I shook my head with a smile and started the car, heading home.

Friday, Broward returned. I rode up the elevator, noticing brand-new carpet beneath my feet, nervous about seeing him. I felt that something had changed between us since he'd told me about his wife, but that might have been me feeling paranoid because of my actions with Brad. The wing buzzed with activity all day, everyone working on the normal work-load plus the documents related to the mediation settlement. Brad called my office around 3:00 p.m. I smiled when I saw his extension show up on my phone.

"Yes?" I said coyly.

"Got dinner plans?"

"No, but I don't plan on doing anything more with you until I can make a decision about us."

"You mean you want to skip the cheap talk and go straight to the threesome?"

"Theoretically speaking," I said.

"Well, I need to find out what you want so I can set it up. We can either do that over the office phone lines or you can bear the pleasure of my company for some brief time...."

I thought for a minute. "Fine. How about breakfast at your house this Monday? Then we'll do the dirty deed on Satur-day night."

"Why Monday? Why not Saturday or Sunday?"

"No. I want my weekend. Plus," I added wickedly, "I want to meet Martha."

The weekend passed quickly, mostly due to an MTV *Real World* marathon, during which I watched the entire season of *The Real World: Hawaii* and ate about nine bags of butter pop-corn and three DiGiorno pizzas.

Monday morning I rang Brad's doorbell at 6:30 a.m. I was dressed in a gray knee-length pencil skirt and black sleeveless sweater. I had black pumps on, cute but not too sexy. The door was answered by an African-American woman in her fif-ties, my height, but about two hundred and fifty pounds. The woman was dressed in a faded red shirt, jeans and white tennis shoes. She crossed her hands over her huge breasts and made a show of looking me up and down, blocking the doorway.

I gave her my friendliest smile. "Good morning. You must be Martha."

"Uh-huh." She lifted her chin slightly, then twisted a bit, calling over her shoulder while she kept her wide body blocking the doorway. "Bradley! That girl is here for breakfast!" She turned back to me, her face unmoving, holding her bodyguard pose till Brad appeared over her shoulder. He patted her and she moved, begrudgingly, taking a few steps back and continuing to stare at me. *Talk about the gestapo.*

I stepped inside and offered my hand to her. "I'm Julia." She looked at my outstretched hand as if it was a piece of diseased meat. Finally, with Brad staring at her, she shook my hand, her grip loose and uninterested.

"Nice to meet ya," she muttered, then turned and waddled into the kitchen.

Brad smiled at me, stepping forward and giving me a quick kiss. "Brace yourself," he whispered in my ear.

We sat at the island counter, Martha on the other side of us, loudly banging pots and pans and doing a lot of muttering under her breath. From my seat next to Brad I could smell the soap from his shower, and see a small nick where he'd cut himself shaving. Martha said something that included my name and turned to look at me.

"I'm sorry, what was the question?"

"Your eggs. How do you want them?" she barked, giving me a strong look that indicated what she thought of my intelligence level.

"Scrambled, please." I shot Brad a dismayed look and he tried to hide a grin under his hand. I poked him under the counter.

Martha served us at the counter. She had prepared eggs, bacon, grits and biscuits. The woman might have been a tad prickly, but she could cook. I dug in.

"I'm going upstairs. I'll let you two eat and be back down after you leave for work. Just scrape the plates and put them in the sink."

"Will do. Thank you, Martha," Brad said, spreading grape jelly on a biscuit.

I smiled and waved goodbye to her. "The food is delicious."

She glared at me. "Thank you, miss." Ripping her apron from around her neck, she hung it on a hook by the door and left, the screen door closing with a loud smack behind her.

Brad and I looked at each other, then burst out laughing. "I told you," he said, starting to choke on his bite of biscuit. "Part of that is irritation that I asked her to come in early—to accommodate your ridiculous need to arrive at the office by seven-thirty. She doesn't like to conform to anyone else's schedule."

"And you *pay* her? Is it just me or is she like that with all of your women?"

"She's like that with any woman, though she's only met a few. Most of the time I try to keep them away from her."

"I can see why!" I took a big gulp of milk and fanned myself, trying to clear her hostility from the air.

"Okay, getting down to business," Brad said, scooping up a pile of eggs. "Have you decided what you want to do on Saturday?"

I blushed, and focused on my breakfast plate. "Are we sure Martha's gone?"

Brad raised himself off his stool and leaned over till he could see through the double window above the sink. "Yeah. I can see her sitting on her balcony."

"Okay. In Vegas, what I did with the girl from the strip club..." I trailed off.

"Montana," he prompted.

"Right. Montana. That turned me on, but not because of her, though she was really hot. What turned me on was, ah, the group of people. Around us. Like, watching."

"Okay. That's good to know. So you liked to be watched. Do you want a group of people watching?"

"God, no—not right now at least. I was thinking just you, me and someone else, for starters."

"Okay. So you want to be with a girl or a guy?"

I looked up from my *ohsoexciting* grits and bit my lower lip nervously. "I'm thinking a guy. Is that...okay?"

"Of course." He spooned eggs into his mouth as if we were having a completely normal conversation. *For him, maybe it is.* "Do you want to go to a club and pick a guy, or do you want me to give you a choice?"

"Well, if it's at a club, we won't know anything about the person, right?"

"Right."

"Is there anybody you've done this with before? That you could...use again?"

He kept a straight face and considered my question. "I have a guy that you might like. He's good—quiet and respectful— very...ah...well-endowed."

I tried to keep a neutral look on my face and nodded. "Then let's go with him. I just want someone who knows what they're doing, since I don't. And someone who isn't, you know, sleazy or dirty."

He leaned over and kissed me gently, so gently I felt pain at the quick release; I wanted more so badly. "So we're good to go, Miss Campbell," he whispered.

I shoveled eggs into my mouth and looked at him nervously. *Good to go. I guess.*

Thirty-Two

I knelt on the floor, a pillow underneath my knees. Blind-folded, I listened intently, waiting for a sign of what was to come. Only the hum of the hotel air conditioner met my ears. Seconds passed, then a minute. Finally, I heard the door open and then click shut. Footsteps, muted on the carpet, behind me, I felt, rather than heard, a male presence pass by my side and come to stand in front of me. Close, so close. I leaned backward slightly. The sound of a zipper being drawn down filled the silent room.

"Relax." It was Brad's voice. Deep and strong. For the first time, I appreciated his strength, his control. I leaned forward, wanting the connection of his cock in my mouth, my hands reaching out to grab his pants. He seized my outstretched hands, pulling me to my feet instead, and moved me back-ward till I felt the bed behind me.

"Lie down. Facedown."

I obeyed, all of my senses alert, listening for him, the un-known, anything. I heard the crackle of lit candles and smelled their fragrance mixed with the lavender scent of the expensive sheets I was lying on. I felt a flow of air and then felt a second presence in the room, though I can't explain how. Someone got on the bed; it sank beneath his weight, the springs sighing softly in the dark. I stiffened, not sure what was about to happen, my eyes wide beneath the blindfold.

A hand touched my calf and I flinched, surprised at the contact. Then I relaxed. The hand ran up my leg and I felt another hand, this one on my other leg. Briefly, the hands stopped, disappearing, then touched me again a few moments later, this time with the lubrication and warmth of massage oil. I felt a third and a fourth hand, rubbing my arms and back. They moved in slow, unrushed strokes, lingering and teasing, running down the sides of my body, grazing the sides of my breasts. I groaned softly, enjoying the wonderfully strange feeling of four hands on my body.

In the darkness, a man's voice said, "God, she's hot." It wasn't Brad's voice. *The stranger.*

One set of hands wrapped underneath my stomach and moved up, sliding under my body. They cupped my breasts and gently squeezed, kneading, and I moaned again, louder this time, and rose off the bed slightly, wanting more. I was pushed down and the hands on my breasts released, roaming up the sides of my body. I felt my legs being pulled apart till I was wide-open, exposed, and my breath hitched a little in my throat. There was silence and no touches for a moment. I tensed, imagining them circling me, looking at me, my thighs parted wide, nothing covering me, open for their examination.

Fingers ran up the inside of my calves, past the backs of my knees, my thighs, and then to the slit between my legs. They grabbed my ass and gripped the cheeks firmly, spreading them. I felt warm breath hit the tight pucker of my ass and blow, then the hot air moved lower to my open slit, and wetness pooled there. A finger followed the breath and ran from my ass to my pussy, and back again, gently rubbing, teasing, making my stomach curl, my pleasure grow. I moaned and tried to push against the finger, wanting, needing some kind of penetration. The finger dipped inside me for a brief moment, and was then gone again. I panted, and arched my butt up in the air, offering my slit to whoever was in between my spread legs. Someone moaned, and then a face was pressed to me, a hot, wet pulsing sensation—*tongue*—on my clit, and dipping inside me. I bucked on the bed, grasping the sheets, my mouth opening in silent ecstasy.

There was a voice in my ear, quiet and strong. Brad.

"Is this okay?" he asked, his voice husky. I nodded furiously, my hands reaching out till I felt his muscled skin. I gripped it tight. He moved out of my reach and I moaned. The mouth between my legs was doing incredible, twisted things to me, and I felt my body flexing and arching in the swells of pleasure. I pressed harder against his mouth, his face buried in me, and bit my bottom lip. I heard a zipper in the darkness, close to my head. The tongue on my clit slowed, then stopped. I spread my legs farther, begging with my body for more.

"Flip over." Brad's voice again. Authoritative. I instantly complied, desperate for more stimulation. There was a slight breeze, and I heard a door click shut. My eyes snapped open under the blindfold.

"Julia, it's been fifteen minutes. Do you want to stop?" Brad's voice came through the darkness to me. He sounded far away, over by the door.

I had never heard a more ridiculous question in my entire life. "No," I gasped.

He moved closer, his voice now close. "Do you want to take it to the next level or keep it here?"

"Next level," I whispered, almost moaning the words.

He moved. I heard fabric rustle and floors creak, then there was a flicker of air and the stranger was back. The door clicked shut again.

On my back I waited, unsure of what to do. Hands came again, two at my head and two at my feet. Strong, confident. The two at my head ran down my arms, squeezing them gently. The ones at my feet spread my legs wide and played with my soaking-wet pussy, gently cupping me and sliding a finger in and out. A hand grabbed one wrist, then the other, and held them above my head. A hot mouth nibbled my neck, kissing and sucking, traveling down to my breasts, encircling a nipple and gently tugging on it. I bucked against the man holding my arms back and raised my chest, finally wrenching a hand free and grabbing the back of a head, hair coarse and unfamiliar, holding his mouth against my nipple, his tongue teasing and torturing it, then guiding him to the other one. The fingers in me stilled, then withdrew. I froze, the head under my hand also moving away, then I felt the bed move as both men climbed up onto it.

Their weight on either side of me, I reached out and felt them kneeling near my waist. One was clearly Brad, the one on my left. His thick, muscular thighs gave him away. I explored with my other hand, curious about the second man. His lower thighs were thinner, average, with hair lightly covering them. Tentatively, shyly, I moved my hand higher on his bare thigh till I brushed—wait. I frowned and paused. That couldn't have been… I moved my hand again. It was. His cock. But in a place I didn't expect it, much lower than it should have been. Jesus. The cock was thinner—not the huge girth of Brad's, but ridiculously long, easily over ten inches. Circus cock. I heard Brad chuckle, and I tried to fix the shocked look I must have had on my face. Bolder, I moved my hand over the shaft, grabbing it tightly. It was rock hard, and his hand was still wrapped around its base. He released himself and I stroked slowly, then firmly and more confidently. My other hand moved on Brad, stroking him also, loving the feel of both of them hard in my hands at the same time. They shifted down on the bed so that they both hung above my blindfolded face. While I jacked them off, their hands roamed, one traveling over my tits and neck, one reaching down between my legs. It was Brad's hand on my breasts. I realized that after he cupped my face, turning it to him, and leaned over, brushing my lips with his. Then his mouth opened and his tongue dipped into mine, softly, sweetly, then stronger, passionate, possessive. He ended the kiss and rubbed my swollen lips with his fingers.

The hand at my legs rubbed lightly, so lightly it almost tickled, over my mound, focusing on the wet nub that was my clit, then a little harder, strumming it insistently. I ground against his hand, his fingers creating a swarm of sensation, an aching in my core. I whimpered, forgetting them in my hands, focusing on the growing pleasure, the building need. I was close, so close, when Brad moved. He left my side and then I felt him at the bottom of the bed, his warm, large body between my legs. He raised my legs, pointing my feet to the sky, and tested my wetness with his finger.

"God, you're so wet," he breathed, removing his finger. Seconds later, the thick, stiff head of his dick bumped, then slid into me, filling me in every way. I gasped. The second man tightened his grip on my breast, and Brad moved slowly, sliding in and out of me in an excruciatingly slow movement that only left me wanting more. He felt too good in me, it was unfair how perfectly he fit inside me—almost too big, almost painful, but overwhelmingly wonderful. I groaned and brought the hand holding the cock close to my mouth, licking my lips. The man above me gasped, then pressed his dick against my open, wet mouth.

"Please," he said, his voice thick.

I obliged, sucking it hard, forcing the length of it down my throat and gagging on its length. Gagging on the cock made me wet, lubricating the thickness inside me. I sucked urgently, wanting both of them, everything, all at once. The stranger grew even harder in my mouth, and his fast breaths fueled my arousal. I put his ten inches as far down my throat as I could, wanting to feel the base of him against my lips.

Brad groaned between my legs. "You look so fucking hot," he ground out, and quickened his thrusts, burying himself inside me with every stroke. The increased speed and the friction from his width caused me to contract inside, and I could feel the swells of pleasure starting to grow. I continued my attack of the stranger's cock, sucking and pumping, increasing speed. I reached with my other hand, grabbing his balls—*hairless*—gently tugging them. Without warning my orgasm came, exploding within me strongly and suddenly, and I yanked my mouth off the stranger, crying aloud and arching my back, pointing my feet, the orgasm ripping through my body, taking every coherent thought out of my mind. I heard the man above me moan, and the slick sound of him jacking off, hard and fast above my face.

"I'm about to come," he said, his voice quickening.

"Julia—where do you want it?" Brad's voice came from between my legs, where he continued his relentless fucking, hard and fast.

"On me, please." I squeezed my breasts, arching and offering them to him. As my body shook from Brad's thrusts, the cum rained, covering my breasts and hands, spraying my throat. I felt a few drops hit my lips and I licked them, tasting sweet cum. I pulled my hands to my mouth, greedily licking the drops off my fingers and sucking them hard. Brad groaned and yanked his cock out then, moving swiftly up on my body until I felt him in front of me. I heard him rip off his condom and I reached forward eagerly, found his cock and sucked it quickly, jacking off the swollen shaft with my hand. It twitched hard, and powerfully, and he came, filling my mouth with thick, hot squirts. I swallowed hard and fast, continuing to jack him off until I was sure he was empty.

Thirty-Three

Rule 7: Once it is over, leave quickly. We will want to be alone. No goodbyes are necessary.

I lay back, weak, euphoric, letting go of Brad's cock. My legs, which were bent, flopped straight, limp and useless. I felt the bed lighten by one body. There was the familiar breeze of air—the door—the sound of it shutting, of steps in the outside hall. I felt the remaining weight on the bed, and worried for a brief moment that it was the stranger. Then the edge of my blindfold was pulled off my head. My eyes opened to darkness and it took a moment for me to see in the candlelit room.

Brad was lying on his side, his muscular torso emphasized by the shadows, looking ridiculously tempting despite my sated state. I turned on my side so that we were facing each other. He smoothed my hair back and smiled at me.

"Well?" he said softly.

"Well…" I said in response, with a lazy smile.

"What'd you think?"

I thought for a minute, playing with his chest hair with my fingers, scooting closer to him and exploring the ridges of his upper body. I searched myself for a pang of regret, for guilt, for diminished self-worth, and felt nothing but extreme sexual satisfaction. I stretched luxuriously and Brad's eyes traveled down, feasting on my swollen nipples and my shaved, still-wet crotch. He bit his lip and gave me a suggestive look. I rolled my eyes, pushed his hand away and covered up with the sheet.

He yanked it back, eliciting a strangled protest from me, and pulled me close to him, his hot skin heaven to my cold body. He wrapped a strong leg around me, holding me prisoner, his scent overtaking me, and I inhaled it deeply, wanting more than he could ever physically give me.

He leaned forward and kissed me lightly, then tilted my chin up, looking into my eyes. "Tell me. Did you enjoy it? Are you gonna take off running now?" His eyes were concerned, vulnerable, pools of dark need, the most exposed I had ever seen him.

I wanted to leave him hanging and play coy, but in his vulnerability I saw possibility—that he could care, that he could be mine, wholly and completely. If the night's experience was any indicator, this lifestyle, this arrangement, was something that I could not only deal with, but could enjoy, could want, could need.

His question hung unanswered in the darkness. His hands tightened on my chin as he tensed, waiting for a reply.

Am I going to take off running?

"Straight to you, baby," I whispered. "Straight to you."

A tentative smile started on his lips and grew till it stretched across his face. He released my chin and leaned forward, kissing me, grabbing the back of my head. Our kiss started out celebratory, but our naked bodies pressed together, the energy between us exploding, and everything changed, like everything else about our relationship, in an instant. His hand gripped my ass, squeezed it hard and pulled me even closer, flush against his cock, already hard and ready.

And there, in the quiet room with the candles casting crazy silhouettes on the wall, my eyes now able to take everything in, we made love, sensually and slowly, until the candles burned out and the wax became cold. In the kisses, caresses and erotic pleasures, we celebrated the unknown future.

★ ★ ★ ★ ★

Find out what happens next for Brad and Julia....
The sequel to BLINDFOLDED INNOCENCE
will be available soon from Alessandra Torre and Harlequin HQN.